"What the hell are you doing here?" Jess growled.

This was no place for a woman, let alone this woman.

"Saving your butt," she growled right back, pulling one of the sleeping bags from her stack of supplies.

She paused when she turned to spread the opened bag on the ground next to where Jess sat. "For heaven's sake, you can stop staring at me like that," she snapped. "I haven't grown two heads since you last saw me."

Since he last saw her.... It seemed like yesterday instead of two years. The last time he'd seen Gina Michaels, she'd been standing in the middle of her living room with tears streaming down her pale cheeks.

After all this time he could still hear her shouting that she never wanted to see him again. So what was she doing here, saving his hide?

Dear Reader,

There's a nip in the air, now that fall is here, so why not curl up with a good book to keep warm? We've got six of them this month, right here in Silhouette Intimate Moments. Take Modean Moon's *From This Day Forward*, for example. This Intimate Moments Extra title is a deeply emotional look at the break-up—and makeup—of a marriage. Your heart will ache along with heroine Ginnie Kendrick's when she thinks she's lost Neil forever, and your heart will soar along with hers, too, when at last she gets him back again.

The rest of the month is terrific, too. Jo Leigh is back with *Everyday Hero*. Who can resist a bad boy like T. J. Russo? Not Kate Dugan, that's for sure! Then there's Linda Randall Wisdom's *No More Mister Nice Guy*. Jed Hawkins is definitely tough, but even a tough guy has a heart—as Shelby Carlisle can testify by the end of this compelling novel. Suzanne Brockmann's TALL, DARK AND DANGEROUS miniseries continues with *Forever Blue*, about Lucy Tait and Blue McCoy, a hero as true blue as his name. Welcome Audra Adams to the line with *Mommy's Hero*, and watch as the world's cutest twin girls win over the recluse next door. Okay, their mom has something to do with his change of heart, too. Finally, greet our newest author, Roberta Tobeck. She's part of our WOMEN TO WATCH new author promotion, and once you've read *Under Cover of the Night*, you'll know why we're so keen on her.

Enjoy—and come back next month for six more top-notch novels of romance the Intimate Moments way.

Leslie Wainger

Leslie Wainger,
Senior Editor and Editorial Coordinator

Please address questions and book requests to:
Silhouette Reader Service
U.S.: 3010 Walden Ave., P.O. Box 1325, Buffalo, NY 14269
Canadian: P.O. Box 609, Fort Erie, Ont. L2A 5X3

UNDER COVER OF THE NIGHT

ROBERTA TOBECK

Silhouette®

INTIMATE™MOMENTS®

Published by Silhouette Books

America's Publisher of Contemporary Romance

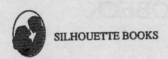

SILHOUETTE BOOKS

ISBN 0-373-07744-0

UNDER COVER OF THE NIGHT

Copyright © 1996 by Roberta Tobeck

Dear Reader,

And who says dreams don't come true?

After years of writing and editing, and millions of dreams, I've finally published my first book. I'm so excited that you have chosen to be a party to this celebration!

Having long enjoyed reading stories laced with romance, it was only natural that I should want to write them, as well. I found, however, that reading a book is much easier than actually writing one. But once bitten by the writing bug, there is no cure. So I wrote, rewrote, stared at the ceiling, wrote some more, then repeated the whole process until my characters came to life and a story developed.

With the continual encouragement of my husband, and the support of my writing group, I reached the end of my first book and sent it off to Leslie Wainger with bated breath. Would it receive an amicable reception? I needn't have worried. I received more support and encouragement...and the realization of my dream.

So sit back, relax and join me in a stirring romantic adventure while Gina and Jess entangle themselves deep within the confines of the jungle....

Sincerely,

Roberta Tobeck

Acknowledgments

For Roland, with love, for his unending faith in me.

A special thank you to Judith Duncan for her encouragement and direction, and to Ray Fenton for taking the time to guide me.

Thank you to the members of the Tacoma RWA and my critique group for sharing their knowledge and for helping me fine-tune my skill.

I would like to dedicate this book to the memory of fellow writer, Rhonda Music.

Chapter 1

Dark. Pitch-black dark.

Dark that covered like a shroud, enveloping completely, smothering all light. The oppression grew day by day. The only way for Jess Knight to survive was to draw within himself, close his eyes and dream of freedom, sunshine and cool breezes.

The only way to escape the fact that he was lying half-naked on a cold dirt floor in a small cell God only knew where. Escape the awful stench that filled every corner and seeped into his skin until a hundred baths wouldn't erase the odor.

But in the end there was no escaping the endless nightmare that held him as captive as the four stone walls of his small cell. Nor could he escape the questions that roared through his head like a freight train out of control, driving him slowly out of his mind.

Why had he been thrown into a cell that was barely large enough to allow him to lie down? And why had he been stripped of all human dignity and held in total darkness for

more days than he could remember? His jailers fed hir
slop a dog wouldn't touch. There wasn't a bed, or even
blanket to ward off the chill that seeped up from the dir
floor.

In the absence of facilities, he was forced to use or
corner of his cell for a toilet, adding to the foul smell in th
airless dungeon.

Jess knew there had to be a reason why he was bein
treated worse than a wild animal, but none came to mind

The creak of the slowly opening cell door interrupted h
thoughts and announced the return of his jailers. He a
most welcomed their arrival. A reprieve from the dead
silence that accompanied the total darkness would near
be worth the pain their visits usually brought.

His dignity demanded that he stand and meet his er
emy face-to-face, instead of cowering on the floor like
whipped dog. He would be damned if he let anyone, e
pecially his jailers, see him groveling on the floor, but th
pain racking his body from their last visit made it almo
impossible for his body to obey his mind's command. E
sheer will, and the pride that had sustained him, he rose
meet his enemy.

A small beam of light pierced the darkness, then slow
surveyed the dark cell before coming to rest on hir
Though his eyes were unaccustomed to the light, Jess fac
the unseen intruder through the darkness with raw dete
mination.

Jess could barely suppress the groan he felt rising fro
deep in his gut when the light was extinguished, plungir
the cell into total darkness once again. His preoccupatio
with the loss of light kept him from hearing the intrud
move across the small cell. It was a gentle touch on his ar
that alerted him to the position of his visitor.

Jess pulled out of reach, as far as the stone wall wou
allow. Again the touch came, more insistent this time. B

fore he could pull away, gloved fingers curled tightly around his wrist, preventing his escape.

It took only a brief struggle against his intruder's hold to exhaust his small reserve of strength. He was far too weak to put up much of a fight. In his condition, it was all he could do to remain upright while his assailant tangled gloved fingers in his filthy beard, further trapping him.

A slight tug brought his head down until he could feel soft material brush his cheek, moments before he felt warm breath on his left ear. Even through the stench, he could smell the clean outdoor crispness that surrounded the unseen person. Jess had dreamed of that clean smell often since being locked in his filthy cell. The scent of sunshine, fresh air...and woman. The last thought was so farfetched that he discarded it as foolish and concentrated on inhaling deeply to savor the precious fragrance. For the moment, he forgot his fear of the unknown intruder.

He was so lost in drinking in the clean aroma that he was startled when a soft voice spoke directly into his ear.

"Jess Knight?"

Stunned, he didn't realize the voice wanted his confirmation until the fingers tangled in his beard gave a slight tug. He answered with a hesitant nod as he wondered what kind of test he was going to be put through this time.

"Can you walk?" the voice asked, whisper-soft.

Once again, Jess slowly nodded.

"Keep very quiet. Don't make a sound. Understand?" The intruder's whisper was so soft that Jess had to strain to hear. He answered with another nod.

"Do exactly as I tell you, and we'll get you out of here. Understand?"

This time it was difficult for Jess to confine his response to a simple nod. The blood suddenly pounding in his head made thinking almost impossible, and he still wasn't sure his guards weren't playing some kind of cruel joke. But he wasn't going to take any chances, and he slowly nodded for the fourth time.

His beard was finally released, and he strained to see his rescuer in the darkness. He could make out no more than a small, dark shadow.

"Hold on to my belt, and stay very close." The voice reached out to him through the darkness. "We don't have far to go, but silence is very important." Without waiting for an answer, the shadow started forward. "Let's go."

Jess reached out to grasp the bodyless voice as it moved away, grabbing hold of what he thought was a belt. His heart thudded in his chest at the chance he was taking, but anything was better than dying like a rat trapped in a hole. The soft voice had him in its spell, leading him on. He would willingly follow it anywhere, as long as the journey started with his release from this hellhole.

In his haste to vacate the small room, Jess brushed against the cell door. His racing heart stopped, almost painfully, when the creaking hinges echoed like the screeching of an owl in the dark. He forced his bare feet to keep moving across the packed-dirt floor as his labored breathing thundered in the total darkness. Sweat ran down his bare back in rivulets as he tensed, waiting for someone to jump out at any minute and drag him back into captivity.

When his rescuer didn't pause, but confidently continued on, Jess drew a deep breath in an attempt to control his rapid breathing. With concentrated effort, he relaxed his fierce hold on the belt.

Suddenly, cooler air surrounded Jess, prickling his damp skin. They were near the door! The slight form leading him had been right; there hadn't been far to go to reach the outside... and, possibly, freedom.

The cold sweat now covering his bare chest had nothing to do with the sudden draft rushing through the crack around the door. Raw nerves had his breath coming in ragged spurts and his muscles so tense that he was ready to snap by the time the shadow led him the short distance to the door. He wasn't ready to accept the truth of his freedom yet.

Trying to keep up with the dark form, Jess tripped over a body lying on the floor, temporarily losing his hold on the belt. Rushing to regain his grip, he didn't waste time worrying about the man's condition. More than likely he was one of the guards who had visited him in his cell. All thoughts of the guard vanished when he got his first glimpse of stars through the outer door as it was pushed open.

Jess looked up through the narrow opening and saw the dark sky overhead. Night. How many times had he wondered whether it was day or night?

Releasing his hold on his rescuer, he stumbled up the few steps that separated him from the freedom beyond. He had no more than reached the last step before he was jerked off his feet, landing facedown in the dirt.

His fledgling hopes plummeted. Now the punishment would begin. For one split second Jess debated the feasibility of continuing to fight the inevitable. If he antagonized the guards enough, they might put an end to his torment.

The thought passed as an old adage flitted through his tired mind: Where there's life, there's hope.

He wasn't ready to surrender. He'd left too much unresolved in his life. His need for answers had been his sole reason for being in this godforsaken jungle in the first place.

Jess's muscles bunched in preparation for the blows he knew would come. When nothing more threatening than a hand, one he recognized, tugged on his arm, he carefully raised his head. The hand encouraged him to rise to his knees. He slowly complied, maintaining his guard.

"Stay low," the now-familiar voice hissed in his ear. "Follow me."

Quickly surveying the campsite, Jess was astounded to discover that he'd been held in nothing more than a small opening in the ground. Where he'd expected to see a prison yard, he instead saw the remains of a farmhouse, all but overtaken by the surrounding jungle. All that remained was the underground cellar where he'd been jailed, and a clearing where his guards had set up their camp around a rustic well.

Everything was quiet, as the men slept nearby. Jess wondered how many guards there were as he hurriedly stumbled after the dark shadow.

The night was black as ink, but the few stars peeking out between the clouds helped relieve the darkness with a promise of light. The breeze was cool and clean. Even the smell of rotting jungle vegetation was welcome, after the stench he had lived with for days. He filled his lungs with the cool air that was causing goose bumps to rise on his sweat-soaked skin.

The need to reach the safety of the jungle before they were discovered was a priority, but he took a moment to savor his newfound freedom. A sharp tug on his arm prodded him along. His desires would have to wait.

Crouching low, Jess followed the slight figure leading him away from the cellar, panting with the effort to keep up. With every step, he shot searching glances over his shoulder. His ears roared with the strain of listening for sounds of the discovery of his escape. He didn't breathe easy until they were swallowed up by the dense foliage that surrounded the old farm.

Jess stopped as soon as he was out of sight of the camp and leaned against the base of a large tree. He wrapped his arms around his throbbing ribs, sucking air into his tortured lungs. God, he was weak. He wouldn't make it much farther.

In the dim light under the thick overhead growth, he watched his rescuer scan the surrounding trees. Jess could see only a slim, dark shadow carrying a gun. Straining to see through the darkness, he could make out the size and shape of the shadow, and neither gave him much comfort.

The dark figure reached no higher than Jess's shoulder, making him just over five feet tall, with a slight build the bulky army fatigues couldn't mask.

That left Jess with only one disquieting conclusion. The small shadow that had entered the hole in the ground and safely led him out could be no more than a boy.

Jess wasn't the least bit encouraged.

Just then, another slim figure, not much taller than the first, silently slipped out of the jungle to rendezvous with the shadow. He was dressed in camouflage fatigues, and a ski mask covered his face, like the first boy's. He was also carrying a gun and a large pack.

Kids! They couldn't be more than teenagers. Being a trained government agent didn't necessarily mean he knew all there was to know about rescue operations. And as his boss had heatedly pointed out, he didn't know anything about the jungles of Central America. But being saved by a couple of kids was a blow to his pride—the only thing worse being saved by a woman. Not that he was about to complain. His pride could withstand the blow, as long as they got him away from that stinking hole.

After finishing his whispered conversation, the shadow gave Jess's arm a sharp tug, drawing him deeper into the shelter of the trees.

The rough, vine-covered ground made travel difficult, and Jess labored to follow the two boys. But then, running through the jungle in his bare feet wasn't the ideal way to ensure a speedy escape. He knew keeping up was going to be a major problem if they had far to go. So was exhaustion. Jess could feel the burst of energy that had gotten him out of his prison quickly depleting. He hoped to God they had come prepared with some sort of transport, or chances were he wasn't going to make it. The two boys surely couldn't carry someone of his size for very long.

Jess was so lost in his efforts to put one foot in front of the other without falling that he didn't notice that his rescuers had stopped until he ran into the back of his small shadow.

The pause allowed him to rest his spent body against the nearest tree. He watched as his rescuers had another whispered conversation, completely ignoring him again.

It was plain that his shadow was the leader. It was equally plain that the boys weren't in agreement. He could only make out a few of the words passing between them, but the intensity of the argument made him wonder whether they knew what they were doing.

Jess felt a sudden tingling of fear. They were so young. He had to concede they were more knowledgeable about the area than he was, and they'd done a good job so far, but he was uneasy about letting two boys take responsibility for his life.

Granted, he had no idea where he'd been taken after four goons barged into his hotel room and dragged him out of his bed, but, damn it, he should be in command. Relying on someone else went against his instincts. And right now, his gut feeling was to strike out on his own.

Only once before had he gone against his instincts and it had cost him the life of his best friend. It had been an expensive lesson. One he'd never forgotten.

Casting the boys another searching look, he found them watching him. Their argument must have been resolved. The dim light under the trees didn't allow Jess to see their eyes, and their faces were still covered with masks, but he could feel them studying him. Not knowing anything about his rescuers added to Jess's uneasy feeling.

Until that moment, it hadn't occurred to him to question their reasons for rescuing him. His freedom might not be their goal, as he'd first thought. Maybe they hadn't come to rescue him so much as to steal him away from his guards for their own purposes. There were different factions fighting in these jungles, and Lord only knew which group had been holding him.

They evidently knew who he was. Quite possibly, they belonged to a rival group and had rescued him just to use as a pawn for their cause.

"Who are you, anyway?" Jess growled, gathering his rapidly dwindling strength. If they represented a rival faction, there wasn't much he could do about it, but he wasn't going to meekly go into another cell.

When his voice rang in the darkness, both boys quickly motioned him to be silent.

A gloved hand clamped over his mouth. "We're too close for talking," the boy Jess had now dubbed Shadow whispered directly into his ear.

Shadow was pressed against Jess, much the same as when they had been in the cell. He could feel warm breath on his cheek as the soft voice whispered into his ear, once again sending chills down his spine. The same strange feeling came over him, a flitting memory of woman, soft and fresh. He tried to shake it off as the voice continued.

"Who we are isn't important. The important thing is to get you safely out of here."

Looking around, Jess noticed that the taller of the two had disappeared into the trees while Shadow was talking to him. He returned shortly with two more backpacks. He passed them to Shadow, who slipped on one and passed the other to Jess.

"This is for you," the husky voice whispered.

Jess opened the pack and rummaged inside. He discovered pants, shirts and a pair of boots. Pulling out a shirt, he noticed it was his size. Without delay, he quickly donned the khaki shirt before searching for a pair of thick socks. He gratefully slipped on the warm socks and sturdy boots. He would have liked to be rid of his filthy pants, but he wasn't going to take the time to change.

Uncontrollable shivers rocked his body in the cool air, making the clothes doubly appreciated. As soon as the boots were laced and he'd slipped his pack on, the boys silently motioned him forward. Fingers of apprehension played along his spine as he stepped between the two boys. Their generosity with the clothes hadn't alleviated his nagging doubts about their motives. Especially since he'd noticed they hadn't included a weapon, along with the pack.

Even in the poor light, he could tell that they were well supplied with top-of-the-line gear and up-to-date weapons. Whoever they were, they'd come prepared for a successful mission.

Resigned to following their lead, he struggled to keep up as they went deeper into the dense cover of jungle growth. After half an hour of fighting through the tangled jungle, he was grateful he didn't have to carry a heavy weapon. His almost-empty pack was more than enough for him to carry in his weakened condition, and it grew heavier with each step he took. Carrying a gun would only have worn him down sooner.

They halted again. The taller boy slipped into the trees, while Shadow stood guard. Jess found another tree to support him while they waited. For what, he didn't know, and he wasn't sure he cared anymore. Just drawing air into his burning lungs took his full concentration. His head swam from the exertion of just keeping himself upright. He'd gone so long without any form of exercise that he'd grown weak. He would have given anything for a place to lie down.

The unmistakable sound of gunfire cleared his foggy brain. Before it ceased echoing through the jungle, Jess found himself facedown under the vines that grew thick around the base of the tree he'd been leaning against a moment before. He had barely enough time to crawl between the thick vines before Shadow squeezed in after him, shoving him up against the base of the tree and putting his slight form between Jess and danger.

A gloved hand clamped over his mouth. He understood the warning to be silent as they waited, cramped together in the tangled underbrush. Jess's thoughts were running wild, and his heart raced double-time. Had his escape been discovered? God, he hoped not. He might not be in any condition to evade whoever was shooting, but he would fight. He would rather face the guns in the distance barehanded than return to his prison cell.

Long minutes passed once the volley of shots had died, and the silence was tearing at Jess's nerves. He expected to hear the rustle of brush as his guards beat the foliage, searching for him. God, he needed a gun!

A hiss of pain slipped past Jess's tight lips as Shadow pressed close to his battered body. As he recalled his rescuer's small size, another thought flashed through his mind. How were these two boys going to fight off experienced soldiers? They were hardly old enough to take care of themselves.

The question had barely taken hold when a soft whistle sounded close by. Jess was pushed toward the ground, and he assumed the gesture meant he was to remain where he was while Shadow investigated. The boy crawled out of their hiding place without making a sound. After a few minutes, he returned, as silently as he had left, giving Jess's arm a tug, signaling him to come out from under the brush.

"Our ride has been discovered by drug dealers," Shadow whispered, as Jess brushed the rotted vegetation off his shirt. Jess's tight muscles relaxed when he realized it hadn't been his guards searching for him after all.

"We're going to have to hide until you get your strength back. Then we'll hike through the jungle to the coast."

Jess noticed that the taller boy had returned and was standing next to Shadow. Their eyes glittered from the slit in their ski masks as they both turned their attention on him. Were they trying to determine how soon he would be able to make the journey over land? Jess pulled himself upright, ignoring the fiery pain in his punished ribs, as he met the searching looks the boys were giving him. He wasn't going to give them cause to leave him behind. He would keep up if it killed him.

Evaluation completed, they once again ignored him, and held another intense discussion. He couldn't understand what they were saying, but he was getting damned tired of being viewed as a piece of cargo. One thing he could tell. Once again, they weren't in agreement.

"Paco will go ahead to arrange the pickup for ten days from now," Shadow said, turning to Jess. "We'll follow as soon as you've had a chance to rest up." Shadow urged him deeper into the jungle. "Come on, we have to hurry. The shots will have alerted your guards, and someone might start checking to see who the chopper was for."

Paco halted Shadow before they'd gone five feet, and they exchanged a few more heated words. Once again Paco gave Jess a look that he could feel even in the darkness, then silently disappeared into the jungle. While Jess tried to understand the boy's attitude, Shadow gave him a push, indicating that they were to go in the opposite direction. They, too, were soon swallowed up by the foliage.

Jess struggled as they worked their way deeper into the dense growth. Seeing no set trail, he depended on Shadow's knowing where they were going.

After what seemed like hours, they reached a small stream that ran along the side of a steep hill. Through the break in the canopy overhead, Jess could see fingers of light streaking across the sky.

He looked at the top of the hill, visibly outlined in the faint light, and swallowed a groan. The hill wasn't high, but it might as well have been Mount Everest, as far as he was concerned. His strength was spent, and climbing that hill was more than he could manage.

His weakness infuriated him. His insides were churning, and his legs were shaking so badly he could barely stand. It had been hours since he had eaten anything, and what he had eaten had barely kept him alive. And to top it all off, he had a fever. He could feel his skin burn as chills chased through his body. If he didn't rest soon, he was going to humiliate himself by fainting at his rescuer's feet like some Victorian maiden.

Their pace slowed as they reached the stream, allowing Jess time to catch his breath. He swept his hand over his face, wiping away the covering of sweat as his body shook from another chill.

Shadow motioned him forward. "We'll hole up just ahead. Hang on."

They should have been far enough away from the camp that they didn't need to keep their voices down, but the information was still delivered in that same soft whisper, and the husky voice continued to have the strangest effect on Jess.

Slowly Jess followed Shadow across the shallow stream and through the brush that lined the other side. The boy stopped in front of the vine-covered bank. With one hand, he pulled the fall of vines aside to reveal a dark cavern hidden underneath. Their refuge was a small cave in the side of the hill, completely undetectable until the vines were moved aside.

Shadow held the vines out of the way and motioned for Jess to enter the cave. Bending down, he hesitated. The inside of the cave resembled the dark cell he'd just escaped far too much. He'd spent enough time in the ground to last him a lifetime.

A light touch on his arm reminded him that he wouldn
be alone this time, so Jess swallowed his fear and crawle
into the narrow opening. He was surprised when the sma
beam of light followed, relieving the darkness.

The entrance to the cave was only four feet wide, but a
Jess crawled farther inside, the area widened out. Th
ceiling angled upward, allowing Jess to sit upright with
out banging his head, which he did as soon as he was fa
enough inside to give the boy room to follow.

There was even enough room for him to stretch ou
comfortably. With two of them sharing the small space
they would be cramped, but with the vines covering th
opening, they wouldn't be easily detected.

Jess leaned against the rock wall. The cool stone fe
good to his fevered body. He wouldn't have made it muc
farther.

Opening his eyes a mere slit, Jess took in his surround
ings once again. The cave couldn't have been more tha
eight feet square, but with the light on, it looked like
room at a Hilton to Jess. He was surprised to see three fu
packs stacked against the back wall.

Who had forked out the money to pay for the expensiv
gear? The packs were U.S. government issue, all brand
new. Jess knew this type of gear was not easily found dow
here, even on the black market. This rescue was profe
sional. And whoever had planned it had covered all th
bases.

Jess's gaze circled the cave until it came to rest on th
small beam of light. The miniature flashlight cast a warn
halo of light on the ceiling from its makeshift perch atc
some rocks on the dirt floor, giving the boy the use of bot
hands.

Now that they were out of immediate danger, he wante
answers. Turning to Shadow with the intention of d
manding them, Jess was in time to see the ski mask con
off, revealing a mass of short copper curls.

The thick curls shone in the faint light, despite their matted condition from being stuffed inside the stocking hat. Large sherry-gold eyes surrounded with thick, dark lashes looked back at him. Jess's inventory went no further. His Shadow was no boy, but a very beautiful woman. And the last person he would have expected to come to his rescue.

"What the hell are you doing here?" Jess growled. All her skill aside, the jungle was no place for a woman, and especially this woman.

His body was a mass of throbbing pain, while his stomach pitched and rolled as if he had just taken a ride on a roller coaster, its meager contents in danger of making an unsightly reappearance at any moment. He shook from chills until his teeth were rattling, and his head felt as if it were going to explode. He sure as hell didn't need this twist added to his problems.

"Saving your butt," she growled right back, pulling one of the sleeping bags out of the stack of supplies.

She paused when she turned to spread the opened bag on the ground next to where Jess sat. "For heaven's sake, you can stop staring at me like that," she snapped. "I haven't grown two heads since you last saw me."

Since he last saw her... It seemed like yesterday, instead of two years. The last time he saw Regina Michaels, she'd been standing in the middle of her living room, with tears streaming down her pale cheeks.

After all this time, he could still hear her shouting that she never wanted to see him again. So what was she doing here in the middle of a Central American jungle?

Jess hadn't expected anyone to rescue him, let alone Regina Michaels. It would have made more sense if she had been the one who had him thrown into that stinking hole in the first place.

It had been bad enough when he thought he was being rescued by a couple of boys, but it was far worse to find

out that the person responsible for saving his butt, as sh
so eloquently put it, was the person who hated him mos
in the world. The situation would have been laughable, i
he had the energy to laugh.

"You look as great as ever." What an understatement
Jess thought as he ran his steely eyes over her. Even in fa
tigues, with her hair matted to her head, she was still th
most beautiful woman he'd ever known. For two year
he'd avoided seeing her for that very reason. He'd spent a
little time as possible at the Agency's main office so tha
he wouldn't run into her. To no avail. He might hav
avoided seeing her, but he hadn't been able to stop think
ing about her.

Now Jess wanted to know what she was doing riskin
her life in this war-torn country, rescuing him. She migh
be the Agency's top rescue and survival expert, but h
didn't want her in danger—not at his expense.

Jess watched as Gina smoothed out the thick sleepin
bag. How ironic the situation was. Whether she knew it o
not, her dead husband was still guiding both their lives
Just as he'd done before he was killed.

Jess's eyes roamed over Gina's slim form in the bulk
camouflage clothes, slowly returning to her mass of cop
per curls. She was even more beautiful than he remem
bered. And he remembered often. Her beautiful face fille
his dreams—waking and sleeping. There wasn't anothe
woman who could begin to compare to Gina. He knew
Every woman he'd met since he first saw her had failed th
test.

Judging from her stony expression and jerky move
ments, Gina still blamed him for her husband's death.
was ironic that she continued to condemn him, whe
Greg's death was the reason he'd been in that hole in th
first place. If he hadn't been investigating the charge o
treason that now blotted Greg's file at the Agency, he neve
would have been in this stinking jungle at all.

She'd never let him explain the circumstances that had led to Greg's death—not that he could have told her the complete truth. Maybe he never would be able to. Especially since he'd missed his chance to find the man responsible and ended up being held prisoner instead.

Worrying about things in the past that couldn't be changed would get him nowhere, Jess decided. Once he was out of this mess, he would see whether he could pick up the trail again. Right now, he had more pressing problems to concern himself with, such as getting his strength back so that they could get home.

Having to depend on Gina ate at his pride. Being helpless was foreign to him, and he didn't like it. He certainly didn't want her seeing him so weak and defenseless. As another tremor shook his body, he was forced to face the truth—there was no one else. He was so weak, he'd scarcely made it to the cave. Right now, he didn't have the energy to do more than sit up straight.

When he thought of the degrading conditions he'd been forced to endure, his pride received another blow. She shouldn't have been the one to see him in this state. He knew it was only his bruised male pride that made him want to strike out at her, when he should be showering her with gratitude, but why couldn't it have been someone else? Even the two boys he had thought were his rescuers would have been preferable.

"I bet you were disappointed when you discovered I was still alive and kicking," he growled as he watched her finish with the sleeping bag, her movements quick and jerky. She obviously wasn't any more pleased with the situation than he was. "Do I have to worry you'll push me off the nearest cliff before we're out of here?" Her stony silence was aggravating. He wanted to hear her voice. He'd spent weeks listening to himself talk.

Satisfied with the sleeping bag, Gina turned toward Jes The dark look she shot him wasn't encouraging, but least she wasn't ignoring him.

"The temptation's strong, but I've never lost a subje yet, and I don't mean to break my record with you. You' reach home safely. Don't worry."

The words were promising, but the look in her ey painted another picture. The lingering hatred said sh would make him pay. He'd better get stronger, fast, thought as the blackness overtook him, or else he wou find himself alone in the jungle.

Chapter 2

"**F**ool!" Gina muttered, watching Jess's eyes roll back in his head as he slowly slid down the wall of the cave, landing in a heap on the floor. He had finally come to the end of his strength.

Shaking her head in disgust, Gina looked at Jess, lying in the dirt. What was he so worked up about? She had gotten him out, hadn't she? Or was he doubting her ability to get him safely out of the jungle?

Paco had. Of course, he couldn't have known that her unease wasn't because she thought she couldn't do the job, but because she knew who she was rescuing. She had spent the past two years despising Jess for what he'd done to her life.

Kneeling on the spread-out sleeping bag, Gina worked to get Jess onto the thick cover. She watched as his body shook with chills. Straightening his legs into a more comfortable position, she eyed him in the dim light. If he got sick, they would be stuck in the cave longer than the few days she'd planned. And that would put them behind schedule for the pickup. Damn! If only they'd been able to secure the chopper.

Gina sat back on her heels, satisfied she would be able to zip the bag around Jess. Flexing her straining muscles, she ran her gaze down his body. He might have been poorly fed over the past six weeks, but he was still a large man, and rolling him onto the sleeping bag had taken no small effort.

Catching her lower lip between her teeth, Gina took a closer inventory of Jess as he lay sprawled on the open sleeping bag. His filthy hair and beard made him look like a derelict. What she could see of his face was swollen and bruised. There was a raw cut under his right eye, evidence of a recent beating.

Running her slim fingers through her tousled hair, she prayed for fortitude. His clothes would have to come off. And it wasn't going to be an easy task. He was too big for her to easily strip him. Just the thought was enough to initiate a prickling sensation down her spine.

"For heaven's sake," she chided herself. "I don't even like the man."

Directing her mind back to the problem at hand, Gina quickly removed Jess's boots. She set the boots and socks aside before reaching for the grimy pants. They were too short for his tall, rangy body, and they fit too tightly around his slim waist to be his. As she tugged them down, her eyes widened in shock when she found him naked beneath.

Her heart slammed against her chest, and she quickly jerked her eyes upward, tugging until the pants lay in a heap against the cave wall. With shaking hands, she concentrated on removing Jess's shirt. The task was made more difficult when her normally nimble fingers fumbled over the buttons.

Drawing a sharp breath, Gina stared at the vivid discoloration on his ribs. The small beam of light in the cell hadn't allowed her to see the extent of the damage his captors had done to him. In the faint light filtering through the fall of vines, she could see that he had been severely beaten—and more than once. He had moved too well on their trek through the jungle for her to suspect anything was broken, but the severe bruising indicated that some of his ribs had most likely been cracked.

Gina ran her hand over his bruised body, checking for broken bones. She was surprised to see the tremor in her fingers, and clenched them into a tight fist to hide the effect Jess was having on her. She'd thought she would be able to detach herself during the rescue, but it was apparent that she wasn't as immune to his obvious masculinity as she'd thought. She was grateful he wasn't aware of her state of nerves as she continued to work on him. It would have been extremely embarrassing if he'd seen how much his nearness disturbed her.

The extent of the abuse Jess had suffered troubled her. The rebels wouldn't have given him first-class treatment, but he was far too important for them to let his death endanger their deal.

They needed the arms they were asking for as ransom. That had been the sole reason for the kidnaping. Without Jess, their arms deal would fall through. And to get the arms, they needed him alive.

As she cleaned the numerous lacerations on his body, Gina visualized Jess in that dark cell. He'd barely been able to stand, but he'd been ready to face whatever was coming his way. He hadn't been fit to tackle a baby, let alone the men he had expected to come through the door.

Looking back, Gina remembered that she hadn't even been positive that the filthy man leaning against the dirt wall was Jess, he was in such terrible shape. It hadn't been until she looked into his eyes that she was sure. She'd seen that same fierce determination in their gray depths years ago, when he tried to explain how Greg had gotten killed.

When she refused to listen, he'd let her rage at him about killing her husband, without saying a word in his own defense. She'd damned him for being alive while her husband was dead.

He'd had the same look then—as if he weren't going to let anything or anyone beat him down. He had just lost his best friend of seven years, but she hadn't given that a thought. She'd needed someone to carry the burden of blame, and Jess had been the likeliest choice.

For the past two years, she'd rationalized her behavior by convincing herself that Greg wouldn't have taken such risks without Jess's influence. Jess was the reckless, irresponsible one, the one who always let Greg handle the dangerous assignments while he took the praise.

Letting her gaze glide over Jess's battered body, she questioned her wisdom in agreeing to the rescue. For any reason. She'd been with him for only a few hours, and already she was behaving in a way that was out of character. And she had a gut feeling she was in for trouble.

Her examination complete, Gina shook off thoughts of the past and set about sterilizing Jess's infected cuts. There was a large gash on his upper thigh that was festered and swollen. There wasn't much she could do for the wound except apply antiseptic and cover it with a gauze bandage to keep it clean. It was too late for stitches.

At least Jess was in better shape than some of the victims she'd rescued over the years. She'd never had to hike out with any of her rescue victims before. In the past, her connections had gone like clockwork.

She always went into a rescue prepared for any unseen event. If necessary, she could have performed first aid in Jess's cell with the medical supplies she kept in the many pockets of her pants.

Medicines and bandages were necessities she never traveled without. So was a knife that would have made Rambo envious. All her survival gear was top-of-the-line. It was almost weightless, and took up as little space as possible. Gina had quickly learned that there wasn't room for frills when your life depended on what you were able to carry.

She had a reputation for getting the job done that would have remained unsullied if not for the abundance of drug runners working this part of the world. With a little more force than was necessary Gina threw the used cotton swab on top of Jess's filthy pants. Rotating her tired shoulders, she thought of their narrow escape.

The drug runners were worse than the rebels who had kidnapped Jess. They just took what they wanted and killed anyone who got in their way. If the chopper hadn't arrived ahead of schedule they might have been caught in the cross fire while the drug dealers attempted to capture the rescue chopper. Given Jess's weakened condition it would have meant certain death for both of them.

Satisfied she had done all she could for the cuts, Gina put the supplies back in their kit. After taking out a small bottle of medicine, she filled a syringe. The injection was to safeguard against the effects of contaminated water. The doctor had assured her that the supplement would also help build up Jess's strength.

Gina gave the needle a suspicious look. He wasn't sick, but he wasn't healthy, either. The shot wouldn't hurt, so why was she hesitating? Administering injections wasn't new to her; she'd been a licensed paramedic for years. What was interfering with her normal self-assurance was the naked male body sprawled on the sleeping bag, clearly visible in the early-morning light. Jess's rugged body would recover quickly, but it couldn't be too soon for her peace of mind.

With efficient movements, she injected the medicine into Jess's hip before dragging her eyes from his nude body. She quickly threw the sleeping bag over him, soundly rebuking herself for taking advantage of a defenseless man. What was the matter with her? She never gave men a sec-

ond glance. That she would start by noticing *this* man was
particularly disturbing. She knew almost everything there
was to know about him, and what she knew she didn't like.

Jess risked his life time and time again chasing women
and adventure for the thrill of the moment, like some su-
per spy. He had little regard for those around him who
might be hurt by his actions. She knew firsthand what that
cost could be. Hadn't Greg paid with his life?

Jess and Greg had belonged to an elite group that
tracked illegal arms dealers. Most of the arms went to
small, war-torn countries where fighting was a way of life.
If the children lived past infancy, they invariably grew up
to join one of the fighting forces—fighting a never-ending
war. To members of the Agency, arms dealers were men
who grew rich off the blood of innocent people.

It wasn't Jess's job that Gina disapproved of; it was his
cavalier attitude that she didn't like. His involvement with
fellow agent Rita Tanner was a prime example of his selfish behavior. If it hadn't been for Jess's affair with Rita,
Greg would never have tried to save her from the arms
dealers; the rescue would have gone through normal
channels. The fact that Greg had been killed, along with
Rita, and the whole episode classified as top secret, cast
Jess in a suspicious light because the Agency wouldn't have
kept it under wraps if one of their operatives hadn't been
out of line. All she wanted was the truth surrounding the
explosion. It was the only reason she'd agreed to this mission.

Gina blamed the revival of better-forgotten memories
for her pounding heart and trembling hands. She would
accept no other excuse for her unusual lack of professional detachment. Certainly nothing to do with emotions—especially where this man was concerned.

She gave the zipper on the sleeping bag one last tug,
bringing the warm fiber-filled cover up under Jess's chin
to ensure that he wouldn't get chilled. Fingers of early-

morning light filtered through the curtain of vines streaking across Jess's sleeping form. Gina mused that the temperature in the jungle would soon rise, making the warm bag unnecessary.

Stretching her tired muscles, she gave Jess one last look before slipping out of the cave to reassure herself that they hadn't been followed. Once outside the cascade of vines, she turned to survey their hiding place. Even with the morning sun hitting the green foliage, the cave was undetectable.

The abundance of vines and foliage that covered the entrance concealed the cave's hidden recess. Its setting on the edge of the stream was another advantage. No one would be apt to check this side of the stream when the hill rose so sharply out of the water. They were relatively safe as long as they stayed inside. She'd picked this cave, before she went to break Jess out of his makeshift prison, primarily because of its seclusion.

Gina circled the immediate area, making sure they had left no telltale signs of their presence. Unlike the men who had been holding Jess, she wasn't going to let down her guard. Satisfied that she had secured the area, she ducked under the vines and slipped inside again.

She spread her bed near the entrance. From this position she would be able to hear if anyone happened to stumble on their hiding place. Giving the vine-covered opening one last glance, Gina slid into her sleeping bag. With a tired sigh, she let her body relax for the first time in two days.

The rescue hadn't been harrowing—as rescues went. In fact, she reasoned, it had been quite simple. The so-called prison had been a joke, one of the easiest she had ever encountered. Jess's cell had been nothing more than a root cellar for the abandoned farm where the rebels had set up their camp.

The only guard on duty had been sleeping at his post. Overconfident, no doubt. Removing him as a threat had been child's play, a maneuver she'd learned in her first years of training. The main safeguard of the cellar had been its almost invisible location. If she hadn't had prior knowledge of its existence she would have walked right by and never even noticed it.

Of course, the concealment of the underground prison had also been the reason for her easy rescue. The rebels had been so confident that Jess's cell wouldn't be easily discovered, and they had been so lax in their guard duties, that she was able to walk right in and back out with their prize prisoner without working up a sweat.

If the rebels believed they had met the chopper, and were already out of the country, she wouldn't have to worry about them searching the jungle. But until she handed Jess over on U.S. soil, she wasn't going to take any chances with his safety. He was worth too much to the men who had captured him for her to make a mistake now.

Shifting to get a more comfortable position on the hard-packed dirt floor, Gina thought longingly of her queen-size waterbed at home. She fantasized about how soft it would feel to her tired body, how its cozy warmth would be welcome.

Sleeping on the hard ground brought back memories that she would rather have left in the past. Memories of her father, and the rough existence she had endured while living in the wilds of the Cascade Mountains of Washington.

Life had been so special while her mother was alive— before her father's discharge. Her father had been a highly decorated army officer, a general serving with the elite Special Forces—the Green Berets. During his third tour in Viet Nam a gunshot wound had resulted in the amputation of his left arm and a medical discharge.

Years before his injury, just after her mother's death, her father had deposited Gina with his great aunt. After that, she hadn't seen much of him for six years. The time Gina lived with her elderly maiden aunt had been devoid of any affection. Living with the emotionless woman had made her think she'd been abandoned in a barren wasteland.

Expecting things to be different when her father was discharged from the service, she had been dismally disappointed. The father who returned wounded from the war had been nothing like the loving father she remembered. Gone were the smiling face and the warm hugs. He had been as devoid of emotion as his aunt.

Richard Beck had stayed in Seattle just long enough to pack up his daughter, and then he'd moved them both deep into the Cascade Mountains, where Gina had traded one sterile existence for another, this one devoid of any outside contact.

The only time her father knew she was alive had been when he was teaching her the survival techniques he'd taught his recruits in Viet Nam.

She'd learned quickly that to earn her father's recognition she had to be the best at tracking, hunting and living off the land. Eventually, she had learned what it took to be the top survival expert on the government's payroll.

Gina bunched her bag up under her head to make a pillow. Watching the early-morning light through the veil of vines, she shook off her dismal thoughts and sought a couple of hours of sleep. It did her no good to think of her unhappy childhood. All she needed to remember from her life with her father were the things he had taught her.

Sleeplessness plagued Gina as she tossed and turned. Blaming her restlessness on thoughts of her past did little good. She knew what had her mind working overtime. Her father and his lack of love for her weren't the cause. Jess, sleeping a few feet away where she could hear his deep breathing in the early-morning quiet, was solely to blame. His presence disturbed her more than she had expected it would. Her mind was too tired for her to sort out the sudden change in her feelings toward Jess or figure out why he disturbed her so, but she knew she didn't like the influence he was having on her thoughts.

Gina pushed reflections of Jess to the back of her mind. She had ten days to sort through her feelings. To find out what was altering her emotions. Before she left Washington her thoughts had been clear. Now that she'd seen him again, they were muddled.

What she needed was sleep, not a self-analysis of her disturbing emotions. Gina snuggled in her sleeping bag and put her years of training to work. With the discipline she'd learned from her father, she forced her mind to go blank so that she could get a few hours of much-needed rest.

After two hours of tossing and turning Gina was as tired as when she'd lain down. What little sleep she had gotten had been filled with disturbing dreams. Dreams that left her feeling melancholy and reluctant to face the day.

She was hesitant to open her eyes. But while her mind was sluggish, her body was filled with nervous energy. Kicking back the too-warm sleeping bag, she listened to the barrage of noise from outside the cave. The jungle creatures obviously had different ideas about her getting any more rest, as they were going about their daily search for food. The chattering monkeys in the trees, added to the chirping birds, created enough noise to wake the dead.

Forcing her gritty eyes open, Gina could see the faint light filtering through the dense foliage, straining to reach the jungle floor. Enough sunlight streamed through the vines to fill the cave with a weak glow. By the slant of the rays, she surmised that it wasn't quite noon. She knew the amount of light in the cave would increase, but the rear would always be in semidarkness. And when it rained, as it did every day, it would become as dark as night inside.

As the afternoon approached, the increasing temperature would turn the jungle into a steam bath, heating the wilted vegetation on the jungle floor until it emitted its own special odor of rot and decay. Lying on the cave floor, where the air wasn't as muggy, Gina could appreciate the jungle's beauty.

Vivid flowers filled the high branches of the trees, providing natural camouflage for the many brightly colored birds that flitted through the foliage. For Gina, the scene conjured up the image of a dazzling rainbow in motion.

She enjoyed the colorful picture until a low moan coming from the other sleeping bag overrode the sounds of activity in the jungle, drawing her attention. She rolled over to see what was disturbing Jess. There wasn't enough light for her to see him clearly as she reached out and touched his bare shoulder, but his skin was hot under her fingers.

Rising up on her knees, Gina parted the vines to let in more light. Jess was still unconscious. His face and the upper portion of his body, which had been bared when the bag slipped down, were covered with a fine sheen of sweat. Just what she had feared—Jess was burning up with fever.

That was all they needed to delay them. If the fever lasted too long it could rob him of much-needed strength, delaying their departure. The hike through the jungle was going to be difficult enough without Jess being weakened by a bout with fever.

Looking at her watch, she calculated the time that had passed since she'd given him the shot. The injection she'd administered had better begin working soon.

After quickly pulling on her pants and boots, Gina grabbed her rifle and a water pouch from their store of supplies and slipped out of the cave. She paused behind the

cover of some brush and watched the stream below.
Nothing moved. The birds and monkeys were carrying on
in their usual noisy manner, indicating that nothing was
nearby to disturb them.

That didn't mean someone couldn't be hidden within the
dense undergrowth a few feet from where she stood on the
bank. The thick vines and leaves were a good shield, but
they worked both ways. She held her rifle ready as she
filled the pouch with water, remembering that caution had
played a large part in keeping her alive all these years.

Returning to the cave, Gina began the business of
bringing Jess's fever down. She forced some bottled water
between his lips and prepared another injection.

With the afternoon sun hitting the face of the cave, more
light filtered through the vines, giving Gina an even better
look at Jess's battered body. Some of the bruises were fresh
and still vividly colored, while others had faded to a sick-
ening green showing that he had been beaten over an extended period of time. The last beating had been so recent
that some of the bruises were still raw and swollen.

After giving Jess the second injection, she began bath-
ing his fevered body with the cool water she'd gathered
from the stream. She needed to bring Jess's fever down
quickly.

He had been missing for weeks, and she doubted he had
been fed well. The lack of food and safe drinking water
was one thing, but Jess's battered body was a whole different story. She would just have to let the medicine do it
work. In the meantime, she would keep him cooled off
with sponge baths and get as many liquids down him as
possible.

As Gina reapplied another dose of antiseptic to the cut
and abrasions on Jess's body, she was pleased to see a
marked improvement in the few hours since she'd cleaned
and treated them. Except for the deep gash on his upper
left thigh. That cut looked as though it had been made by

a knife. The slash was six inches long, and deep enough that it should have been stitched. In the daylight, the wound looked worse than it had a few hours ago. But there was nothing she could do about stitches. Too much time had passed. So she applied a liberal dose of antiseptic to fight the infection and prayed it wouldn't get worse.

If the knife had moved a few inches to the side, it would have put a permanent stop to Jess's philandering. Gina smiled at the thought of Jess's womanizing coming to an end. No more Rita Tanner. And no more disasters. Her smile disappeared as she turned her attentions to Jess's injuries and away from his social life.

His hair and beard were another problem. They were filthy. A bath was out of the question until he could take care of the chore himself.

Gina heated water on their small propane burner, and, after cutting Jess's beard as short as possible, she carefully shaved his face clean, telling herself she was performing the task strictly for hygienic purposes.

Task completed, she softly drew in her breath as she got her first good look at Jess in two years. In repose, his face lacked the arrogance she remembered. The weeks of imprisonment had honed his features to a fine leanness, pulling his skin taut over prominent cheekbones.

As she studied Jess, Gina wondered why she had never before noticed the strength so evident in his face. Maybe the trials of the past weeks had changed him. No matter what the reason, his rugged handsomeness drew her eyes like a magnet. She said a silent prayer for a speedy end to this mission as she cleaned up her barber's supplies. If she continued to find qualities about Jess to admire she could see nothing but trouble for her in the weeks ahead.

Shaking off her foolish thoughts, Gina got back to the problem of ridding Jess of as much dirt as possible. His hair would have to wait until he could handle the chore himself. She brushed the tangled mess out of his face leaving his wide forehead bare. Even the simple hairstyle didn't detract from the handsome features that held her fascinated. Defenseless, Jess tugged at her heart, but she knew that as soon as he was back to his normal egotistical self he wouldn't be nearly as captivating.

After sponging off Jess's upper body, Gina felt she knew every firm muscle and dark hair intimately. Running the thin cloth over the bulging muscles and across the mat of thick dark hair that covered his wide chest before tapering down his flat belly was proving to be no hardship. Each stroke of the cool cloth made maintaining a semblance of detachment more difficult.

She reminded herself repeatedly that what she was doing was necessary to get Jess's fever down. That she would be performing the chore for anyone who was in the same condition. What troubled her was the pleasure she derived from the simple task...and the amount of time it took to accomplish. She knew better than to waste her feelings on this man. The problem was getting her heart to listen.

Forcing liquids down Jess was a battle. The experience was as effective as a bucket of cold water, ending Gina's fantasies and dropping her back into reality with a thud. Every time she tried to get liquids down his throat he mistook her for a guard and fought her the whole way. She knew she was going to have a mass of bruises to show for her efforts. She eventually grew tired of his resistance until finally he gave in and let some nourishing broth slide down his throat.

By nightfall, Jess hadn't regained consciousness and Gina was totally exhausted. Her hard bed looked as soft as a cloud, and she eyed it longingly. She couldn't take the risk that Jess might thrash around during the night and become uncovered, so she pulled her sleeping bag up around her shoulders and leaned against the wall near Jess's bed. The nights weren't exactly cold, but he might get a chill. She didn't need more to worry about, not even something as common as a cold.

Every day counted, and Jess hadn't made an inch of progress in gaining his strength back. One day had been wasted.

Pain stabbed at his body from a multitude of sources. His head throbbed. His eyes refused to open on his first attempt. He could see no point in wasting energy forcing them since there was nothing to see except darkness. He'd grown tired of straining to see in the total blackness that surrounded him.

He ached in every part of his body. His guards must have paid him another visit. At the rate they were going, he would be finished before long.

The total lack of light and sound preyed on a man's mind until he could imagine almost anything, like chirping birds. Jess's foggy brain balked as he tried to bring his thoughts together.

It was the realization that he really could hear birds that brought Jess out of his bleak thoughts. If he was still locked in his cell, he wouldn't be able to hear the birds. He lay still, keeping his eyes closed as he listened to the sounds.

Jess held his breath, waiting to see whether the chattering birds would disappear, as his previous hallucinations had. When the noise only grew in volume, he slowly pried his eyes open.

Light! Light and noise! The realization brought back the events of the previous night. He was no longer in his tiny cell. He was free!

Ignoring his screaming body, Jess rubbed the lingering sleep from his eyes before slowly reopening them to the golden rays of light filtering into the cave. The shafts of sunlight sliced through the vines, sending bright streamers from heaven. After endless days spent in total dark-

ness, never knowing day from night, the shafts of sunlight
were more priceless than the gold they resembled.

Thank God he was free.

Many times during these past weeks he'd believed he
would never see the sun again. Now he could see the sun
and hear the birds.

He could still smell the stench of his cell, though. Maybe
in time the rankness would fade, but it would be a long
time before he forgot that odor completely. Breathing
deeply, he concentrated on flushing the stagnant air of the
prison cell from his lungs with the cool, fresh air that softly
stirred through the cave opening.

The fresh air was quickly forgotten, along with the
chirping birds and sunshine, as Jess noticed Gina sleeping
beside him. After so many days of darkness, to awaken
and see her lying so peacefully in the soft sunlight was a
sight he would long remember.

An early-morning ray of light fell softly across her coppery curls. Without much effort, Jess could have reached
out and run his fingers through the lush mass. The urge to
move his fingers the slightest bit and feel the thick curls the
sun was turning into a bright tangle was almost irresistible.

Jess could smell the light scent that was exclusively
Gina's. That soft fragrance had tormented his dreams for
the past two years. He liked seeing her face while she was
sleeping, because he knew that when she woke she would
hide behind the guarded look she usually wore when she
was around him. She might have the face of an angel, but
he knew from personal experience that, when provoked,
she possessed the tongue of a viper.

From where he lay, he could see her thick, dark lashes
lying on her sleep-flushed cheeks. Last night it had been
too dark for him to see her eyes clearly, but he knew they
would be a dark, somber gold, and as serious as ever. In

his dreams he saw them burn a bright gold, smoldering with passion instead of hate.

Jess felt a stabbing in his chest that had nothing to do with the multitude of aches and pains left over from the attention he'd received from his overattentive guards. He'd grown used to the pain they inflicted over the weeks he was held captive. This piercing pain was a blow to his male pride. Why did it have to be Gina who'd rescued him? His present situation could only reaffirm her low opinion of him.

His superior at the Agency, Virgil Carpenter, had cautioned him about his lack of wisdom. He'd said rushing off to a country he knew nothing about on the slight chance that he would find Thomas Rico was nothing short of foolishness. But Jess had ignored his warnings and rushed headlong into disaster.

After searching for Rico for two years, he couldn't risk passing up the only lead he'd had for months. Central America was as close as he'd come to catching the man he knew was responsible for Greg's death. Now he had nothing to show for the endless days he'd been stuck in that makeshift prison. And on top of losing Rico's trail, he would have Gina's scorn to deal with.

Rico was most likely a continent away, and the trail would be stone-cold by the time he got back to it. Jess sure had missed the mark this time. Nothing had gone right from the minute he stepped off the plane.

Virgil would be sure to point out that he should have waited for backup—even given up on the chase—since Greg had already been found guilty and the case was closed as far as the department was concerned. The department might have closed his file, with the verdict of treason stamped across it in big letters, but he hadn't believed Greg would disgrace his country by stealing guns from the Agency. Especially when he knew what the guns would be used for. He just couldn't believe Greg had stolen the con-

fiscated arms no matter what his last letter had implied.
According to Greg, Rico had been responsible for the
thefts. So Jess had sworn to find the man and make him
confess.

Besides, the sham of a life he'd been leading for the past
two years had been wearing thin. He was tired of the sly
innuendos and whispered rumors after Greg's death. Virgil had known he wasn't involved and that Gina was in the
clear, but defending their careers from further specula-
tion required Rico's capture. With this in mind, he'd made
the decision to change departments in order to gain more
information on Rico.

Even if he appeared to be nothing more than a glorified
messenger boy for the Security Department, he could have
lived with that—if he had gotten the information he
needed. But in two years he had gotten no closer to his
prime objective—proving that Greg had been used by Rita
and Rico without his knowledge—than he'd been when he
started his search. How was he going to face Gina? He'd
promised himself that he would stay away from her until
he had proof of Greg's innocence—as well as his own.

The tip from Sid Carson was the closest he'd come to
finding Rico, and he'd blown it. Going off on his own in a
country he wasn't familiar with had been a move in the
wrong direction. Getting kidnapped hadn't been his
smartest move, either.

For months he'd been fighting the feeling that he was
chasing a phantom. He wanted to get on with his life. But
until he had the past settled, there could be no hope for the
future. And he wanted a future—one that included Gina.

He certainly wasn't cut out for intelligence work. He was
an investigator who hunted bad guys, not information.
Being stuck in an office or attending social events so that
he could pick up little tidbits of information wasn't his idea
of chasing stolen arms.

If it hadn't been for the wealth of information at his fingertips, he wouldn't have changed departments. But gathering information for the government gave him a clearance that put him in contact with a vast amount of material. And information was what he needed if he was ever going to find Thomas Rico.

Jess watched Gina as she slept, and wondered whether it would make a difference in her feelings toward him if she knew what his mission had been for the past two years. Was she even interested in the reason he was in Central America? Was that why she had agreed to rescue him?

He hardly thought she would have done so out of the goodness of her heart. Not that she wasn't the type of person to help others. Just not the person in question— namely himself. She should have refused. After all, she thought she had good reason to hate him, and until he caught up with Rico she would just have to go on believing the worst. Greg might have been many things, but Jess would stake his life that he wasn't a traitor. He wasn't going to be the one to point a finger at Greg without concrete proof that he had been guilty of selling confiscated weapons to illegal arms dealers to be shipped out of the country. He didn't think Gina would be able to withstand that kind of information about her husband.

Jess hadn't seen Gina during the past two years, but he'd heard plenty about her and her missions. He shouldn't have been surprised to discover that she was behind the ski mask. Her showing up in the jungle with only Paco for backup confirmed what he'd been hearing. She'd gained a reputation for daring the Fates by going on dangerous missions without a full rescue team. She'd been working primarily alone for the past year. Granted, she'd been successful, but a person's luck only held out so long.

Without warning, Gina sat up and looked around, her golden eyes alert. Other than the fatigue shadowing her eyes, she showed no signs that she had just been sound asleep.

Her sharp gaze lit on Jess. Serious gray eyes locked on to surprised golden ones, the time passing unnoticed while they both searched for answers to questions they dared not voice. Gina was the first to break the contact, but not before Jess saw the doubt she tried to hide.

"So, you're finally awake." Gina cringed inwardly at her stupid statement. Of course he was awake. Hadn't she just been drowning in his seductive gray eyes?

Needing something to do, she quickly slipped out of her rumpled bag and focused all her attention on the simple job of rolling it neatly into a ball. After placing it with the supplies, she had no alternative but to face him again.

He didn't look quite as barbaric this morning, with his face clean-shaven. His eyes were clear, and his face had more color. Even his bruises weren't standing out the way they had been yesterday morning. Gina automatically reached out to check his forehead for signs of fever, then quickly dropped her hand when she encountered Jess's steady gaze.

"How long was I out?"

Jess's steely eyes studied her as if she were some hitherto-unknown insect, making her nervous. Her gaze ran over his body, snuggled in the sleeping bag, and she remembered how she'd tended him the day before. Her face heated, and she quickly swung away, answering him over her shoulder.

"We arrived at the cave early yesterday morning. You were worn out, so it's no wonder you slept for so long." Gina knew she was rambling, but her nervousness was hard to hide when she could feel his eyes boring into her back.

"Sleep? I passed out, plain and simple," he growled as he rubbed the morning stubble that covered his cheek. After the first swipe, his hand paused when he noticed that the bristly beard was missing. His jaw tightened. "You couldn't wait until I woke up?" he asked, his voice stiff.

He watched Gina's pale complexion flush with warm color and narrowed his eyes, studying her. Something was making her edgy, even guilty, and he wanted an explanation. His sharp gaze followed her movements as he waited for her to answer. Waiting was something he'd learned to do well the past weeks.

Shifting in his warm bed, Jess searched for a more comfortable position for his battered body as he continued to watch Gina fuss with the packs. He froze when he realized the explanation for her nervousness.

"What the hell?" he roared as he lifted the edge of the bag and looked underneath. He was stark naked! And it didn't take a genius to figure out who had removed his clothes, either.

After his quick look under the cover, he brought his cold gray eyes back to the woman before him. His face darkened.

"What happened to my clothes?" The question was low and guttural, as if the words were being forced out of a too-tight throat.

The clothes weren't important. The pants had been worthless. They'd been thrown to him days after he regained his senses in the dark cell. They'd been old, filthy and much too short, but he had grown dependent on them as his only touch with civilization.

Gina flinched noticeably at his angry tone. "I removed them so I could clean your cuts. Some of them were infected and needed attention. You could have become sick—" Her explanation stopped abruptly when she realized she was rambling again. But he was making her feel like a voyeur caught peeking in a window. It was impossible for her to stand before his dark regard without feeling the power of his anger—and he was still only sitting! She had better get hold of herself. If he could intimidate

her while he was in his present condition, what was she
going to do when he was standing on his feet?

"They haven't been treated for weeks. One more day
wouldn't have hurt," he snarled, his large hands doubled
into fists where they lay on the sleeping bag, as if he
wanted to hit something, or some*one*.

Gina took an involuntary step backward as his frown
deepened and he continued in a terse tone. "I'm sick and
tired of being a puppet for anyone who happens to hold
the damned strings. It's my body! Leave it alone!"

The order was delivered in a near shout that reverber-
ated around the cave.

As the echoes died, Jess drew a deep breath, in a clear
attempt to control his anger. "Where are my clothes?" he
asked, in a tightly controlled voice that held an undertone
of contempt.

Gina stiffened when his tone didn't match her conclusion that he was suffering from embarrassment. Was his
disdain aimed at her? Did he think she had enjoyed stripping him? She frowned at the thought as she felt her face
heat. She refused to be embarrassed about helping him!

She stubbornly kept silent until Jess turned eyes as dark
as thunderclouds on her. Gina pointed to the back of the
cave, where a pile of neatly folded clothes was stacked beside his boots and the supplies.

Without giving her another look, Jess pulled the pile
toward him. The shirt she had given him the night of his
escape was neatly folded on top. He jerked it up and slid
his arms into the sleeves. He began shoving the buttons
into their holes, but Gina's quiet voice halted his movements.

"It will just have to come off again. You might as well
wait until I put some more antiseptic on your cuts before
you dress." Gina turned her back to Jess while she gathered up the medical kit. "I'll have to give you another shot
this morning, too."

"Shot! What shot?" Jess's fingers froze as his head snapped up. His cold stare snared Gina's wary look. "What shot, Gina?" he repeated in a low growl.

"A special prescription ordered by the doctor. He suspected you'd be run down, suffering from dehydration or malnutrition, possibly both. Gina shrugged, as if the shot were of no importance. "I've been giving you an injection twice a day. It's supposed to help you regain your strength quicker. Maybe even fight the infection in your cuts."

"The cuts are fine, so we can dispense with your playing Miss Nightingale," Jess replied tersely, ignoring her instructions by buttoning his shirt.

He wasn't being entirely truthful. Some of the cuts, and especially the one on his left thigh, hurt like hell. Not that he was going to complain to her. He was just plain sick and tired of being at a disadvantage all the time.

"They've improved since I've been putting the medicine on them." Gina could see the stubborn set of his jaw and decided to take a different course. The cuts had to be tended, whether he was willing or not. Especially the one on his thigh. "But they aren't healed yet. If they get infected, and you get sick, it might prevent us from getting out of here. You don't want that, do you?" She didn't look at Jess when she tacked on the last statement. She hoped it would convince him to let her continue treating his cuts without giving her a fight. She hadn't even contemplated that Jess Knight would be modest, and not just contrary.

Modesty was the furthest thought from Jess's mind at the moment. He didn't mind a beautiful woman gazing at his body. What man would? It was the feeling of helplessness that had him squirming. From the moment the four goons burst into his hotel room and dragged him, stark naked, out of his bed, he hadn't had the upper hand. And he didn't like the feeling one bit.

Jess had to admit he didn't want to be the cause of their being stuck in the jungle for God only knew how long, but he didn't want to submit to her ministrations again. The first day, he hadn't been aware of her care. But being awake while she put her soft hands on his body might be more than he could stand. Just the thought had his blood racing.

Giving Gina a calculating look, he started to grin. "I'll tell you what. To make the situation fair, you take your clothes off, too. Then you can play doctor . . . and give me the shot."

The more he thought about it, the more Jess liked the idea. He'd always thought she was the sexiest woman he'd ever seen. Getting her naked would be a pleasure.

Gina stiffened, momentarily ruffled by Jess's remark, before she cocked one eyebrow at him. She wasn't going to dignify his crazy request with a response. And she wasn't going to blush, not if it killed her. As she reached for the edge of Jess's sleeping bag, she was startled when his hand snaked out, grasping her wrist, his hold preventing her uncovering his body.

Raising her eyes, Gina met Jess's intent gray gaze. What she read in his smoldering look flooded her cheeks with bright color and held her more firmly than his hand on her wrist. She could see the heated results of his comment in the fire that burned in those gray depths.

Jess cursed himself for a fool. His reckless suggestion had backfired. Instead of the stupid remark relieving the situation as he had intended, the image it had conjured up sent a shaft of heat to his groin. It had been a long time since he had been with a woman, but he knew that wasn't the reason for his instant response to *this* woman.

She had always had this effect on him. Only before, he had been able to control his responses when he was around her. He'd had to. She'd been his best friend's wife. This time, his defenses were down, and his big mouth was all it had taken to set him off.

Still holding contact with Gina's wide golden eyes, Jess released her wrist while he slowly pulled the bag away from his body. He turned his head for a moment, breaking his visual hold on her, so he didn't see the color flood her face or her eyes widen in panic before they flew up again.

Gina's embarrassment quickly turned to outrage as she turned away from Jess. Picking up the medicine kit, she carelessly dropped it onto the sleeping bag.

"The shot can wait until later, since you're feeling so damned improved."

The contempt in her voice stabbed the air as she grabbed her rifle and left the cave.

Jess saw her pass across his line of vision as he looked through the curtain of vines, watching the mist rising from the damp jungle floor as the sun heated the wet vegetation. The red staining his cheeks was from shame. For some insane reason, he'd wanted her to see what she did to him. What he hadn't expected was the self-loathing he felt at the cheap stunt. This time, he deserved her disgust.

Chapter 3

Green leaves shielded the sun from the small outcropping where Gina sat watching the entrance to the cave. Her perch was in the shade, but she felt as though she were sitting in a sauna. Her shirt was plastered to her back, and a rivulet of sweat ran down between her breasts. She knew she would be cooler in the cave. The dirt floor and stone walls kept out most of the sweltering heat—but Jess was in the cave. After the embarrassing episode that morning, she'd had no desire to return to those close confines. The atmosphere had only gone from bad to disastrous from the moment she awakened to find Jess's cool gray eyes watching her.

Regaining her usual composure so that she could return to the cave to fix Jess breakfast had taken more time than she cared to remember. Not only had his obvious arousal shaken her, but the thought of Jess watching her as she'd slept lent an intimacy to their confinement that she was far from comfortable with.

Nothing had changed between them. She still blamed him for her husband's death...or did she? Where was the doubt coming from? She hadn't changed her opinion of him just because he had taken a little rough treatment. She certainly wasn't going to let his condition cloud her judgment. As soon as he was on his feet again, she knew he would revert back to the same old Jess. Hadn't his actions that morning proved that his outlook hadn't changed? He was still a man with a roving eye who chased after anything in skirts. According to Greg, Jess had kept a harem of women around the world. She would be smart to remember that when she started getting soft in the head about him.

She didn't care what excuses Jess came up with. As far as she was concerned, he *was* responsible for Greg's death. And for her being alone for the past two years. All she was interested in now were the facts surrounding Greg's last mission. She needed to settle his death once and for all. That was the reason she'd agreed to come to Central America and rescue Jess from the rebels...wasn't it? Her doubts were driving her crazy. Suddenly, learning about Greg's death didn't seem as important, now that she'd seen Jess again. When she thought about how Jess's botched mission had gotten Greg killed, she couldn't seem to dredge up the same raw anger she'd felt just last week, when Virgil requested that she come looking for Jess.

Nothing had changed. Jess was in this mess because he was still the same irresponsible, adventure-seeking agent he had been two years before. Virgil had admitted as much when he said Jess had gone to Central America on his own. Hadn't Greg continually told her how Jess was always off seeking excitement and letting someone else pick up the pieces? So why had seeing Jess again, having his life depend entirely on her, put him in a different light?

Her confusion was a major part of the reason she was sitting outside again. Where she could keep her eye on the entrance from the vantage point of the ledge, instead of inside, where it was cooler. There was no need for her to stand guard out here. She had given the area a thorough inspection before she returned earlier. They were as safe as they could be in a combat zone, but she wasn't ready to return to the cave yet. Standing guard was a valid reason for being outside. It wasn't as if she were running from Jess.

Eyeing the clouds gathering above the trees, Gina knew her stolen moments of solitude were coming to an end. The daily torrent of rain would be coming soon, soaking everything in its path. She told herself she'd better get a move on, or she would be soaked through before going ten feet.

After the fiasco earlier in the morning, Gina wasn't going to do anything to encourage Jess's sexist behavior. The tension between them had been so thick while she was preparing their breakfast that it grated on her nerves. A good old-fashioned yelling match would have been preferable to the dead silence that filled the cramped cave.

Gina laid all the blame for making their situation impossible squarely on Jess's shoulders. If it hadn't been for his smart remark, they would have been able to tolerate the ten days they were forced to spend together. Now she couldn't see how they were going to spend the few days before Jess could travel, confined in a small area, without dire repercussions.

Jess's uncalled-for remark only heightened the unwanted attraction that was building in her—one she had been fighting ever since she'd removed his clothes. Gina had examined her feelings a hundred times since that morning, but she hadn't come up with a single reason why she should be attracted to a man she'd spent the past two years hating. Nothing made sense anymore.

The first raindrops fell, jarring Gina's thoughts back to her present location. Jumping up from her hiding place, she quickly brushed off the seat of her pants and pulled her clinging shirt away from her damp skin as she grabbed her gun and made a mad dash for the cave.

Jess was bored. He might be free of the dark hole, but he was still trapped. His battered body held him prisoner in the cave as much as the locked door had held him inside the cellar. Until he was stronger, he was also dependent on Gina, and that was a condition that grated.

The morning had dragged. He longed to have someone to talk to. Not that Gina would have talked to him if she had been there. And he didn't blame her. He'd spent the time he hadn't been napping running through an impressive list of foul names he felt fit his actions that morning. His mood hadn't improved one bit.

The asinine remark about her getting naked had sent lightning bolts shooting through his body, to center in his groin. Just thinking about his reaction to the thought, even hours later, reignited the fire, making him realize how much he deserved each name he had called himself . . . as well as some he hadn't even thought of at the time. He had no one except himself to blame for being such a fool as to let his imagination run wild and ignite the very situation he had been trying for years to avoid.

He could still feel his reaction to Gina's touch when she'd finally returned to give him his shot. A task she'd enjoyed, no doubt.

Advertising the response to his suggestion had probably confirmed Gina's misconceptions about his life-style. He'd heard some of the things Greg had told her about his many women.

His first chance to show her he wasn't the louse she'd been led to believe and what did he do but reaffirm every lie Greg had told her? He couldn't have acted more like an ass if he'd planned to.

Jess appeased himself with the weak excuse that he had been caught off guard. But that didn't absolve him for the crude display of his aroused condition. Gina didn't deserve to be treated in such a coarse manner. His insulting exhibition was a poor way to treat the person who had delivered him from hell. Especially when he'd had no hope of anyone coming to his rescue.

The seedy excuse for a hotel where the rebels had grabbed him was the last place anyone would have expected him to be staying. He'd been looking forward to the solitude while he waited for Sid to contact him. He'd needed to rethink his life. To seek a more positive direction for his future. He'd needed something that would put some meaning back into his life. Something he could believe in again.

Most of all, he'd needed to know whether he was doing the right thing in keeping the truth from Gina while he searched for Rico. And was he doing it for the right reasons, or were his motives purely selfish? He'd had plenty of time to sort out the answers during his solitary confinement. He had to admit that his reasons were partly selfish. He wanted to find out the truth so that he would have something to give her besides Greg's tarnished reputation. The selfish part was what he hoped to gain by the truth—Gina.

He'd wanted some time alone to think. That was a laugh. He'd gotten more time alone than he bargained for.

Jess's brow knotted when he realized he still didn't know why he had been kidnaped. Regardless of whether Gina was still talking to him or not, he was going to get some answers when she returned.

The rain began to beat down outside, like someone playing a set of drums, interrupting Jess's thoughts. The covering of clouds had cast the cave in deep shadows. He hadn't noticed the growing gloom inside the cave; it matched his mood.

Loosening two more buttons on his shirt, Jess pulled the sweaty garment away from his body, seeking a little of the rain-cooled breeze. When the rain stopped, the slight relief from the humidity would disappear as quickly as the rain had begun.

Jess didn't have long to wait for Gina's return. She ducked into the cave just minutes after the rains began in earnest, her khaki shirt plastered to her body, leaving little to Jess's imagination. His body's reaction to the provocative shape outlined by the soaked shirt brought forth a new string of curses under his breath.

Without giving Jess as much as a glance, Gina went to the back of the cave and began rummaging in her pack. She was in the shadows, but Jess had no trouble seeing her movements as the soaked shirt slipped off her pale shoulders, falling to land at her feet. A thin pink tank top, as wet as her shirt, was all she was wearing underneath. Realizing she wasn't through undressing, Jess quickly turned to watch the downpour outside the cave, and longed for a cold shower.

The light rustle of clothing that he heard over the drumming rain was pure torture as he mentally visualized Gina's body being revealed to his hungry eyes. Drawing in deep breaths of humid air, Jess tried to direct his thoughts to the questions he wanted answered, instead of to the back of the cave, where he could still hear Gina stripping out of her wet clothes.

He succeeded so well that he didn't realize she had finished dressing until he heard her rummaging through the supplies. He chanced a quick look in her direction, letting out the deep breath he hadn't realized he was holding when he saw she was fully clothed.

Gina turned to find Jess's quiet gaze on her, and once again she felt a coil of tension run down her spine. Had he enjoyed watching her change her wet shirt? She'd reached the conclusion, as soon as she had left the small ridge above the cave, that she couldn't sit around in wet clothes.

She'd had little choice but to change. And there had been nowhere else for her to change but the cave.

Giving a slight shrug of her shoulders, dismissing Jess, Gina set about fixing lunch. She lit the small propane burner. At least the rain would keep anyone from looking for them for a couple of hours, she reasoned. And the light would help dispel the gloom. Maybe even help lighten the mood. Something hot to eat couldn't hurt them, either.

Jess watched as she lit the little burner she had used to fix their breakfast. He welcomed the way it illuminated the cave with a warm glow. He appreciated the light, after spending so many days locked in darkness.

His brows drew together as he thought about all the days he had spent in total darkness. Having light was such a small thing. Most people never gave it a second thought. But Jess knew he would never take light for granted again. The beatings he could have withstood until his guards went too far and killed him, but the constant darkness would have driven him crazy before much longer.

And how had he thanked his rescuer? By making crude remarks that had embarrassed both of them and caused tension that would make the days they were forced to spend cramped together unnecessarily uncomfortable.

Jess didn't know how to begin to apologize, but he did know the apology wasn't going to be easy if she wasn't even talking to him. She had carefully avoided looking in his direction ever since she'd entered the cave.

"You wouldn't happen to have a pizza and a beer in that pile of supplies, would you?" he casually asked.

The ridiculous question was almost drowned out by the riot of driving rain, but the absurdity of the request caught Gina's attention. She slowly raised questioning eyes in Jess's direction where they met his and held.

"Sorry, you'll have to make do with dehydrated stew and instant coffee," she answered simply before turning back to the preparation of their meal.

"What I'm trying to do is clear the air between us." Jess said, raising his voice to be heard over the pounding rain. "We're going to be together for the next ten days, and I got us off to a poor start." He hurried on before Gina could voice the comment he saw forming. "I'm sorry about this morning. I was out of line, and I wouldn't blame you if you refused to accept my apology."

He didn't expect her forgiveness—and wasn't asking for it. He just didn't want the next ten days to be spent in a cold-war atmosphere. "I assure you, it won't be repeated."

As Jess's voice trailed away, Gina shot him a quick glance. She was torn between his straightforward apology and her desire to keep the boundaries that had gone up that morning in place. She was troubled by her mixed feelings, and until she had them sorted out she needed all the protection she could get from whatever was growing inside her. She'd counted on the emotional space that anger would give her to keep her distance. In their confined living quarters, she couldn't put much physical space between her and Jess.

Glancing at him through her thick lashes, Gina was startled to see the hopeful look in his clear gray eyes. Her acceptance of his apology was important to him, and he wasn't afraid to let her see it.

"Don't let it bother you. I've already forgotten about it." The flip answer was an outright lie, but she wasn't about to admit it to him. Let him believe what he wanted. As of right now, she was determined not to let him get to her again. He could save his games until he was back home.

Then why, said a small voice inside her head, *are you shaking so*? Gina scowled as she pushed the irritating voice to the back of her mind and focused her thoughts on preparing their simple lunch.

She darted another quick look in Jess's direction, only to discover that he was engrossed in running his long finger through the soft dirt of the cave floor, as if in deep thought.

Jess raised his eyes to find her watching him. "I'd like some answers," he said softly.

His quiet voice startled her, but she gave a quick nod, granting permission, before turning back to preparing their lunch.

"How long was I in that hole?"

"You were gone for forty days." Gina kept her answer simple. She wasn't sure how much she should tell him about his capture, though Virgil hadn't cautioned her to keep quiet about the ransom.

Gina looked at Jess as she waited for more questions. If she had been locked away for that long she would have a book full of questions waiting for answers.

"Forty days?" Jess said almost to himself, in wonderment. "Do you know why they grabbed me? As far as anyone knows, I'm an investigating agent these days. I haven't worked in the field for two years. I have no political value for any government." He had racked his brain the entire time he was imprisoned, trying to understand what anyone would want from him. Each time he had come up empty-handed.

If the rebels had been after information, why hadn't they interrogated him? Other than a few obscure questions during the first beating, they hadn't seemed interested in what he might know. Of course, there was little he knew that would be of interest to anyone in this area. His assignments had always been centered in the Middle East, not in Central America.

Jess's eyes narrowed as he watched Gina. She appeared to be trying to decide just what she should tell him. He felt his anger ignite at the thought. Granted, they were in different sectors, but his clearance level was equal to hers, and he was about to remind her of that fact when he noticed that she'd obviously reached a decision.

"I'm not too clear on the details myself, since I don't usually need to know all the facts when I'm sent on an assignment. But this situation was different." Gina paused when she realized what she had implied. Judging by the look on Jess's face, he'd caught the implication.

"You don't have to tell me that you refused to come when you were first assigned this mission. I'm surprised you accepted at all." Jess's dry tone let her know that he was aware of her opinion of him.

Gina shrugged, dismissing Jess's comment. She'd never attempted to hide her disapproval from him, so why start now? "I took the assignment because there were extenuating circumstances I couldn't overlook. Virgil knew I would turn him down flat, so he brought in the big guns when he came asking for my help. He brought Thomas Knight with him."

All signs of humor left Jess's face, and he snapped to attention like a raw recruit facing his drill sergeant for the first time. Gina had been informed by Thomas Knight that he hadn't seen his son for five years, so she wasn't surprised by Jess's reaction to the information.

Jess couldn't believe what Gina was telling him. The last time he saw his father there had been all-out war between them, and their parting hadn't been a friendly one. To think that his father had aided Virgil in getting him rescued wasn't just surprising, it boggled the imagination.

"What possessed Virgil to seek help from my father? Come to think of it, how did Virgil know where I was?" Jess asked.

"Virgil didn't go to your father. Your father went to Virgil. He received a ransom demand for you from a group of rebels. He notified Virgil before he agreed to pay the ransom. Hearing what they were demanding, Virgil wasn't about to let your father pay the price. He suggested they try to get you out instead." Gina paused, thinking about the argument she had witnessed between Virgil and Thomas Knight. "Your father wasn't going to let you die in a Central American rebel camp, and Virgil wasn't going to let your father pay the ransom. They were at a standoff. So they agreed to have me come in and get you out."

Gina thought about the carrot that Virgil had dangled before her to get her to agree to the rescue. After her unexpected response at seeing Jess again, she thought it best to keep that bit of information to herself for now.

"What would my father have that the rebels would be interested in? If money were the issue, Virgil wouldn't have objected." Jess wouldn't have thought his father would put out any of his hard-earned money to ransom what he termed an ungrateful, hardheaded son. He had to give him credit, though, for making the effort to see him rescued.

He loved his father. Thomas Knight was the only family he had. But their last argument had been bitter, and final. It also hadn't been their first. And with both of them being too stubborn to back down, they hadn't seen each other for years.

To Thomas Knight, there was only one serious pursuit in life that was worth his time—the pursuit of more money. He had enlarged the small loan business he'd inherited from Jess's grandfather into a multistate conglomerate within a few years. Then he'd invested the profits in so many businesses that Jess had long since lost track.

He'd never taken Jess's career seriously, and when Jess refused to join Knight Industries the blowup had resulted.

"Guns." Gina cleared her throat to gain Jess's wandering attention. His file didn't go into his personal relationship with his father beyond listing Thomas Knight as his next of kin. But knowing that his father had played an active part in his rescue didn't seem to sit well with Jess, if his dark frown was any gauge.

"What did you say?" Jess asked, still trying to determine what his father hoped to gain by paying his ransom. If his father thought for one minute that he was going to buy him away from the Agency, he was in for a big disappointment.

He glanced up to find Gina staring at him, her arms folded across her chest.

"Jess, are you interested in this or not?" she asked, not relaxing her position.

"I'm interested. What were you saying?"

"About the ransom. It seems the rebels wanted the guns your father's munitions company makes. They had been trying to buy arms from him for months, without success. Then you accommodated them by walking right into their hands. They used you as leverage to gain what they wanted."

"What company are you talking about? I don't know about any munitions company." He might not know about a company that manufactured guns, but he vaguely remembered his guards asking about arms during their only interrogation. His answer had angered them enough that they had almost beaten him to death.

"The plant in Texas your father took over a couple years ago that manufactures weapons for the military. Needless to say, the government wasn't about to meet the rebels' demand. That's why Virgil came to me instead of going through the proper channels. This mission is strictly off the record, and totally financed by Knight Industries. In other words, Thomas Knight is running the show."

Jess found it hard to believe that his father would go out of his way to help him, but he could see him wanting to run the operation. Then again, Thomas Knight was a very possessive man who didn't let go of his property easily. That was how he'd amassed a fortune out of one small company. And his father believed his son was his personal property.

His father's attempts to run Jess's life had been the source of their main disagreement. His father hadn't understood Jess's wanting to be his own man and had fought to mold him into the person he wanted. In response, Jess had joined the military to spite his father's attempted domination. He'd realized that their inability to get along would prevent them from ever working together, and in his stubbornness Jess had searched for a way to strike back at his father. Joining the army had seemed to be the perfect way.

Jess had realized later that his joining the army was the best thing he could have done for himself. He'd had to grow up quickly in boot camp. He had ceased to be the son and heir of Thomas Knight, millionaire, and had been simply Jess Knight, private. The change had been disconcerting at first for someone who had enjoyed the benefits of his parents' wealth without having to lift a finger. But he'd soon learned the satisfaction of self-accomplishment, and that life had far greater meaning when you earned your place by your own efforts.

His father's involvement in his rescue had an understandable explanation, but it still left one unanswered question. Why had Gina come to his rescue? Given the way she felt about him, she should have been pleased that he had gotten himself into a situation he couldn't get out of. He'd been aware of her feelings about him ever since he'd met her. She'd never tried to hide how she felt about him, not even before Greg had been killed. Her dislike of him had always puzzled him. What had been even more puzzling was Greg's answer when he'd asked about Gina's attitude toward him. Greg had given the weak excuse that Gina disapproved of his life-style.

The confusing thing was, Jess's life-style wasn't at all unusual. Since his break-up with Serena Dayton, he kept his relationships to a minimum. He didn't want to chance repeating his experience with Serena. By choice, he lived a very solitary life. His work left him very little time to date, let alone lead the swinging bachelor's life Greg's statement had suggested. He was on the move so much he never had the time to form a lasting relationship. That was one of the things he'd envied Greg—he'd had Gina to come home to.

"Why did they beat you, Jess?" Gina asked, interrupting his thoughts.

"I guess you could say it was my fault. They wouldn't tell me why they'd grabbed me, so I wasn't going to answer their questions." Jess smiled as he shrugged dismissively. "It's not too wise to mouth off when the odds aren't in your favor. Especially when you're in no position to defend yourself."

"That was all? You mouthed off, so they beat you?" she asked, her disgust coming across loud and clear. "Why didn't you just keep your mouth shut and spare yourself all that pain?"

"The first beating put me out for days. I lost track of time then. After that, they'd show up every couple days and use me for their entertainment. A few punches and kicks and they'd leave. They weren't trying to do any serious damage. I think they couldn't resist the temptation of a little sport. It also kept me in a weakened condition, so I couldn't escape. Not on my own at least." He smiled at Gina as he thought of what would have happened if she hadn't shown up. "By the way, thank you for getting me out of that hell."

"Don't thank me. It was your father who paved the way. He put up the money. I just did the fetching," she said irritably, brushing off his thanks as a warm feeling seeped through her.

"You did a great job, and I'm very grateful. I'd just like to know why you accepted the assignment. Granted, I'm grateful that you were the one they chose—you're the best. But given your feelings toward me, I find it a little strange you would risk your life to save mine.'' Jess's piercing gray eyes were watching every emotion that flitted across Gina's beautiful face. She didn't let much show, but some things were impossible to keep inside—like pain and sorrow.

Jess felt his heart sink at Gina's stricken look. He was sure that if he could see her downcast eyes, he would read in them a repetition of the accusations she had once hurled at him.

"There isn't anything to explain. Virgil asked me to help your father, and I agreed. So just let it drop, okay?"

Without looking at Jess, Gina turned away to set a small coffeepot on the burner while she dished their lunch of dehydrated beef stew into tin bowls. Silently she handed the meal to Jess. She didn't feel up to discussing her reasons for taking the mission right now, and she hoped he would take the hint and let the subject drop.

She was surprised when she didn't feel the sudden stab of pain that usually accompanied thoughts of Greg. Worse was the realization that she'd ceased to associate Jess with Greg's death. That thought made her feel disloyal to her dead husband. All she felt when she thought of him now was regret. Didn't she owe him more than that?

She settled against the wall of the cave, her lunch balanced on her lap, and darted a quick glance in Jess's direction. When she found him still intently watching her, she made a quick grab for the bowl of stew, as it threatened to slip onto the dirt floor. Gina lowered her eyes to her rapidly cooling lunch. She no longer had an appetite, but she made a big production of preparing to eat. One quick glance told her she hadn't fooled Jess for a moment, and she tensed as she waited for him to continue with his questions.

She didn't have long to wait. He set his uneaten lunch on the ground, drew his long legs up and balanced his forearms across his knees. He never once took his eyes off her.

"I'm waiting for a real answer, Gina,
etly.

He recalled her mentioning that Virgil had tempt
with something she couldn't pass up. He disregarde
money without a second thought. Gina wasn't merce-
nary; he would stake his life on that. So it had to be something personal. The only thing personal that drove Gina
was the answers surrounding Greg's death. Answers Virgil knew Jess had.

"Virgil said you had the answers to the questions I've
been hounding him with for the past two years," Gina
softly answered. "Why no one will tell me what happened
with Greg."

Finding out he'd guessed right didn't make Jess feel the
least bit superior. He could—if he'd wanted to—have given
Gina the answers she sought anytime in the past two
years—at least, the answers that were in his report. But
those were "facts." The facts that said Greg had been a
traitor selling confiscated arms to gunrunners. Jess certainly didn't want to pass that information on to Gina. He
himself had found the facts impossible to believe. Even the
letter Greg had sent before he was killed hadn't completely convinced Jess that Greg had done everything he'd
been accused of.

Laying out all the information that had been gathered
against Greg would prove he hadn't been involved in
Greg's death. But taking into consideration what that information might do to Gina had stopped him two years
ago—as it stopped him now.

Greg had been Gina's entire life, outside of her job, and
he didn't know what she would do if she found out Greg
had been branded a traitor by the Agency, to which he'd
devoted ten years of his life. Jess didn't want to be the one
to destroy what memories she had left.

"Are you sure you're ready to hear the truth? You refused to listen two years ago, when I tried to explain." Jess

held his breath. If she said no, it would mean she was still in love with Greg. And he didn't want to hear that. If she said yes, he was in danger of destroying any chance he might have with her by telling her about Greg's affair with Rita, and the events that led to the charge of treason on his record.

Either way, he stood to lose her before he even started winning her. And winning her love was becoming more important each day he spent with her.

Chapter 4

Did she want the truth? If Jess had asked her that question a year ago, she would have jumped at the chance. Just two weeks ago, she'd let Virgil Carpenter bribe her into rescuing Jess with the promise of answers to the questions that had plagued her for the past two years.

Would she be able to let the past rest when she knew all the details? Perhaps the question she should ask herself was whether she wanted to hear Jess declare his love for Rita. Gina didn't understand a love that powerful. Thinking about Jess's love for Rita made her heart ache with envy. What would it be like to be loved that fiercely?

Sighing, Gina rubbed her throbbing temples as she admitted to herself that it was past time to get on with her life. The truth was the only way she was going to get Jess out of her mind. After two years of blaming him for her loss, she needed some peace. And the only way for her to gain that peace was to hear all the facts, then put the past behind her. But did she have to hear them right now, when she was feeling so exposed and unsure?

"I'm not certain what I want anymore," she finally answered.

Running her slender fingers through her wet curls, she searched for a reason she could use to postpone hearing a confession from Jess. When nothing came to mind, she admitted defeat and slowly plunged forward.

"After I got over the shock of Greg's death, I had a burning need to know all the facts." She looked out at the pouring rain, her lunch forgotten where it sat on the cave floor, along with Jess's. "I often wondered why Greg left that day, when Virgil hadn't contacted him. He'd been moody and unresponsive for days—not at all like himself. Then he up and left without saying anything. I knew you must have gotten into trouble again and Greg was helping you out of a jam." Gina shot Jess an accusing glance. "Just like he'd done a dozen times before. That's why I didn't want to listen when you came to the house," she whispered as she resumed watching the steadily falling rain.

"By placing all the blame on you, I didn't have to accept any of the responsibility. I'd known for a while that something was wrong between us, but I didn't want to admit it . . . even to myself." Gina realized her voice was devoid of expression, and she'd forgotten Jess's presence as she continued delving into her past.

"We married for the wrong reasons. I think Greg viewed me as more of a prize than a wife, at the beginning, but once we were married that changed. The blame wasn't all his. I was just as guilty. I used him to fill the void in my life. My father had been dead for less than a year, and I was feeling lost and alone. I'd been with the Agency for three months and was still in training when I first met Greg. He was so bright and dynamic. I'd never met anyone like him before. He swept in like the promise of spring after a hard winter. I thought he was everything that had been missing in my life."

Gina heaved a small sigh, feeling again the force that had surrounded Greg—before reality set in. "But that was all it was, a promise. One that never materialized." It had taken only a few short months for her to realize that the man she'd believed Greg to be was a figment of her dreams.

"We didn't have much of a marriage. All the times he said he had to be away...I knew that wasn't because of his job. After the passion had worn off, he just found life with me boring. After a while, a pattern evolved where he only returned when he had no place to go. We shared a house, no more.

"It wasn't until the Sangers built their home down the road that I started examining our relationship. After seeing their marriage, I started thinking there should be more to mine. Julie Sanger had it all, a loving husband who came home every night and a sweet little girl. That's when I began to want a family of my own." Gina paused, drawing a deep breath. "But by that time it was too late. Greg was gone."

She thought about all the wasted years of her marriage—wasted even though neither of them had seemed unhappy with the arrangement. In a way, the marriage had filled a need for both of them, until she had started to want something more.

She didn't blame Greg for his lack of interest in her. She wasn't a person who inspired lasting love in anyone. Even her father had found it difficult to spend time with her until his military career ended and he had no place else to go. And even then, he'd never loved her.

She realized she'd focused all her energies on blaming Jess for her loss. Passing the blame had been easier than admitting to herself that she had been a failure. Now she knew she had to accept her part in her failed marriage... and in Greg's death.

Gina's head snapped up when Jess covered her clenched hands with his. The warmth of his fingers was in direct contrast to his icy scrutiny.

Blinking her eyes as she chased away the visions of the past, she was startled to find Jess hunched down in front of her. His cold gray eyes bored into hers as if he were a hawk inspecting its kill. She realized that he'd said something but she hadn't caught it.

"What did you say?" she managed to ask as she attempted to pull her hands from his tight grasp.

"Why the hell did you stay with him?" Jess's growl ricocheted off the stone walls as he released her hands and resumed his position on the dirt floor. "Why didn't you divorce him?"

She stared at Jess in wide-eyed amazement. She couldn't believe the resentment in his voice—let alone his question.

"I never thought to," she answered absentmindedly, as she tried to comprehend the motive behind Jess's question. Greg had been his best friend. If he was going to choose sides, it stood to reason he would stand by Greg, not his wife. "Why do you ask?"

"It's not important." Jess waved her question away. "You never answered my first question. Are you ready to hear the truth?"

Still watching Jess with troubled eyes, Gina had no problem answering the question to herself. Telling Jess was another thing altogether.

Her answer was yes. It was time to hear the truth, and put the past behind her. She hoped she could find the courage to accept her part in her failed marriage and move on. Feeling sorry for herself wasn't going to change the past. She had plenty to be grateful for, a fulfilling job she liked and a beautiful home. She led a full life, even if it wasn't the life she wanted. She needed to start looking to the future, not the past.

Gina looked toward Jess. "The truth, as you put it, won't change the fact that I owe you an apology. I shouldn't have blamed you. I should have realized right from the start that Greg knew the danger he would be getting into when he chose to go."

Jess felt a deep disappointment when Gina did no more than return her attention to the falling rain. Her answer left too many things unsaid, too many of his questions unanswered. Especially the question uppermost in his thoughts: What were her feelings for Greg?

By her own admission, she hadn't loved her husband as a woman should. He remembered all too well the sad-eyed girl she had been when he first met her. He had just returned from a long mission and had been shocked to learn that Greg had married. Less than two months later, Greg had already been interested in Rita. An interest that soon became more than simple flirtation.

Gina's admission gave him hope, but he didn't want to jump the gun without knowing what he was getting into. Taking the coward's way out went against his ethics, adding to his feelings of guilt. But once he started telling the truth he would have to reveal everything. And he didn't think she was ready to accept him, or his feelings, just yet.

"Is that what you believe, or what you want to believe?" Jess asked cynically, taking his sour mood out on her. Maybe the question would annoy Gina enough to take that damned bruised look from her face.

Had he been doing her an injustice by keeping Greg's true character from her? Greg had been his best friend for years. He might have had a problem being loyal to one woman, but he'd been a good friend. He'd also been a good partner. They'd covered each other's backs more than once. He knew he wasn't aiding his cause by letting her believe that Greg had been rescuing him, but it went against his conscience to paint Greg as all bad.

Gina ignored the tone of Jess's question as she raised her head to find smoky gray eyes watching her intently. They narrowed as she studied him, as if he were preparing for a blow. "I just feel there should be a plausible reason why everyone doesn't want to talk about that night. It's like a conspiracy, with everything pointing back to you. That was why I agreed to get you out. To see if you could put the past to rest. But the answers don't seem important right now."

Jess's scornful look goaded her into striking out. "I have one question, though," she stated, her voice filled with reproach. "Was Rita worth risking your life for, not to mention getting Greg killed? Did you love her that much?"

Hearing the questions echo around the cave, Gina was appalled at her boldness. That wasn't what she'd come all the way to Central America to learn. She was wandering into an area where she had no business. What appalled her even more was her burning need to hear his answers. The realization left her reeling.

For some reason, the thought of Jess loving Rita enough to risk everything for her was disturbing. She'd known about Jess's numerous flings. Hadn't Greg delighted in telling her of his escapades often enough? According to Greg, Jess never stayed with one woman long enough to form a close attachment. Evidently Rita Tanner had been the exception.

Gina shot Jess a quick look through the curtain of her thick lashes and found his eyes trained on her. At least he didn't look furious, she thought as she quickly lowered her own eyes. Now that she thought about it, she hadn't heard anything about Jess's women for the past couple of years. Was he still pining for Rita?

Jess's heart jumped against his ribs, as if it were trying to escape the confines of his chest. The implications of Gina's question were hard to believe. She still thought he and Rita Tanner had been involved. He couldn't believe no one had set her straight. Either she never listened to gossip or everyone had been careful to spare her feelings. He'd known she was well liked, but until now he hadn't realized just how well.

Why had she asked the question? Jess needed to see her face. With her head bowed, all he could see was a mass of damp curls. He wanted to see her eyes, to be able to judge what she was thinking.

Jess reached out to raise Gina's face. His hand froze in midair, halfway to its destination, when he realized he was back where he'd begun. Not only did Gina know nothing about the charges that had been brought against her husband, she also didn't know that he'd been having an affair with Rita. What would learning the truth do to her?

Gina chanced another quick look through her lashes, only to encounter an agonized look on Jess's face. Did he still love Rita so much that even now it was painful for him to talk about her? She'd met Rita Tanner only once at the Agency. She was a beautiful woman, so Gina understood if he were still in love with her.

Not wanting to hear the answers anymore, she grabbed their uneaten lunch and turned away. She made a big show of cleaning up while keeping her back to Jess. It wasn't like her to intrude. She didn't know what had prompted the questions in the first place. Drawing a deep, steadying breath, she realized she owed him another apology. If she wasn't careful, she would be making a habit of apologizing to him.

Her apology was forgotten, as the rain stopped as suddenly as it had begun, filling the small cave with a tense silence.

Even the birds and monkeys that had been so noisy earlier were quiet. The silence held both Jess and Gina spellbound long enough for the tense moment to pass.

Gina took advantage of the distraction to quickly change the subject. "Do you think you're strong enough for a short walk this afternoon?"

She needed to get out of the confines of the small cave. Before this mission was over, she was going to have developed a good case of claustrophobia. Anyway, she wasn't ready to face Jess's declarations of love for Rita. She also needed space to analyze her strange reaction. Her feelings came too close to jealousy for comfort.

Jess watched Gina's unusually stiff movements as she busily put the lunch things away before stirring instant coffee into the water heating on the small burner. He couldn't see her face, but the look he'd seen in her eyes before she turned away gave him plenty to think about. The most important question that came to mind had to do with Gina's reasons for asking about Rita Tanner. The thought gave him hope and brightened his mood.

Gina's eyes were drawn to Jess as she handed him one of the tin cups of coffee. His eyes trapped hers as he accepted the coffee. Time hung suspended until the need to draw a breath forced Gina to turn away.

Taking her cup of coffee, she settled in the opening of the cave. As she sipped the hot brew, she analyzed the tender look she'd seen on Jess's face. Her mind whirled as she unconsciously rubbed her tingling fingers, still warm from Jess's touch.

What had he been thinking? she wondered. Had she given away more of her feelings than she was prepared to share? What she needed was some time to get her thoughts in order again. She had understood her emotions before she left home, but ever since her first glimpse of Jess, standing so proud and alone in that dark cell, she didn't recognize herself anymore.

Jess watched as Gina sat staring out into the jungle as if the activities going on outside held her complete interest. He smiled to himself as he recalled the confusion that had filled her big golden eyes moments before. Confusion was better than her hatred.

Jess lightly ran his fingers over a soft curl on Gina's cheek, startling her. Apparently she hadn't heard him sit down next to her. The cave entrance was too small for her to put any distance between them, but as she turned her head she managed to put a few inches between them. Jess let his hand drop to his side. Taking in her defensive look, he accepted her change of topic and answered her question.

''Getting out in the sun sounds great.''

Judging by the look on Gina's pale face, he knew he'd made the right decision in changing the subject. Clearing up a two-year-old misunderstanding was going to take more than a few words. He also knew that convincing Gina to trust him wasn't going to be easy.

Before she was going to even listen to him, she had to learn to trust him. He was going to have to accomplish that feat in the few days before they reached the sea. He hoped a week was going to be enough time. One thing he was sure about—she wasn't going to freely grant him any more time alone with her once they were home.

An unspoken truce made their short walk enjoyable. They stopped at the river first, where Jess gratefully peeled off his shirt and, using the bar of soap Gina handed him, lathered his head and chest while Gina stood guard. Cupping his hands, he splashed water over his hair, washing away the dirt that had gathered in the thick strands.

Feeling cleaner than he had in weeks, he picked up the gun Gina had given him before they left the cave and followed her along the secluded trails she'd discovered around the area. The short walk along the stream gave Jess his first taste of what the trip ahead would be like.

The route was easy, but before they'd gone half a mile his shirt was soaked with sweat, and his rifle felt like a lead weight. He wasn't going to complain. Even with the overpowering humidity, he enjoyed the walk. The sunshine and fresh air were worth the sweat and the strained muscles.

When their walk was over and Gina turned toward the cave, Jess followed on lagging feet. He didn't relish returning to the small, dark refuge, but he was more than ready for a rest.

"God, I'm beat," Jess groaned as he leaned his rifle against the wall and dropped down to sit on the cave floor. Resting his tired body against the wall next to the rifle, he leaned his head back. His legs felt like rubber bands, and his shirt was soaked with sweat, but he couldn't suppress a smile. It felt good to be using his muscles again.

Gina poured a cup of purified water for Jess. As she handed him the cup, she carefully examined his flushed face for any signs of a returning fever. Satisfied that he was just hot and tired, she turned her gaze to his clean hair.

Thick black strands fell over his forehead, catching her attention. She longed to thread her fingers through the unruly swath to test its texture now that it was no longer caked with dirt. As she watched him down the cup of water in one long swallow, she recalled the picture he'd presented as he bent over the shallow stream, his broad back bared to the sun's rays as he splashed water over his upper body. Her mouth had gone dry as her eyes followed the tracks of water that ran down his back and disappeared into the waistband of his pants.

Stricken by her train of thought, she quickly turned her attention to the birds she could see flitting through the trees. In another minute she was going to be drooling over Jess like some simpleminded female at a male strip club.

Unaware of the turmoil plaguing Gina, Jess finished the water and set the cup aside. He gratefully rolled his tired body onto his sleeping bag and fell asleep almost instantly.

The next couple of days passed routinely. When they weren't walking through the jungle to build his strength, he was either sleeping, eating or getting his daily shot. Gina didn't tend his cuts anymore. Since the morning he'd shot off his mouth, she'd left that task to him. A wise decision on her part. He liked the feel of her soft hands on him when she administered the shot far too much for her to continue attending to his battered body. As it was, just the thought of her touching him was enough to fire his blood.

With Jess's strength rapidly returning, the tension between them mounted. The only letup came when they left the cramped cave for a short trip to the stream or when Gina made her daily check of the area. The atmosphere between them was growing more intense each day. The unspoken subjects of Greg and Rita hung between them like a ghost, crowding the small cave.

Jess's thoughts, constantly centered around Gina, were turning more erotic by the hour. Whether she was in the cave, where he could watch her as she did the few small chores that kept their living area habitable, or in the jungle on one of their walks, where he watched her shapely hips sway before him—leading him along like the proverbial carrot dangling on a stick—she was continually on his mind. If they didn't get out of the cave soon, he was going to go mad.

Her essence lingered in the humid air, surrounding him like a cloud. Her unmistakable scent filled the cave until he couldn't sleep at night from aching to hold her.

His fingers burned, even days after the all-too-brief contact with her velvet skin and silky hair. The brief touch hadn't been nearly enough. He wanted to explore all of her softness.

Without any more beauty aids than a hairbrush, Gina was still the most beautiful woman he'd ever known. And she was slowly driving him out of his mind. Remaining civilized around her was becoming impossible.

Gina's heart pounded each time she looked in Jess's direction. She could feel his smoldering eyes on her almost like a physical touch, watching her every move.

For the past three days she'd felt him watching her, with hooded eyes like a big cat waiting to pounce. She knew what she would see if she dared look into those seductive gray eyes . . . passion, hot and dangerous.

It wasn't that Gina had never seen passion in a man's eyes before. It was her response to this man's desire that frightened her. Her heart thudded against her ribs, making breathing almost painful, and her legs felt like butter melting in the hot sun.

Gina wasn't sophisticated enough to hide her reaction, and she knew Jess read her like a book. She had no experience in the modern games of love that men and women played. All she could do was pray that he would rein in the desire she could see burning in his eyes whenever she looked in his direction. She didn't know whether she would be able to refuse him if he lost control.

Gina glanced at Jess, her eyes widening as she saw the fire flare in the depths of his eyes. She looked away nervously as she racked her brain for a topic that would direct Jess's thoughts away from her. In desperation, she blurted out a question that had been hounding her.

"With all your family's money, why did you join the Agency?"

Gina could feel her cheeks heat at her rudeness. Her tongue was making a habit of speaking without her brain's consent. His career choice wasn't any of her business, no matter how much money his family had, and judging by the look on his face, he didn't appreciate her probing. Her question did divert his attention, though. He was no longer looking at her as if he could eat her for lunch, instead of their rations.

Jess silently agreed that talking would be safer than spending his time just watching Gina. Anything that might help to take his mind off the constant ache throbbing through his body was welcome. Even though he understood her tactics, he would have preferred it if she'd chosen a different subject. His past wasn't a topic that was open for discussion.

His smoky eyes flashed a firm but gentle warning. He might not be proud of his reasons for joining the Agency, but he didn't need Gina, or anyone, pointing out his faults. He'd had plenty of time to analyze his life during the past few weeks. He would be the first to admit that changes were in order. Changes *he* would decide on.

The daily rainstorm droned on, keeping them confined inside. Jess watched Gina as her nervousness grew the longer they sat in silence. He hid a wicked smile, knowing he was the cause of her fidgeting. He didn't feel the least bit guilty about making her nervous, though. He'd been fighting a burning ache for days, which her nearness incited. Each day it was becoming more difficult for him to keep his hands off her.

Each night he dreamed of making love to her in a thousand different ways. Each morning he would wake aching for her, that ache was becoming a constant companion. Just watching her simple, graceful movements around their camp only fed his frustrations.

He knew Gina held a position with the Agency that was an unusual one for a female. Her reasons for joining a male-dominated profession would prove to be intriguing, and possibly diverting.

His eyes narrowed. "Why did you?" he asked, returning her question.

Gina gave a start when Jess's voice turned dangerously soft. She wasn't surprised that her rude question upset him. His allowing his anger to show was unexpected, though. The only times he'd been sharp with her had been when he first discovered who'd rescued him—and again when he'd discovered she had undressed him after he passed out.

She quickly diverted her thoughts from that first day in the cave. The last thing she wanted to think about was his naked body. She didn't want him remembering the incident, either. To deflect his anger, she decided to ignore both his tone of voice and the fact that he had answered her question with one of his own.

"It's no secret," she quietly stated as she shrugged. "I had a skill, and Special Services was the only place where I could put it to good use."

Jess's brows shot up in surprise at her quick answer. He'd expected her to ignore his question as he'd ignored hers. But since she had answered, he wanted to hear more than her too-short response had told him.

"Where did you get this unusual skill?"

He was intrigued enough to forget his irritation at her intrusion into his personal life. And his thoughts of making love to her were—for the moment—sidetracked as he waited for her answer.

Gina shot Jess a withering glance. He blithely responded by arching one dark brow inquiringly as he waited. Turning away from his shrewd gaze, she bit her lip to stifle a grin. Talk about double standards... She was limited as to the questions she could ask, while no topic was taboo for him.

"Do you mean unusual because I'm a woman?"

Jess was startled by her question. He knew delaying tactics when he saw them.

"No, I don't mean because you're a woman." He mimicked her tone, letting her know what he thought of her question. "It's just not training most women receive so young."

Gina hesitated. The years she'd spent with her father in the wilds of the Cascade Mountains weren't something she readily discussed with anyone. Even Greg hadn't known of the loneliness she had suffered all those years. Her best course of action was to stick with her prime rule: Keep the answer simple and to the point.

"My father was a Green Beret. He taught me survival."

Jess's dark frown let her know he was far from satisfied with her continually brief answers. He could see by the shadows that clouded her eyes when she mentioned her father that there was more to her training than she was letting on. The only concern he had now was whether he had the right to intrude on her privacy to get the answers he wanted.

Gina watched as Jess leisurely stretched his long legs and grinned at her. The easy shrug of his shoulders—as if he were saying, "What the hell?"—had her bristling. She wasn't going to feed his curiosity by elaborating on her answer, even if his grin *could* melt the North Pole in winter.

"Is survival training what fathers are teaching their daughters nowadays?"

When she refused to answer his mocking question, his grin turned to a frown. He'd hidden his eagerness to know everything he could discover about her behind the sarcastic question, and he wasn't pleased with the silence he received.

"I'm sorry. I just wondered why your father would give you such unusual training," Jess prompted seriously, all traces of humor replaced by a determined expression.

Gina lowered her eyes before Jess's steady gaze. His resolute look told her without doubt that he would wait the rest of the day for her to explain. But delving into her past was something she customarily avoided. And she didn't want to begin with someone who couldn't possibly understand.

Impatiently Gina pulled her drifting thoughts together as she looked out at the pouring rain. When she transferred her gaze to Jess, she could see the gleam of interest in his eyes. Maybe he was the one person who could understand the loneliness of her téen years, after all. He'd had a sample of loneliness himself.

She turned her attention back to the desolate weather. She wouldn't be able to look into those piercing gray eyes while she exposed a time in her life that had created a void that could never be filled.

"There isn't much to tell," she said hesitantly, as the memories she had avoided for years floated through her mind. "My father was a career soldier. After my mother died, he devoted his life to his career, leaving me in the care of his elderly aunt until I was twelve. Then he lost his left arm in Viet Nam and was discharged.

"Losing his commission almost destroyed him. When he finally came to get me, he was withdrawn and bitter. We moved to a cabin high in the Cascade Mountains, where he taught me the skills he'd spent his life teaching the recruits under his command. I was an apt pupil, and the training gave him a reason for living."

Her answer hadn't been as brief as she had planned, but it would have to do. She wasn't ready to share any more of herself with Jess right now. Maybe she never would be.

Her to-the-point statement was accompanied by a look that punctuated the terse words—plainly stating that she wasn't going to elaborate further.

Her misery was so acute that Jess could almost feel it across the small space that separated them. The sorrow in Gina's beautiful golden eyes was unmistakable. Telling the story had upset her. His mind was burning with more questions, but he wouldn't badger her any more for now.

The dark shadowed sadness was the same look that had been there years ago, when he'd first met her. He was still puzzled as to the cause, and he was determined to solve the puzzle . . . soon.

Chapter 5

It was their last day in the cave. Jess was fit enough to make the hike, so they would leave in the morning for the coast. But today they would take a trial run to test his strength, like a dress rehearsal before the opening night of a play. The path Gina chose was dense and required that she hack their way through the vines and thick foliage with a machete.

Jess carried his pack and the gun he kept with him whenever they were away from the safety of the cave. During their previous outings, they'd never run across any signs that there were other humans in the jungle, but Gina never let down her guard.

Following Gina, Jess listened to her husky voice with half an ear as she told him about the dangers in the jungle. Survival was her area of expertise, and he wasn't so macho that he had to be the leader just because he was a man. She held the key to their safe escape from the jungle, and he was well aware that their lives depended on her knowledge.

Besides, with her in charge, Jess was free to walk behind her and enjoy the scenery before him. The graceful swing of her hips as she cleared their trail filled his line of vision and held his interest captive. Her clothes certainly weren't the attention-getter. They hid more than they displayed. It was what the masculine attire covered that captivated him. Just guessing what was under the coarse shirt and heavy pants kept his imagination working overtime as she hacked away at the thick vines crossing the trail. He watched her shirt pull tight, outlining her slim waist and curving hips, with each swing of the machete.

Jess hadn't seen Gina dressed in anything other than khakis for years. And except for the quick glance he'd had of her as she'd changed her wet shirt, he had no real idea of the figure hidden under her fatigues. Watching her in the shapeless garb, he let his imagination run wild. Without question, she would surpass his dreams when the time was right. And he had no doubt he would be gaining first-hand knowledge of her shapely body in the near future. But for now, he would settle for using his imagination, even though he knew he would be spending another uncomfortable night as erotic thoughts of Gina plagued him in his dreams.

The response of muscles that had gone soft over the past weeks encouraged him as he flexed his shoulders to feel their stinging response. The long walk was going to stretch his muscles to their limits. He smiled, welcoming the exertion.

The humidity was exceptionally high and rapidly drained his strength, but he wasn't about to complain. Wiping his sweaty face on the sleeve of his shirt, Jess searched the sky through the overhead canopy of trees for a sign of the daily rainstorm.

They were headed away from the cave, and the walk back would be long and hot, but he was in no hurry to return to its tension-filled confines. The pack he carried contained a simple lunch, and judging by the sounds his stomach was emitting, lunch couldn't come too soon to suit him.

As if reading his thoughts, Gina stopped to wait for Jess to catch up. Turning, she caught her breath at the sight he made. His shirt, soaked with sweat, clung to his broad shoulders. He had unfastened the buttons to his waist, baring a wide expanse of sweat-covered muscular chest matted with crisp dark hair that she remembered all too well. Just watching his long-legged stride cover the distance between them quickened her pulse.

For the past hour, Gina's mind had been focused on the trail and the surrounding area. Listening to the jungle for any unusual sounds took her full concentration. She'd been able to forget, for a short time, Jess's stirring virility. Now her hand pressed against her stomach as the sudden reminder of his rugged masculinity set butterflies loose inside.

All it took was a glimpse of his raw masculinity and she was caught in his web all over again. One sign from Jess and she would be joining the ranks of the women in his life—and his bed.

"Ready for some lunch?" she asked past the tightness in her throat as he joined her on the trail.

"Starved. I could also use a breather. I have a way to go before I'm back in condition," he said as he wiped the sweat from his forehead with the tail of his shirt.

Gina frowned as she thought about Jess's candid response.

His honesty was so out of character for the man she'd thought she knew. He was constantly behaving in ways that were contrary to everything she'd heard about him from Greg.

Where was the man Greg had complained about for years? The man who put his own comfort above others'? Jess never hesitated to say if he was tired and needed to rest, but he didn't expect her to cater to him. His behavior was so unlike the picture she'd formed of him that he constantly kept her off balance.

The men she worked with at the Agency were always eager to demonstrate how tough they were. But Jess far surpassed them without the least bit of effort, or egotism, on his part. He didn't feel the need to constantly prove his virility in actions or by bragging.

Setting aside her confusing thoughts, Gina led him to a clearing along the stream, where the water backed up behind a fallen tree to form a clear pool. In the shaft of sunlight that reached the water through the treetops, the glen looked like a little bit of Eden.

Jess gazed longingly at the clear water. It was too perfect. A serpent had to be hiding in this paradise somewhere.

"Is this a mirage, or is it real?" he asked, letting his gaze sweep the small glen before it came to rest on Gina's smiling face.

"It's perfectly real. I discovered this place the first day I arrived in the jungle." Gina's smile turned impish. "Although I took a shorter route to get here."

Seeing Jess's gathering frown, she rushed on. "As far as I've been able to tell, no one else has been here. We should be safe while we have lunch."

Gina's eyes sparkled with a mischievous light that held Jess spellbound. Her face was alive with excitement. He could see that she was bursting to tell him what further surprises she had in store for him. He was just as determined to wait and enjoy the changes in her before he gave in and asked her to explain.

The moment stretched as the sparkle in Gina's golden eyes intensified, capturing Jess. The beautiful glen paled beside her transformation. He'd always thought she was beautiful, but with her eyes lit with humor and excitement she was more breathtaking than ever. A shaft of sunlight turned her thick curls into a red-gold halo around her face, and her smooth skin bloomed with an inner radiance.

He could tell that she was waiting for him to ask why she had brought him to the glen. And he would do just that—but not yet. He wanted to draw out the moment. To enjoy her transformation to the fullest.

Jess felt the intensity of the familiar pull of desire that had been his constant companion ever since he'd awakened to find her sleeping beside him. He could feel the driving need being tempered by softer feelings as he watched Gina's delight at something so simple as giving him a surprise.

He didn't intend to delve into those softer feelings until they were out of danger and safely back home. If he was smart, he would keep his mind on getting out of the mess they were in instead of dreaming about making love to Gina. When the truth about Greg came to light, there was every possibility that Gina wouldn't want to see him again. Not that he was going to let that possibility deter him.

Jess finally relented. "All right, I give up. What surprises have you got up your sleeve that have you looking so proud of yourself?"

Just as he'd suspected, Gina's eyes brightened even more, and her smug look turned into the first genuine smile he'd seen since she removed her ski mask. It far outshone the midday sun. The lesson he'd learned from Serena which had initiated his steadfast rule about never entrusting his heart to a woman again was the farthest thought from his mind.

Unconsciously he lifted one hand and slipped his fingers around Gina's neck. Closing the distance between them, he joined her in the shaft of sun spiraling down through the trees that bathed her in its golden glow.

Gina filled Jess's thoughts as he pulled her closer—so close he could feel the rapid beating of her heart. He watched as her pupils dilated until all he could see was a bright golden ring. Jess felt himself sinking into their depths without the least thought to self-preservation.

Gina's humor fled as she watched in fascination as Jess drew near, his smoky eyes smoldering as they captured hers. Her entire being was filled with anticipation as she nervously moistened her dry lips, unintentionally drawing Jess's hot gaze to their moist fullness.

She tingled as she heard Jess groan her name deep in his throat seconds before his lips touched hers. Her pounding heart beat an erratic rhythm as he slowly brushed his mouth across her soft lips, capturing the moistness her tongue had left behind.

When she didn't protest the kiss, Jess gathered her closer, his arms circling her trembling body. He slid one large hand down her back until it came to rest on her rounded bottom. Lifting her, he pressed her hips tightly against the juncture of his thighs, bringing forth a pleasure-pain that was intense.

Holding her in his strong arms, Jess intensified the kiss until she parted her lips, letting his tongue explore the sweet recesses of her mouth.

Gina's hands were trapped between their bodies. Her palms tingled where they pressed against Jess's warm flesh. She was aware of the strength and warmth of his bare chest as her heartbeat throbbed in her ears. Slowly she traced his firm muscles and the soft swirls of hair that lightly coated his chest as his tongue slid past her parted lips, stealing her breath. Her shocking response to his kiss didn't deter her, as she slid her hands over his shoulders and threaded her fingers through his thick hair, holding him tight.

The kiss was endless. He couldn't get enough of her sweetness as he ravaged her soft mouth. He could feel her straining to get closer, even as he tightened his embrace, meshing their bodies. He longed to feel her silky soft skin against his burning body without the barrier of clothes separating them.

With that thought in mind, Jess eased his hand between their bodies to gently cup her full breast. His heart stopped as he felt the tight bud straining for release through the coarse material.

Quickly unbuttoning Gina's shirt, Jess pushed it aside. All that separated him from his goal, as his hand enclosed the soft mound again, was the thin cotton top.

Jess captured Gina's soft moan inside his mouth as his thumb brushed the throbbing peak back and forth, causing her to arch her back, filling his hot palm with her riches.

Blood pounded in Gina's brain, and her knees threatened to give out. If Jess hadn't been holding her so tightly, she would have melted at his feet when his hand closed around her straining breast. She was bombarded with sensations she'd never experienced before. The intensity of her feelings frightened her, but not enough for her to end the magic yet.

Despite the sunlight, uncontrollable shivers racked Gina's body as she felt her shirt slide down her unresisting arms and land at her feet. She knew she should put a stop to this madness, but her body reveled in the touch of Jess's hands as he traced a trail from her waist to her straining breasts as he raised her thin cotton top.

Grasping Jess's strong shoulders as the only anchor in a rapidly spinning world, Gina was pleased to feel his warm skin under her fingers instead of the coarse shirt. Throwing her head back, she worked her fingers against the firm muscles as Jess caressed her bare breasts. All thoughts of ending the barrage of sensations that were rioting through her body faded into the sensual mist that filled her mind.

Jess looked down at Gina's flushed face and felt his heart stop at the picture she presented with her kiss-swollen lips and the throbbing pulse at the base of her throat. He slowly eased her down onto the moss-covered bank. Dancing sunspots dotted her full breasts where they lay exposed to his hungry gaze. There was an added shimmer to her golden eyes, like a light in a dark night, that invited him to take her higher. Just the thought of how high they could soar together overwhelmed him.

Easing his tense body onto the ground beside Gina, Jess ran his fingers down her flushed cheek until she raised her passion-filled eyes. Slowly he lowered his head until his lips brushed hers, as softly as the dew kissing a rose. Her instant response was all the encouragement he needed to deepen the kiss with an intensity that rocked him.

The burning hunger of his kiss had Gina straining for more, until she was astounded at her own eager response to the touch of his lips. He was driving her crazy. She pulled him close, drinking in his musky scent.

She *wanted* him. She'd never *wanted* before. It was that awareness that brought her to her senses. The magnitude of her feelings was overpowering. Too much. Too fast.

Jess felt Gina tense in his arms as she slowly untangled her fingers from his hair. His arms tightened around her, pulling her closer. For a moment, he wanted to protest her withdrawal. He hadn't had nearly enough, but he wasn't about to force her, either.

He loosened his hold until their lips parted, and he gently ran tender kisses over her flushed face, waiting for her to open her eyes.

When she did, the need to pull her back into his arms was so overpowering his muscles shook. Her eyes were the color of dark honey, and filled with the passion he had long dreamed of seeing in their golden depths.

She wanted him. She had been as lost in their kiss as he had been. The knowledge made his heart pound anew.

Gina saw the smoldering fire reignite in Jess's dark eyes, and quickly rolled out of his reach. She willed her trembling legs to support her as she rose to her feet, pulling her cotton top down with trembling fingers. She searched his face for signs of anger and was surprised when she could detect only tenderness in his watchful eyes.

She felt cold and alone without the warmth of his strong arms, and for one long second she thought about stepping back into the haven of his embrace. To prevent any further foolish action, she grabbed her shirt and focused her mind on the reason they were standing in the sun-dappled glen.

"Bath," she managed to whisper past the tightness in her throat as she hastily rebuttoned her shirt.

When Jess's eyes didn't waver from her flushed face, Gina cleared her throat to try again, thinking he hadn't heard her. "A bath," she managed to say, a little louder this time.

Shaking his head, Jess drew his hungry gaze from Gina's kiss-swollen lips. "What were you saying about a bath?" he murmured.

Gina could feel her cheeks heat even more, and without conscious thought she ran her tongue over her tender lips—tasting Jess. And judging by the fire she could see flare anew in his eyes, he knew it.

"I...uh...thought..." Gina stopped to clear her throat again before rushing on. "I thought you might like to have a real bath. All you've been able to do is splash around in the stream. This pool is deeper, and the water should be warm enough for you to enjoy," she was babbling. Jess's intense regard was making her nervous.

Jess let his eyes linger on her flushed face and pouty lips a moment longer, until what she was saying sank in; then he turned his attention to the clear pool.

"A bath was one of the fantasies I had the most while I was locked in that filthy hole in the ground. That, and a good steak." Jess grinned when he heard Gina release a deep breath. He'd picked up on her attempt to redirect his thoughts. Anyway, a bath sounded damn good.

Gina backed up a couple of steps, putting a safe distance between them. "Well, I can't get you the steak. You'll have to settle for cheese and crackers. But I *can* provide you with a bath. And you can stay in as long as you like."

Jess watched as she slowly retreated. He would let her have her space, for now.

Wasting no time, Jess dropped down onto a rock beside his discarded pack and pulled off his boots and socks. As soon as his shoes were off, he reached for the button on his pants, but then he remembered that Gina was standing behind him. Turning, he was surprised to find she was no longer there but had disappeared into the surrounding foliage.

Not that he was modest. He just didn't want to further embarrass her. He quickly removed the rest of his clothes and, without hesitation, dived into the shallow pool.

Crossing the pond underwater, Jess resurfaced on the far side wiping water from his face as he stood in the shallow pool. The pond was small. He could cross it in a couple of strokes, but it was cool to his hot skin. Dunking his head underwater, he ran his fingers through the long strands before snapping his head up, sending water flying in all directions.

Throwing back his head, Jess let out a hearty laugh. He hadn't felt this good in months. All he needed was some soap and he would feel almost human again.

The thought had no sooner slipped into his mind than he felt a splash in the water near his right hip. He looked up to see Gina at the edge of the pond, holding a small plastic bottle in her hand.

"I thought you might be able to use these. You'll have to search for the bar of soap," Gina said, laughing as she tossed the small bottle into the air and watched as it landed with a splash in front of Jess.

Shampoo! And a bar of soap, if he could find it. He sent Gina a quick grin of thanks before diving underwater to find the soap, giving her a quick glimpse of his tight white buttocks. When he resurfaced, victorious, with the bar of soap in his hand, she smiled and gave him a thumbs-up.

"Would you care to join me?" he asked with a rakish smile.

Gina felt her heart skip a beat at the thought. She had to force air into her lungs before she could answer, but she was already shaking her head and backing away. "I'll...uh...go," she stammered, her vocal cords frozen, "er...scout the area. Be back soon."

Jess watched Gina fade into the jungle. He saw the pile of clean clothes she'd left on the rock beside the pack and smiled at her thoughtfulness. After pouring a generous amount of shampoo into his hands, he rubbed them together, working up a lather. Vigorously, he undertook the job of washing his hair.

Gina slipped behind a large fern so that Jess couldn't see her, and turned to watch him for a few moments. She watched the flex of his muscles as he shampooed his hair, and let her imagination run wild. There could only have been one outcome if she'd joined him in the small pond. The thought had her resolve weakening another notch until she brought her wandering fantasies under control.

Staying in the glen would have been pure foolishness. She didn't have the experience to casually engage in sex with Jess without being hurt. The magnitude of the sensations he had aroused in her with a mere kiss was more than she could handle. Surviving his complete possession was a risk she wasn't prepared to take.

Just watching him in the waist-deep water while he lathered his magnificent body with the small bar of soap had her heart in her throat and her blood soaring through her veins. His body had been something to see when he was half starved and beaten. Since he'd been eating and exercising, his shoulders and chest had filled out until he was even more devastatingly virile than ever. And he seemed so unaware of his masculine appeal.

Forcing her eyes away from Jess as slivers of sunlight filtered through the tree branches overhead like spotlights on a stage took enormous willpower. Directing her thoughts to scouting and away from Jess's sexy body, Gina moved deeper into the jungle. But no matter how hard she tried, each time she closed her eyes, she could see Jess waist-deep in the clear water, his wet skin gleaming.

As she slowly threaded her way through the tangled vines surrounding the small glen, Gina's thoughts turned to Jess's pleasure in the first bath he'd had in nearly two months. Arranging a bath for Jess had been easy. The obvious enjoyment he derived from the simple diversion was worth any amount of trouble.

The kiss was another thing entirely, Gina thought as she came to a halt. She didn't wonder why Jess would kiss her. The reason was obvious. He'd been without a woman for so long that he'd simply gotten carried away. Her reaction to his kisses was what troubled her.

Gina felt her face flame as she thought of his heated kisses. It wasn't as if she'd never been kissed before. A kiss had just never had such a powerful effect on her before. She'd never thought of herself as a passionate person, but Jess's kisses and caresses had awakened a part of her that she hadn't known existed. Maybe she'd reacted so strongly because she hadn't been kissed for so long. The next time— What was she thinking of, the next time? There wouldn't be a next time.

That didn't mean she couldn't hold on to the memory of Jess's heated kisses. Or remember how his large hands had explored her body, leaving a trail of fire in their wake. She couldn't see anything wrong with enjoying the feelings Jess's passion had invoked, as long as she kept everything in perspective.

Smiling to herself, Gina realized she felt better than she had for years. She commenced her patrol with a light heart. She knew the feeling wouldn't last, but she was going to savor—

Cigarettes!

Her heart stopped, along with her feet, as she froze in her tracks. There was no mistaking the acrid smell of tobacco smoke. Someone was in the jungle! And near enough that she could smell the smoke from a cigarette.

As she lifted her head like a frightened doe catching a scent on the wind, Gina's heart pounded against her ribs as she checked the direction of the smoke. It took a moment to get her bearings, and when she did, she felt the blood freeze in her veins.

Whoever was in the jungle was too close to the clearing. Jess wouldn't be anticipating trouble; he was relying on her to guard him—as he should. Only she'd been meandering around with her head in the clouds, instead of paying attention to her job. To make matters worse, she'd been letting her mind wander in a direction she knew was hopeless.

Her distress eased when she determined that the smoke was coming from somewhere in front of her. That put her between Jess and the unknown intruder. With luck, she would be able to slip back and get Jess out of the clearing before anyone stumbled onto him.

Quickly Gina turned to retrace her steps as a prickling sensation along her spine alerted her to a closer danger. That danger appeared in the guise of two armed men as she rounded a large tree.

In no more than a second, her gaze slid over the two men. They were dressed in a combination of camouflage and rough peasant garb. Their intense, dark eyes were hard, and their weapons were as outdated as their clothes were mismatched.

Drug dealers. She was sure they weren't army.

Surprise held them spellbound until Gina ducked into
the underbrush in the opposite direction from Jess and the
pond. She could hear the men giving chase as she led them
deeper into the thick undergrowth. She darted through the
foliage, hearing the men shouting in Spanish for her to
stop as they crashed through the jungle after her.

She would never be able to evade them if she continued
making as much noise as they did following her. With that
thought in mind, Gina dropped to her knees and crawled
under the nearest bunch of ferns before making a sharp
turn to her left.

From her position on the jungle floor, she could feel the
men stomping through the bushes like a herd of ele-
phants. They passed her, and she changed direction, rapidly crawling through the vines and debris that covered the
ground. All too soon they would know she'd slipped away,
and they would retrace their steps in search of her.

Gina crawled through the dense underbrush as quickly
as possible, her rifle cradled in the crook of her arm. When
she decided she'd gone far enough, she stood and quickly
turned left again. Taking care to leave as faint a trail as
possible, she slipped silently through the foliage, pleased
to hear the men still thrashing through the brush in the
opposite direction.

The caution she'd exerted to keep from being heard or
leaving a trail took time—time she couldn't spare.

The short distance Gina had to backtrack to get to Jess
was the longest distance she'd ever covered. With every
step she expected to hear a shout of discovery, either from
behind her or from the clearing. She gave a small prayer of
thanks as she ducked under the vines that separated the
pool from the jungle and found the glen empty except for
a partially dressed Jess.

Jess finished tying his boots and stood to reach for his
clean shirt. He smiled as his newly exercised muscles pro-

tested the movement. He didn't mind the twinges of pain; nothing could dash his good mood after his refreshing bath. He felt magnificent. Even the protest of his sore muscles was welcome after weeks of forced inactivity. He tested his shoulders as he slipped his shirt on, wincing as his bruised ribs protested the sharp movement. They were healing well, and gave him less trouble each day. He was ready to tackle the hike to the coast.

A frown furrowed Jess's face as Gina broke through the wall of greenery. His good humor evaporated. His unbuttoned shirt forgotten, he watched her race toward him. Something was wrong. He could see the worry clouding her face as she covered the distance between them at a sprint.

"Get moving! Someone's coming!" Gina ordered.

Jess was reaching for his rifle and pack when he noticed a movement behind Gina. "Coming? They're already here," he said as he watched two men dressed in camouflage step out of the jungle. His blood ran cold when he saw one of the men lift his rifle and aim at Gina's back.

With a powerful lunge, Jess grabbed Gina around the waist with his free arm. The force of his tackle sent them both sailing through the air to land with a thud against the side of the fallen tree that dammed the water in the pond.

His ribs protested the harsh abuse, but Jess didn't give the spear of pain that lanced his side a second thought, pulling Gina behind the fallen tree as bullets splattered around them. Propping his rifle on the tree, he aimed the gun at the spot where the two men had been standing before he tackled Gina.

"Who are they?" Jess asked. He ducked as more bullets peppered the fallen tree, sending chills up his spine. He gripped his rifle tightly, his eyes sweeping the opposite side of the clearing for movement, while fear burned in his clogged throat. He wasn't going to get caught and end up in another hellhole!

"I don't know," Gina said, fighting to draw air into her lungs after being flattened by Jess. "They aren't soldiers," she added after a moment, positioning her rifle alongside Jess's. "My guess would be drug dealers." She thought of the two men who had chased her. They couldn't have discovered where she'd gone yet, which meant these men had discovered the glen on their own.

They didn't have long to wait before they could see movement amid the leaves and vines. Without waiting to see whether one of the men would show himself, Jess showered the jungle with a burst of gunfire.

"I don't like the looks of this," he whispered, keeping his eyes on the moving brush. "We're right out in the open. If they decide to rush us, we're dead."

Gina searched the immediate area for a safer position, a task she should already have seen to—one more area where she'd been lax.

"Always be prepared" was her one unbreakable rule. But with her mind filled with Jess, she hadn't given a thought to the possibility of their being discovered. Chance was all that had saved them. Chance—and a cigarette. She shuddered to think what the men would have found if she hadn't gotten cold feet earlier. She and Jess might have been making love when the men stumbled across the glen.

Beating herself up for not doing her job wasn't doing them a lot of good right now. But in the future, instead of fantasizing about more of Jess's kisses, she was going to keep Jess's safety in mind. Getting him home was the only reason she was in this stinking jungle.

Scanning their surroundings, Gina could find only one avenue of escape. It meant they would have to cross the stream and the open meadow on the other side. She peeked over the fallen tree to see whether the men were still moving in the underbrush. With the tree between them and the pond, she and Jess stood a good chance of escaping.

"We need to get across the stream," she told Jess as she judged the open space they would have to cross. It was a good thirty feet, but if they stayed low, the large tree would give them some protection.

Following the direction of Gina's gaze, Jess turned a questioning look toward her. "We'll be sitting ducks out there."

"I know, but we have no choice. What if those men are just waiting for backup before they charge us? You said it yourself, we're wide open here. A few strategically placed guns and we'll be done for." Gina could feel the nerves along her spine crawl as she scanned the area in front of the tree. "We can't stay here."

Jess's discarded pants were lying in a heap on the flat rock next to the pool. Evidently he'd only had time to pack his shirt. They would have to leave the pants. He would just have to make do without an extra pair. At least he was dressed, she thought, turning back to him. Almost, she corrected herself, as she noticed that his shirt and pants weren't fastened.

From where she was sitting, she could see far too much of his naked chest. Her fingers tingled when she noticed the covering of dark hair, still damp from his swim. The thick mat narrowed as it disappeared beneath the open waistband of his jeans. Dragging her heated gaze away from all that exposed masculinity, Gina swallowed to relieve the dryness in her throat.

"You'd better finish dressing," she said in a tight voice, turning to slip the pack over her shoulder as she watched for any sign of movement across the glen. "We're going to be moving fast."

When she was sure Jess had fastened his clothes, she glanced his way. "We'll slip into the pond and follow the tree across to the other side. Once we're out of the water, we won't have cover. Stay as low as you can." Gina slid into the pool, careful to keep her gun above the water.

"And stay close," she added as she began wading across the pond.

Jess watched Gina disappear into the clear water before he followed her into the pond, holding his gun above the water. This wasn't what he'd had in mind when he invited Gina to join him in the pool.

The water was shallow enough that they could easily touch bottom. The fallen tree gave them a handhold, as well as protection. They reached the far side without incident.

Gina crawled onto the opposite bank and crouched next to the base of the fallen tree. When Jess was beside her, she rose enough to see the clearing. When nothing moved, she motioned Jess to follow her. Crouching low, they raced for the protection of the jungle.

Just as they reached the cover of the trees, shouts rose from the clearing. The bullets that whizzed past their heads added a burst of speed to their feet.

Once they disappeared into the darkened jungle, the shooting ceased. Ten feet into the jungle, Gina came to a sudden stop beside another fallen tree that lay next to a larger one, offering them protection from behind.

"This is as good a place as any," she said as she grabbed a handful of vines and pulled herself up onto the tree. She threw her leg over the trunk, then slid out of sight.

As soon as she peered over the top of the barricade, Jess followed her example and quickly dropped to the ground behind her. The area hidden by the fallen tree was cramped, and even the pack couldn't prevent Jess from pressing tightly against Gina's backside. Her rounded bottom nestled snugly against his sex.

All thoughts of the men waiting in the clearing were swept away by the soft pressure, which reawakened the desire that had run rampant through his body earlier while he'd held her in his arms. Jess's fear of recapture vanished as heat raced through his body.

Stifling a deep groan, he fought to get his raging desires under control. This was no time to be lusting after Gina, he reproached himself. He needed to concentrate, and not on Gina's luscious body.

Gina turned all her senses toward the sound of voices coming from the clearing they'd just left. The heated discussion was too far away for her to make out what they said, but she was certain there were more than two voices. Reinforcements had arrived.

She could catch only snippets from the raised voices. She relaxed when she understood enough to verify who the men were.

"They're drug dealers," she whispered to Jess.

"Are you sure?"

"Yes. I can only pick up a word or two, but from the sounds of their argument, their boss isn't too pleased with his men," she answered as she cocked her head to hear.

The raised voices quieted until she couldn't hear more than muttering. The first few drops of rain bouncing off the leaves overhead obscured any chance of her understanding more of what was being said. Judging by the number of voices, though, their odds weren't good.

Gina looked down at the rifle in her hands and muttered a harsh obscenity that she'd heard fellow agents use when she realized they didn't have sufficient ammunition to hold off an attack for long. If the drug dealers were planning an intense siege, they would soon run out of bullets—and it was entirely her fault.

Gina was rapidly running through a series of solutions she could put into effect to get them out of the mess she'd gotten them into when another round of shots thudded into the tree behind them, overriding the sounds of the falling rain. She and Jess returned a volley of gunfire into the ferns and vines that enclosed their attackers. After another short burst, she paused and signaled Jess to do the same.

"This is all the ammunition we have. We can't afford to be shooting at ghosts."

The increasing rainfall filled the tense silence following the volley of shots with its usual pelting thunder. When fifteen minutes passed without any further sounds, Gina chose another escape route. The heavy downpour had visibility to under ten feet. With luck, they could be back to the cave before the rains ceased.

"They've probably taken cover to wait out the rain. We'd better go now, while we have the chance."

Without waiting for Jess to comment, Gina eased herself over the fallen tree and disappeared into the veil of rain, leading the way back to the safety of their cave.

Chapter 6

Gina's anger, and the shorter route, had them back at the cave in a fraction of the time it had taken them to reach the pond. The rain was falling in a steady downpour, and they were both soaked to the skin.

Entering the cave, Gina slid the wet pack off her shoulders and flung it toward the rear wall, where it hit like a wet sponge before landing on the floor with a loud plop. She was wet and hungry, but most of all she was outraged at her own unprofessional behavior.

In the five years she had been doing rescue work for the government, she hadn't made as many mistakes in all her assignments put together as she had on this single mission. Not one thing had gone right since she had entered that cell and laid eyes on Jess Knight. She knew it was unreasonable to blame Jess for the mishaps, but she didn't recognize herself when she was around him. Nothing like this had ever happened to her before.

Jess watched Gina as she tossed down her pack, then proceeded to prowl the small cave. The confined area was barely large enough for her to stand, let alone pace. From the distressed look on her face, he knew something was troubling her.

"You aren't worried they'll follow us, are you?" Jess asked.

Gina gave him a sharp look. That was all they needed, to be caught in this cave without a way out. The cave was well hidden, but if it should be found, they would be caught like rats in a trap.

"I don't think they know who or where we are, but that doesn't excuse my carelessness. You could have been recaptured," Gina answered, with all the self-disgust she felt.

"I thought you said they were drug runners," he said, zeroing in on her implication that the men in the glen might be rebel soldiers.

"They were," she shot back, turning to face him. She planted her hands on her hips as her golden eyes shot sparks at him. "Don't you think word about your escape has hit the jungle grapevine? If they'd caught you, they would have discovered who you were quick enough. And once they had you, they wouldn't have hesitated to return you to your jailers—for a tidy fee, of course." Gina ran her fingers through her wet hair, sending drops of water flying as she resumed her pacing. "Then again, they just might have shot us both and been done with it."

Jess's eyebrows rose as he digested her comments. "You blame yourself for those men stumbling onto us?"

"Of course I blame myself. It's my job to keep you safe. I should have been more alert," Gina snapped as she took another turn around the enclosed area. "Some protector I turned out to be."

Jess caught Gina's hand as her next turn around the cave brought her past where he was sitting. The low roof of the cave didn't allow him to stand, so, with a sharp tug on her hand, he pulled her down beside him.

"They could just as well have come upon us anytime when we were outside these last few days. You couldn't know where they might be."

Jess held on to her hand, preventing her from resuming her pacing. He watched a muscle flex along her cheek as she continued to ignore him. She was going to carry her guilt to the extreme. He didn't hold her responsible. Hadn't she come in time to warn him? Things could have turned out much worse. Talk about being caught with your pants down...

He could understand if she was feeling the aftershocks of fear. Hell, his blood had turned to ice when he thought the guerrillas had discovered them.

And if telling her about his fears would remove the tight expression from Gina's pale face, he would gladly share his feelings. Fear wasn't something he usually brought into a conversation. Not that he was ashamed of being afraid. Any agent worth his pay felt the chill of fear. Fear kept him on his toes when situations got tight. Lack of fear was a sure sign an agent wasn't long for this world.

"I might not have known where they were, but I knew it was possible we might run into them. I should have been paying more attention. I should have been doing *my* job."

Gina tugged on her hand, without much success. Jess didn't understand, and she wasn't going to fill him in. It was bad enough that she'd behaved without her usual professionalism. She didn't have to compound her guilt by discussing her behavior with Jess.

If she hadn't been so lost in her fantasy about him, picturing him swimming naked in the clear pond, she would have had her mind on the constant dangers lurking in the jungle. If it hadn't been for the cigarette smoke, she might have walked right into the drug dealers' arms. And where would that have left Jess?

Ever since she'd removed that ski mask, revealing herself to Jess, she hadn't behaved with her usual competence. There was no valid excuse for her past behavior. But from now until she delivered Jess to the boat that was waiting for them off the coast, she was going to behave like the professional she knew herself to be.

To start with, she would keep some distance between them. Seeing their clasped hands, she made a choking sound and jerked her hand away as if it had suddenly been charged with a thousand volts. She scrambled to her feet.

Jess watched Gina nervously dust off the seat of her wet khaki pants as if they were made of the finest wool. She studiously kept her eyes on anything in the cave but him. He didn't understand her attitude, but if she was going to revert to treating him as if he had leprosy, he wasn't about to try to prove otherwise. Whatever her problem was, she could damn well sort it out by herself. He was cold, wet and hungry, and he'd had enough of her senseless behavior.

Completely ignoring Gina as she stood gazing out the entrance, Jess fished through the supplies for a change of clothes. Having succeeded, he peeled out of his wet ones, dropping them in a pile on the dirt floor.

When he was dressed in dry clothes, Jess retrieved the pack Gina had tossed in the general direction of the supplies in a rare show of anger and emptied it on the floor. The simple lunch of fruit, cheese and crackers was soggy but still edible, and he settled against the stone wall of the cave to eat their forgotten lunch.

Gina watched as Jess sorted through the contents of the pack, rescuing their lunch. The small bottle of shampoo and the bar of soap were missing from the contents scattered on the floor. They had been left beside the pond, along with Jess's pants. They might as well have left a calling card for the drug dealers. Just one more black mark to be chalked up against her on this mismanaged mission. At this rate, it would be a miracle if she got Jess back to the States in one piece.

She needed to get out! If she didn't burn off some energy, she was going to explode. It was too confining inside the cave, and since she was already soaked to the skin, a little more water wouldn't be noticed.

"I'm going to make sure we weren't followed," she said.

Without waiting for Jess to comment, Gina picked up her rifle and silently slipped out of the cave, disappearing into the wet foliage.

No one could have followed them in the heavy downpour. Even if the forgotten bath supplies and clothes were discovered, the rain would keep anyone from knowing where they'd gone.

Gina took her time circling the surrounding area. The rain had turned into a steady drizzle that showed no signs of stopping anytime soon. She was dripping wet and chilled clear through. The sun had dropped behind the treetops, casting the jungle in shadow. It would be dark soon. Reluctant or not, she had no choice but to return to the shelter of the cave.

She dreaded facing Jess. *He* might not hold her responsible for almost getting them caught, but she felt enough guilt for the both of them.

What was the matter with her? She'd given up dreaming years ago. Nothing good ever came of dreams; experience had taught her that. And to top it off, she had been daydreaming about Jess Knight, a man she had disapproved of for years. How could she have let her dislike for him slip her mind, even for a little while?

The shadows were deep by the time Gina reached the cave. The inside was shrouded in darkness, but the little light that filtered through the vines showed Jess was still awake, sitting where he'd been when she left. The pack and its contents had been put away, as had the remains of their lunch.

"Where the hell have you been?" Jess growled from the shadows as a clap of thunder rumbled through the jungle.

His disposition didn't improve when she ignored him and headed directly to her pack at the rear of the cave. He fumed as she sorted through the pack until she found dry clothes to replace her soaked ones.

"Now why did I expect her to explain?" Jess asked himself out loud, since she hadn't answered. Not that he expected her to explain what she'd been doing. The question had run through his mind so many times as he watched it grow darker by the minute with no sign of her returning that there had been no holding it back. He was glad she was here, safe and sound, but her arrival didn't relieve the fury gnawing at his gut.

He watched as Gina removed her boots and socks. Standing with her back to him, she stripped out of her khaki pants and shirt—as if she were alone in the cave. She wore only the pale cotton top he remembered from that afternoon by the pool. A pair of almost-nothing panties peeked out from under the tank top. The outfit suited Gina's personality perfectly—khaki on the outside, silk and lace underneath.

Jess held his breath as her wet tank top joined the pile of clothes on the floor. His eyes were riveted on her slim back and hips as she stepped into dry pants and slid them up her trim thighs before reaching for a dry top to go under her shirt.

This was hell, Jess thought as he watched Gina dress. His heartbeat rivaled the thunder as he remembered touching the velvet soft skin that had been unveiled before him. He both cursed the dying light and perversely wished for complete darkness.

He wanted to see more of the shadowy figure emerging like a butterfly from a cocoon. Then again, he didn't want to see her at all. Watching her outline in the dusky light as she removed her wet clothes had been pure torture as he mentally visualized what his eyes couldn't see.

Jess didn't think the situation could get worse until a flash of lightning illuminated the inside of the cave as Gina lifted her arms over her head to pull on a dry top. Jess had a clear view of one full, pale breast.

The view lasted only a fraction of a second, but even after the streak of lightning had disappeared, returning the cave to darkness, he could still see the womanly form that had been highlighted by the brief light, as if she were posing for an artist. With her arms raised above her head and her body arched, her breast had thrust forward as if waiting for a lover's caress.

He was in for a rough night. Jess's blood was running hot, and his nerves were taut and in need of a release. And if he couldn't get the release he desired, there were other ways of easing tension.

"What were you doing out there so long? Didn't it occur to you that I might be concerned?" Jess fired the questions off so quickly that Gina didn't have time to do more than send him a startled look before he plunged on. "The jungle is full of armed men, or don't you remember? You shouldn't have been running around out there by yourself."

Jess knew he'd gone too far as soon as the words were out of his mouth. One look at the fury gathering in Gina's gold eyes as she stepped out of the shadows confirmed his mistake.

It was safer outside than in here, she thought to herself. She'd felt Jess's eyes burning into her back while she'd changed. With a forced boldness, she'd convinced herself it didn't bother her in the least, and continued dressing with him watching her every move. He had stripped in front of her without hesitation. Let him see how it felt.

"Running around out there, as you put it, is what I do. I was safe out there. I was doing my job, out there." Her voice rose with each word, until she was nearly shouting.

"You might have thought you were safe, but you know it was dangerous, even in the rain." He saw the mutinous set of her jaw and felt like shaking some sense into her stubborn head. "You're courting danger, aren't you? That's what you've been doing for the past two years. What do you have, a death wish? Do you want to join Greg so badly you'd go looking for danger?"

"No, I don't have a death wish," she shot back at him, disregarding the anger that had turned his face to stone. "I do have a job to do, and up until now I've been lax with that job. Well, I won't be anymore. Until you're safely back in the States, this mission is going to be completed *by the book.*"

"Does that mean you're going to be pulling a disappearing act every time something happens that you have no control over?" Jess ground out the question as she turned to the food pack, assuming the argument was over.

She dropped the flap on the pack and returned her attention to Jess. His words sounded too much like an accusation for her peace of mind. He had come too close to the exposed nerve that had been plaguing her while she was tromping through the wet jungle. Her only recourse was to strike back, even though she didn't feel she had a defense.

"I was safe *out there,*" she repeated, facing him with both hands on her hips. She rushed on, preventing him voicing any further criticism. "There weren't any distractions out in the jungle this time to take my mind off my job." She saw the thrust strike home, and heedlessly plunged ahead. "There aren't going to be any more distractions in here, either."

"What do you mean, distractions?" The angry question hardened his features as he rose from the floor. "There were two of us in that glen, if I remember right. I wasn't the only one—" Jess's words halted as he struck his head on the solid roof of the cave. "Son of a—!"

Gina watched, wide-eyed, as Jess dropped back to the floor holding his abused head. He looked at her with a sardonic expression that sent her temper soaring.

"What are you accusing me of now?" Gina's nostrils flared with fury, and her eyes glowed in the fading light as she faced him.

Jess gave his head one final rub before he abandoned it to glower at Gina. "I'm not accusing you of anything. You're the one that's throwing accusations around." His temper was reaching the boiling point. "You were just as hot out there in the glen as I was. Without much more persuasion, I could have had you, and you know it."

Gina glared at him with burning, reproachful eyes as the color mounted in her cheeks at his crude remark. She was so furious that words escaped her. She wanted to strike out at Jess, wanted to make him feel the pain that was ripping at her heart, but he had come too close to the truth for her to retaliate. She might be behaving like a coward, but retreats seemed the better course of action.

Grabbing the pack Jess had used to carry their lunch to the pond, she dropped it on the floor at his feet.

"Get your stuff together. We'll be leaving at first light—rain or shine."

Turning away from the reproach in Jess's eyes, Gina gathered the pile of wet clothes together and dumped them against the back wall, out of the way. Their supply of clothes was quickly diminishing. They would have to make do with what they had. The heavy wet clothes would never dry in the drizzling rain.

Gina didn't so much as glance in Jess's direction as she gathered together what she needed to fix their meal. As far as she was concerned, there was nothing more to say. She brought out the small propane burner and started their dinner.

She could feel his eyes watching her every move in the soft glow of the burner, though it was not the same as the past few days. She knew that if she looked in his direction, his eyes wouldn't be filled with the fire of desire but with the heat of anger.

The rest of the evening passed in silence, while she sorted through their supplies, selecting what they needed for the excursion to the coast. She loaded the packs, the heavy one for her and a lighter one for Jess.

When Gina had finished packing their gear, she rolled out her sleeping bag, still avoiding looking at Jess. He was lying on his bed with his head pillowed on his arm, not even pretending he wasn't staring at her. In desperation she turned out the burner, plunging the cave into darkness.

Sitting on her sleeping bag, Gina removed her boots and socks, before casting a glance in the general direction of Jess's dark form. She wrinkled her brow as the picture of him standing in the small pond replayed in her mind. Her breath caught in the back of her throat, and when she swallowed, it sounded overly loud in the quiet cave. She forced the image from her mind as she unfastened her pants with shaky hands. Removing them, she slid into her sleeping bag.

Gina lay in the dark, listening to Jess's breathing as it slowed and he drifted off to sleep. She had walked for miles that day, and she should be exhausted, but her mind wouldn't shut down so she could sleep. There were too many questions crowding her mind. Was someone even now searching for them? The rain would cover their tracks, but there were other means of following them. Broken branches, or places where she had cut their trail through the dense brush. Mashed ferns and vines that told of their recent passing.

The sooner they were on the move, the safer they would be. And the sooner she could hand Jess over to his father, the happier she would be. She wanted nothing more than to be back home in the Cascade Mountains, snuggled in her cozy waterbed, with this mission—and Jess—far behind her.

A clap of thunder interrupted Gina's thoughts. Rising up on one elbow, she listened as it rolled through the jungle. The worst of the storm was still a long way off, but the building pressure promised to make this the first real storm since they'd been in the cave.

Another clap of thunder rumbled through the night, followed closely by strong winds. The powerful winds drove the rain, pounding the tree branches before forcefully hitting the ground. Gina could hear the wind pick up momentum, driving the rain even harder against the cave's vine-covered opening.

They were in for a killer storm. At least her worries about someone being out looking for them were eased. No one in his right mind would be out in this mess.

She snuggled deeper into her bag, letting the sounds of the rain and wind lull her to sleep. The fierce storm would have kept most people awake, but it was like a lullaby to Gina. She drifted quietly off to sleep.

A few feet away, Jess never stirred as the storm drew closer.

Darkness! He was in that damned stinking dark hole again. He had to find a way out! He didn't want to die in that filthy hellhole. The need to escape drove him, stronger than ever. But it was so dark!

Thrashing around on the floor, Jess tried freeing himself from the bindings holding him down. They had tied him! They hadn't tied him before. Why now?

A loud clap of thunder rumbled through the floor of the cave, bringing Jess out of one nightmare and into another. Darkness surrounded him, and demons ran wild in the black void. He'd been rescued. How had he come to be back in his cell? There was only one explanation. They had been captured. But when had the rebels captured them?

Them?

Gina!

Where was Gina?

Struggling with his bonds, Jess attempted to sit up as he called her name. What had they done to her?

While the thunder had lulled Gina to sleep, Jess's cry woke her instantly. As she sat up, she could hear the savage wind and rain pelting the ground outside the cave entrance. She could also hear Jess fighting his sleeping bag like a man fastened in a straitjacket. Throwing back her own sleeping bag, she shivered when the cool night air struck her bare legs below the tail of her shirt as she went to Jess.

He fought her touch as he had during his fever. He seemed unable to hear her calling him as he fought some unseen enemy.

"Jess, wake up! It's Gina!" she called out, trying to get hold of his flailing arms.

She couldn't see Jess as he thrashed around on the floor, but she could feel his sleeping bag tangled around him as he fought its confinement and her. She needed light, but she didn't want to leave Jess to start the burner.

As if hearing her thoughts, a bright flash of lightning lit the interior of the cave long enough to bring Jess out of his nightmare. Relief flooded through him when he could see that he wasn't in a cell. As the light died out, he recognized the soft voice calling to him.

Gina was safe!

He reached out, pulling her close, and wrapped his arms around her slender body. Jess buried his face in her sweet hair.

"You're safe," he breathed into her ear. No matter where they were, they were still together.

"Jess?" Gina called softly, attempting to untangle herself from his tight hold.

"Everything is going to be all right, Gina. Just let me hold you," Jess answered weakly, tightening his hold on her. He could feel Gina's arms slowly wrap around him, and their warm contact was welcome.

All too soon, she pushed against his shoulders for release. But he wasn't ready to release her. She belonged in his arms.

The wind howled as it swept through the trees, driving the heavy rains. The full fury of the storm had passed, but it could still be heard in the distance as it rolled through the jungle. The howling wind and pounding rain were no match for the pounding of Jess's heart beneath Gina's ear.

She could hear trees snapping like twigs under the strong winds. They were safe from the wind and falling trees, but Gina wasn't sure she was safe from the charged current building in the confines of the cave, a current that might prove even more dangerous than the storm raging outside.

The sounds of the storm faded as Gina struggled to gain control. Her face was still pressed against Jess's firm chest. Pulling her arms from around his neck, she gave a feeble push against his shoulders in an attempt to free herself. She no longer had control of her own body. She was being ruled by the desire firing her blood.

The nightmare had left Jess more shaken than he cared to admit. Holding Gina in his arms had eased the last traces of tension from his body, replacing it with another need, more insistent than the need for simple human contact.

Jess pulled Gina tight against his bare chest. The sleeping bag had fallen to settle around his waist, leaving his upper body bare to cushion her full breasts. He felt her halfhearted attempt to free herself, but she felt too good to release just yet. She was so soft and fresh, like rain-washed sunshine. Her scent had been driving him mad ever since the morning he'd awakened to find her sleeping in a shaft of sunlight.

Holding her closer, Jess softly burrowed his head in her soft, fragrant hair as his hands caressed her back through the thin cotton top. He could feel her heartbeat increase as his movements made her aware of their intimate position.

She resumed her attempts to pull out of his embrace. Tightening his hold, Jess slowly slid his hand up Gina's back, burying it deep in her thick copper curls. Holding her in a firm grasp, Jess hungrily covered her soft lips with his suddenly starving mouth.

There was no gentle persuasion in his kiss. It was as intense as the storm that raged outside. The heat of Jess's firm mouth left Gina without the desire to resist as she kissed him back with equal hunger.

After her first startled reaction to Jess's kiss, Gina ceased to fight the attraction that had been building from the moment she removed the filthy, ill-fitting pants from his battered body. Her thoughts had led her down this path on more occasions than she cared to remember.

Jess had been dreaming of Gina's kisses for years, but dreams were no comparison to the real thing. The kisses they'd shared that afternoon at the pond had only sharpened his desire. Spending endless days aching to touch her had sent his desire for her spinning out of control. The fire heating his blood prompted him to rush forward, to take before she could change her mind, but his heart wanted more than the quick release of the moment. With that thought, Jess tempered his hungry kisses.

His hands eased their hold as he pulled Gina's soft body even closer. He didn't give the bunched-up sleeping bag more than a passing thought as he drew Gina down on the soft cushion it made, to rain light kisses on her swollen lips.

He breathed a quiet sigh when he felt her resistance pass completely, to be replaced with a passion that burned as hot as his own. There was no turning back. Jess's hands traveled over her curves, through the thin top, as his mouth fed on her sweet nectar. His need to touch her silky body was strong as he reached for the bottom of her shirt, only to encounter creamy warm skin where he had expected to find the coarse pants she habitually wore.

The feel of her satin skin sent his heart rate soaring. His chest tightened, and he fought to catch his breath. He wanted to see her...to watch her face soften with desire and her eyes burn with passion when he loved her. Jess slid his hands over her softness, up her slim waist under the light tank top, to capture the treasure he knew he would find there.

Jess groaned deep in his throat as his hand closed over one firm breast. Lifting the full globe in his hand, he kneaded it gently before running his fingers lightly across the smooth skin. His pulse quickened as he felt her breast swell to his touch. He took the hard peak between his thumb and finger and gently tugged, causing Gina to arch upward, moaning softly.

Gina's ardent response was more than he could stand as he quickly rid her of her top before removing his own clothes. The throbbing in his lower body was driving him out of control. He ground his teeth, trying to hold back his rampant need in order to ensure that Gina was ready for him.

Gina's experience in passion hadn't prepared her for the shudder of pleasure that had rippled through her body when Jess palmed her breast. Nor for the sweet fire that had raced to her womb when he softly tugged on her nipple. He'd lit a fire only he could control—and she was burning!

She didn't need the slow foreplay that would build the sensual tension. She was more than ready for Jess's total possession. Their foreplay had begun the first moment they looked into one another's eyes again.

Jess covered Gina's soft body with his naked warmth, snuggling himself between her trembling thighs. His breathing was labored, as if he had run for miles, and his straining muscles twitched with the power of holding his passion in check.

"Oh, God," Jess groaned as he searched for her mouth in the dark. If only he could see her. Her full breasts were pressed to his chest, their pointed tips burning his skin where they touched. He wanted to see her face as he entered her, to see the passion build as he finally made her his.

"Please," Gina moaned, low in her throat. She had been waiting a lifetime for Jess. She didn't want to wait any longer. "Now, Jess!" She pulled on his shoulders, encouraging him to take what she was offering.

Gina's soft pleas nudged Jess over the edge, and his need for control was forgotten as he hastily removed Gina's last remaining garment from her body, leaving her bare and waiting for him. He slid into her silky wetness. She welcomed him with a shudder of pleasure as he sank deep.

She was warm and wet. He had never felt as complete as he did at that moment, buried deep inside Gina.

His hot breath fanned her cheek as he held her tight. "I've dreamed of this for so many years, but my dreams couldn't compare with reality."

Jess moved deeper. Gina clung tighter. Together they shared a rhythm that pleased them both.

Together they flew as close to heaven as a mortal could fly.

No matter what tomorrow brought, Jess knew he would never experience this miracle again without Gina. And as he settled her in his arms, pulling the sleeping bag around them, he also knew that Gina was the only woman for him. He loved her beyond reason.

Now if he could just convince her that she loved him.

Chapter 7

Silence.

The only sound Gina could hear was the water dripping onto the jungle floor from the rain-soaked trees. The storm had run its course.

Opening her eyes, she peered from beneath her thick lashes to find the cave still shrouded in darkness. It wasn't daylight yet.

Snuggled in the warm cocoon, Gina enjoyed the early-morning peace until a drop of water splashed onto her face. She wiped the moisture from her face with the corner of the sleeping bag, discovering that the bag was already damp. The dripping must be what had awakened her from her dreamless sleep. Reluctant to leave the warmth of her sleeping bag for the cool early-morning air, she turned her head away from the dripping water.

The view that met her had her eyes opening wide in shock before they snapped shut. She must be having a bad dream. She would open her eyes and Jess would be sleeping in his own bed, not hers. Gina knew it was wishful thinking. When she reopened her eyes, she knew he would still be sleeping beside her. What was worse, *she* was sleeping in *his* bed—not hers.

Seeing him peacefully sleeping next to her brought back the events of last night's storm. Gina felt her face heat as she recalled her behavior during the night. How could she have let this happen?

Careful to leave Jess undisturbed, Gina quietly slipped out of the sleeping bag, flushing again as the cool air hit her naked body. Searching in the dim light for her clothes, she pointedly kept her eyes from straying toward the rumpled sleeping bag.

After hastily pulling on her clothes, Gina turned to reach for her boots and froze with her hand in midair. The sight that greeted her chased all thoughts and self-recriminations from her mind.

Their secluded cave was far from the safe haven it had been. The storm had been so fierce that the vine covering the opening had been ripped away, leaving them completely exposed to anyone who chanced to pass by. Giving herself a mental shake, Gina grabbed her boots and slipped her feet into them without delay. They had to get moving. As soon as full daylight broke through the trees, any passing patrol could easily see their camp.

Gina turned away from the exposed opening and nudged Jess with the toe of her boot. When he didn't stir at the first nudge, she was tempted to use a little more force. If she hadn't been so engrossed in their lovemaking, she would have noticed when the wind tore their covering away, leaving them like sitting ducks.

In all fairness, she couldn't hold Jess entirely responsible. She hadn't put up much of a fight. She had all but begged him to make love to her.

Who was she kidding? She could remember actually begging.

She remembered his touch, too, like fire on her flesh. His kisses had released something wild in her that she had never known existed. She had whimpered and begged for more, and when he'd given her more, she still hadn't been satisfied. She'd been searching for something just out of her reach, something she instinctively knew he could give her.

She had cried out his name when he showed her the heights her body was capable of reaching, before she floated back to earth and the safety of his arms. She hadn't recognized the woman Jess had set free in the dark hours of the night. Nothing had prepared her for the riot of emotions that she experienced with Jess. A stranger was living inside her. Someone so totally alien to her concept of herself that she didn't know how to accept the woman she'd become in his arms.

She'd convinced herself that she wasn't a passionate person. That she didn't need a man to complete her life. Even as she tried to reassure herself that she still didn't need one, memories of the past night sent aftershocks skittering down her spine. Jess had shattered that theory when he showed her a splendor that far surpassed her wildest dreams.

Gina looked longingly down at Jess, who was peacefully sleeping on the rumpled sleeping bag. His hair was tousled, as if she'd just run her fingers through the thick mass. His face was covered with a dark stubble. He looked wonderful, and so powerful that she ached inside.

She couldn't be sorry for last night. But she had been a fool to let things get far enough out of hand for last night to happen. Not that she had stood a chance of holding him off. From all she'd been told, Jess was a master at getting women into his bed—far more sophisticated women than she had ever thought of being. To him, she was simply child's play, someone to fill the gap until he was back home.

That last thought had Gina nudging Jess with the toe of her boot, more forcefully than necessary to wake him, bringing him awake with a grunt of pain.

Served him right! She would let him know she wasn't going to be so easy in the future. And she certainly wasn't going to let him think that last night held any special meaning for her. They'd had sex, plain and simple—even if the little voice in the back of her mind was laughing its head off at her description of the passion that had passed between them. There had been nothing plain or simple about it. *Explosive* was a better description.

"Wake up. The storm ruined this place for hiding out. We need to move." She shot the words out like bullets from a machine gun, not caring whether he was fully awake or not.

Jess sat up and looked out the entrance of the cave, the damp morning air making him shiver. Gina was right; this was no longer a safe hiding place. He could see downstream for at least half a mile. They might just as well hang out a flag advertising their position.

When Jess turned his attention back to the cave, he found Gina covering the surplus supplies with vines. He watched as she kicked the pile of their discarded clothes under the vines before turning to find him watching her.

"Get moving, Jess. We haven't got all day." She shot him a reproachful look along with the terse order as she opened a pack and pulled out the burner. "Coffee and field rations are all you're getting for breakfast," she added, knowing that they both needed nourishment for the trek ahead, and that the cave was still the safest place for them at the moment.

Jess quickly shoved the sleeping bag aside and reached for his pile of clothes. In short order, he was dressed and pulling on his boots. As he fastened the laces, he watched Gina fire the small burner. The glow from the flame didn't dispel the dark look on her face. He could find no trace of the woman he'd loved during the night.

He would have bet anything her disposition had nothing to do with his not helping. More than likely, her anger was generated by what they'd shared during the night.

One thing he did know—this wasn't how he had expected the morning to start. He'd had visions of waking with her all soft and warm in his arms. Of telling her how much he loved her. And of sharing soft kisses and maybe making love to her in the daylight, when he could see her as he loved her.

Tugging the laces of his boot tight, he filed his fantasy away for a later time and moved to the entrance of the cave.

"I'll bring back another load of vines," he said as he grabbed the machete from where she'd leaned it against the wall. Receiving no answer, he eased out the entrance and headed for the stream.

Winning Gina wasn't going to be easy, he thought as he looked at the devastation around him. He would certainly have a fight on his hands. But if she had come easily to him she wouldn't be worth having. And she *was* worth having—and worth the fight.

Picturing the fight ahead, Jess grinned to himself as he headed for a fall of vines the storm hadn't ripped away. As he swung the machete, he wondered how long she was going to ignore him. He finished chopping an armload of vines and returned to the cave, where he was met by the smell of hot coffee.

"That coffee sure smells good." He looked toward Gina as he dragged the vines in behind him, but she kept her attention focused on the rations she was pulling from the pack.

Jess shrugged as he piled the vines on top of the supplies. So much for friendly conversation.

Gina poured the steaming coffee into cups. She set Jess's cup next to the carton of field rations, carefully keeping her gaze away from his.

"Hurry up and eat. I want to get this stuff packed and get out of here," she ordered as she picked up her plate and sat near the entrance, her back to Jess.

The rain had begun again, but she wasn't going to let that keep them from leaving as soon as they were ready. She couldn't take spending another hour in the small cave, let alone an entire day. They would just have to make do tromping through the rain. Getting wet wouldn't hurt them. They would be wet in a few minutes from the dripping trees, anyway.

When they'd finished eating, Jess silently watched Gina pack their last supplies from his customary spot along the wall. After rolling up his sleeping bag and folding his damp clothes, he hadn't bothered to suggest that he help. All his attempts at conversation had been met with silence. She'd spoken only to issue sharp, clipped orders. He would let her simmer a while before he brought up the subject of last night. He wanted to give her time to adjust to the change in their relationship before he stated his intentions.

"Are you ready?"

Jess looked up to see Gina holding his pack out to him. Accepting it, he gathered up his rifle and followed her out of the cave, then slipped the pack over his shoulders. It was far from light, but he could tell that his wasn't as heavy as the one Gina was fastening on her back.

Jess arched a dark brow at Gina as he hefted his pack. "You've got this packed a little light, don't you?"

Without expression, Gina turned away from Jess's potent appeal. His lean features drew her like a magnet, which only served to arouse her anger again.

"We'll see how you do today carrying a lighter pack. If you manage without any trouble, tomorrow we'll even the packs out a little more." Gina turned toward the trail, the subject closed as far as she was concerned. She had more pressing problems to think about than the weight of their packs. Such as, how she was going to spend five more days with Jess and keep her thoughts off her response to his lovemaking. Such thoughts would be perilous to her concentration.

Jess caught Gina by the arm, halting her departure. "Gina, you don't have to carry everything. We can share the weight."

She twisted her arm out of his grip and stepped back, putting some space between them. After a brief glance at Jess, she turned away. "We'll do things my way," she said abruptly, unable to hide the undercurrent of anger in her voice.

How could he look so unaffected by the momentary contact? Even through her heavy shirt, her arm burned where his hand had touched her. If she was going to continue reacting like a frightened deer each time he came near her, she was in for a rough five days. She didn't know who she was more furious with over her strange behavior, Jess or herself.

"You're just being stubborn, and you know it," Jess called after her as she turned away.

"I'm not being stubborn," Gina said, turning back to confront him. "What I'm doing is my job. We have days of hiking ahead of us. You'll need your strength."

"We both know what this has to do with, and it isn't my strength that's in question." Jess felt little victory when Gina's face flushed bright red as she caught his implication.

Without comment, Gina turned her back on him. "The weight of my pack is no problem. I've carried heavier," she said through gritted teeth.

"To hell with the packs!" Jess nearly shouted as he grabbed Gina by the shoulders and gave her a sharp shake. "This whole morning—the silences, the sullen looks—has nothing to do with the storm or the packs. This has to do with last night—with you and me!" Another shake accompanied his last words before he set her free.

"I don't want to talk about last night," she said, carefully moving out of his reach. "That was a mistake. Anyway, this has nothing to do with that. What this *is* about is today, and the days ahead. What we need to do right now is get moving before a patrol passes by and discovers the cave."

Drawing a deep breath, Jess fought to control the urge to shake her until she admitted that their lovemaking had been special, not a mistake. He had no choice but to leave that discussion until they were safely out of the jungle.

"What are you trying to prove, Gina? That you don't need anyone—especially me? And who are you trying to convince, me or yourself?"

"I don't need to prove anything to you or anyone else. I'm just doing my job. And that job is getting you to the rescue boat on time." She shot him a murderous look before turning to go once again. She didn't want Jess to see how close to the mark his question had struck. After last night, she needed to assert all the self-discipline her father had drilled into her to keep from falling back into Jess's arms.

Not bothering to see whether he was following, Gina started down the short embankment toward the stream, calling over her shoulder, "Get moving, Knight, we have a long way to go today." She could hear Jess muttering behind her, but all she caught of his words was something about doing things her way. She wasn't sure anymore whether "her way" was the right way. Especially when it caused such an empty feeling in her chest.

They fought the jungle for hours. The whole time, the rain fell in a steady drizzle, making passage through the dense undergrowth miserable. Gina slapped a hanging vine out of her way with more force than was necessary, getting drenched for her efforts. Not that a little more water would be noticeable. She was already soaked to the skin. Just one more aggravation to add to a day that had gone from bad to worse right from the moment she woke up in Jess's arms.

At least they were back on their original schedule. If Jess didn't have a relapse, they should meet the boat on time. Letting go of a hanging limb, Gina gave an unladylike snort. If last night's performance was any way to measure his fitness, he would make the trip without any problems. Ducking under a limb, she deliberately let the soaking wet branch swing behind her.

Gina cast a quick glance over her shoulder at the object of her thoughts in time to see him barely escape a drenching. He didn't appear to be tiring, but this was just their first day. And he was carrying a light pack.

He'd been right about the argument over the packs. And now that she'd had time to think about it, she knew she'd overreacted. For some reason, she'd felt the need to prove that she didn't need Jess's help. That she could do this on her own.

Their disagreement over the distribution of the supplies might not have set a companionable mood, but Gina wasn't looking for companionship. She wanted to keep her distance.

Anyway, why had he all of a sudden decided she couldn't do her job? Just because she'd been foolish enough to make love with Jess, that didn't change her abilities to make decisions.

All of a sudden she had been reduced to "female" and was unable to know what was best for their survival. Typical male thinking. Well, he could just think again. They needed to take every precaution. Jess didn't realize how difficult, or how long, the hike to the coast was going to be.

Gina slashed at a heavy vine, her anger increasing. If he thought she was going to suddenly become the helpless woman to his macho male, he had a surprise coming. She swung again, taking out her frustrations, along with her unreasonable accusations, on the helpless vine.

He should realize that the humidity drained the strength out of a healthy body, she thought, giving one more hearty swing that sent a shower of water flying. Any fool would understand how important conserving his strength was to the success of their mission.

Breathing heavily, Gina swiped at the moisture beaded on her brow and prepared for another swing at the thick foliage. She was so busy maligning Jess that she almost lost her footing on the slick ground. The constant drizzle soaking the vegetation-covered ground made movement precarious. She would be better off thinking about a place where they could dry off instead of letting Jess occupy her thoughts.

The light rain showed no sign of letting up any time soon. Anyway, they were going to have to stop. If she could find suitable shelter, they could wait out the weather and dry out a little. But the idea of being cooped up again with Jess for any amount of time was something she couldn't face right now. So they pushed on, with Gina hacking away with the machete and Jess silently following.

Tackling an unusually dense patch of vines, Gina's muscles strained as she felt the drain on her strength. She was going to have to give in and find a dry place where they could rest. Jess had to be feeling the humidity as much as she was.

Putting all her strength behind one last swing before admitting defeat, Gina cut through the foliage. The added momentum of her forceful swing threw her off balance and sent her flying through the opening she had just cut in the heavy growth. The added thrust sent her careening down a steep incline on the other side of the wall of vines.

The machete flew out of her hand as she hit the ground with enough force to knock the breath from her body. She slid down the rain-slick ground, gaining momentum as she went. Reaching out, she attempted to grab hold of the passing undergrowth, or anything else she could get her hands on to help slow her downhill run. She was moving so fast and the vines were so wet that she couldn't grab hold. She flew down the slope. God only knew where her headlong flight was going to land her.

Gina's roller-coaster ride ended when she flew over the edge of a bank, to be suddenly snapped back and dropped to the ground with a thud. Her head struck the bank with enough force to daze her.

Slowly regaining her senses, Gina rubbed her abused head as she looked around her. Terrified, she couldn't prevent the scream that tore from her throat. Frantically she pushed herself against the dirt-and-rock wall behind her and looked around. Her startled eyes were met by a vast empty space.

She was sitting in a pocket left by an uprooted tree. The pocket was hanging on the side of a gorge, with nothing between her and thin air but a small patch of ground. The storm had turned her perch into a puddle of mud. Sheer luck was all that had safely landed her on the small ledge in the first place.

Holding on to a protruding root, Gina looked up. Her eyes grew wider when she saw that she'd dropped a good ten feet to land on the small ledge. The only thing that had prevented her from flying over the edge of the overhang was the shoulder strap on her pack. It had caught a remaining root sticking out of the bank and slammed her back against the dirt wall. The thick mud had softened her landing, but her head still rang from its collision with the packed earth and rocks of the bank.

Wrapping both hands around the root, Gina cautiously looked over the edge of her perch, loosening a section of the rain-soaked ground in the process. In horror, she watched the clumps of mud plunge thirty feet straight down, to join the uprooted tree in the rock-studded, raging river directly below.

Gina closed her eyes and leaned her head against the muddy bank, silently saying a prayer of thanks. Taking deep, even breaths, she waited for her heartbeat to return to normal.

Panicking wouldn't help.

Through her carelessness, she had almost gotten herself killed. She should have followed her common sense and found a dry place to wait out the rain, instead of letting her emotions rule her better judgment. She wouldn't be sitting in a puddle of mud perched on a ledge overlooking a death trap if she hadn't let her hot temper rule her.

As the pounding in her ears subsided, Gina heard Jess calling her name. She could also hear his thrashing footsteps as he followed her trail through the jungle. Her heartbeat quickened. If he didn't slow down, he would fly over the edge of the bank, as she had. And her small ledge wasn't large enough for two.

Jess had watched Gina hacking away at the jungle growth with a vengeance. He would have suggested she let him take the machete for a while, but after her reaction to his attempt to more evenly distribute the packs that morning, he felt he was far safer letting her vent her anger clearing a trail instead of at him—where he was sure she would rather be swinging the lethal weapon.

Standing in the wet drizzle, watching Gina wielding the machete, Jess ran the events of the previous night through his mind. He felt no regrets over making love with her, but he did wish the circumstances had been different. He would have preferred to wait until they were able to clear up the misconceptions about the past.

But when he thought of how she had felt in his arms, all warm and soft, and how her skin had been like satin under his fingers as he ran his hands over her supple body, Jess could feel the heat stir his blood, increasing the effects of the intense humidity.

Making love to Gina had been an experience most men only dreamed about, one that had far surpassed his wildest fantasies. He'd wanted their first time to be special for Gina. He didn't want her wishing last night had never happened.

His reference to their lovemaking when she wouldn't listen to reason and evenly distribute the weight in the packs hadn't improved the situation, but he wasn't going to let her anger deter him. He would just wait until she'd come to terms with their new relationship. He would just have to give her time.

Taking his eyes off Gina's enticing backside for a moment, Jess shifted the guns he was carrying so that Gina could handle the machete and wiped the dripping water off his face. He chuckled when he thought of how close she had come to hitting him with the wet limb. He knew she had let go of the branch on purpose. He smiled to himself when he thought of her childish attempt to get back at him.

When Jess looked back, the spot where she had been standing was empty. All that was left where she had been swinging the machete so viciously was a gaping hole in the foliage. He couldn't see her on the trail ahead, and he could hear nothing through the mist. All was quiet, except for the constant splat of the rain as the heavy drops rolled off the surrounding leaves. She'd dropped out of sight!

Suddenly a piercing scream rent the air, setting him in motion.

Stepping through the opening Gina had made, Jess could see the trail she'd left on the wet ground. He followed the trail of broken, matted vegetation, his heart stopping cold as a wide ravine opened up. With the slope of the ground and the speed she must have been traveling, she wouldn't have been able to stop before going over the edge. Her only hope would be if the ravine wasn't too deep.

Being careful, so that he wouldn't slip and take the same ride she had, he put as much speed as possible into following her trail. Slipping on the wet vegetation made haste impossible, and he took forever to reach the edge of the ravine. The sight that greeted him didn't set his heart at ease. The sides of the gorge were thirty feet straight up and down. Gina couldn't have escaped going over the edge and into the river below.

His heart thundering in his chest, Jess dropped to his knees in the wet grass and let the guns fall to the ground as he leaned out over the rim of the ravine. He halted in surprise. Gina was sitting in a puddle of mud on a small ledge, clinging to a root sticking out of the bank. All that was visible under a heavy coating of mud was her overlarge, golden eyes. She was looking up at him like a little brown owl.

"Are you all right?" Jess asked.

Relieved she wasn't hurt, he was having difficulty holding back the laughter that was building in his chest. The picture Gina made, and his relief at discovering she hadn't gone over the cliff, was making controlling himself impossible.

Seeing Jess leaning over the bank, Gina heaved a sigh of relief—but then she saw the laughter on his face.

"Do I *look* all right?" Gina snapped. She was terrified of heights, a fact he didn't need to know, as long as he was feeling so damned cheerful.

Her head was pounding, and her shoulder ached where she had banged against the bank. And she wanted off this crumbling perch and back on solid ground. She wasn't in the mood for humor, especially if it was at her expense.

Shooting Jess a look that should have conveyed her annoyance and dampened his humor, instead of setting him off again, she added, "I'm just fine. If you think you could control your laughter for a minute, I'd like some help getting out of here."

Hearing that she was unhurt was all the catalyst Jess needed to send his amusement overboard. Rolling onto the wet grass, he laughed until his sides ached. She didn't look half as tough as she would like him to believe while sitting in the mud. Not that he was about to tell her that little bit of information right now. The look she had given him promised retribution.

If she wasn't so put out about his laughing at her predicament, she would have enjoyed listening to the sound of his deep, rich laugh. However, she didn't have the time to enjoy anything. She needed to get off her perch—now.

"Jess!"

Gina's call interrupted his laughter long enough for him to look over the bank. If she thought his laugh was something to hear, the sparkle in his silver eyes took her breath away. Shaking her head to clear her mind of any foolish ideas that might be hatching, she got back to the problem at hand. At least his laughter had eased her fright.

"If you're through enjoying yourself at my expense, maybe you could take a minute and help me off this crumbling ledge before the whole thing slips into the river," she said sourly, failing to see the humor in her situation.

Jess ignored her sarcasm and flashed her a bright smile that lasted until he saw a section of the small patch of mud break loose and slide down the steep wall of the ravine. All humor instantly disappeared as he realized that she could just as easily fall into the river.

After quickly slipping off his pack, Jess lay on his stomach and stretched his arms over the bank.

"Grab hold of my wrists," he instructed as he extended his arms to their full length.

Still holding on to her root, Gina cautiously stood. She had to let go so that she could raise her arms to grab Jess's wrists, but the broken strap of her backpack made her unbalanced. The pack would be too much added weight for Jess to pull up, anyway.

"I'll send up my pack first. Without its weight, lifting me will be easier."

Not waiting for Jess to agree, Gina unhooked the strap holding the pack snug around her waist. When the waist strap was released, the broken shoulder strap allowed the heavy pack to slip off to one side. Gina screamed as the unbalanced weight began dragging her backward toward the edge of the ledge.

"Drop that damned pack!" Jess yelled.

He reached out to Gina, but she was too far below for him to grab hold of her. Feeling helpless, he watched her struggle with the heavy pack.

Gina released the pack, letting the cumbersome weight drop behind her on the muddy ledge as she grabbed for the protruding root. Holding on for dear life, she regained her balance. When she looked behind her, the pack was gone, and so was a good share of the ledge. She watched helplessly as both splashed into the swiftly flowing river. Reluctantly Gina turned back to find Jess holding his hands out to her.

"Give me your hands," he ordered.

Without further hesitation, Gina released her hold on the root and quickly reached up to clasp Jess's large hands. Their strength was reassuring, and their firm hold gave her a sense of security that was out of place, considering her precarious position.

Jess slowly pulled Gina up the rock wall of the ravine by her outstretched arms. She was very light, and under normal circumstances he would have had no difficulty pulling her the short distance, but his injured ribs were screaming in pain at the strain he was putting on them.

As soon as Gina cleared the top of the ledge, she launched herself at Jess, knocking him onto his back in the wet grass. Wrapping her arms around his solid body, she held on tightly.

"Hey! Hold on a minute." Jess sucked in a sharp breath as his ribs loudly protested the additional rough treatment. "I'm sorry about laughing," he said apologetically as he tried to extract himself from her hold.

Having no success at peeling Gina away from his sore ribs, Jess gave up the fight and wrapped his arms around her, relieving some of the strain. "Want to tell me what has you sticking to me so tight?"

Gina's tension eased, and her breathing slowly returned to normal. How was she going to explain her actions to Jess? She felt like a colossal fool for jumping on him the way she had, but she had been terrified.

"Sorry," Gina mumbled, without looking at Jess, as she released her hammerlock on him and eased out of his arms. She lay down beside him in the wet grass and watched the last of the storm clouds pass. "I was scared. I'm not very good with heights." She moved her shoulders restlessly and felt a stab of pain where her shoulder had impacted with the bank. "I guess I panicked."

Closing her eyes, Gina rubbed the goose egg on the back of her head as she thought of the pack, holding most of their supplies, floating down the river. They were on short food rations now, and they didn't have the burner for cooking. All their medical supplies had been in her pack, too. Jess's pack held some supplies, but hers had held the important things.

They were in a fine mess. After making such a big deal over who was more able to carry the heavier pack, she'd ended up being responsible for their being low on supplies. No shelter and few supplies—what a great way to be stranded in a soggy, unfriendly jungle.

Gina glanced at Jess out of the corner of her eye and found him raised on one elbow and looking at her with a definite smirk on his face. Her eyes snapped open as his smile continued to broaden. Was she going to be ridiculed for her fear of heights?

"So you're fallible after all," Jess said, arching one dark brow at her. He quickly changed his mind about teasing her when he saw the look in her eyes. Even fear of retribution couldn't stop his shaking, and he held his throbbing ribs when another fit of laughter threatened.

"You look like a mud owl," he said, a chuckle escaping despite his efforts to hide his humor. "A mad mud owl," he added, seeing Gina's brows draw into a frown. His guess was that she would like to add to his injuries after that crack, but holding back his laughter was impossible given the ridiculous picture she presented. Even in the face of added pain.

"Is everything funny to you?" Gina snapped, her head pounding where she had cracked it against the bank. Let him laugh. At least he wasn't going to needle her about her fear of heights. Her irritation mounted when she remembered his humor while she'd been perched on the ledge. "Don't you realize the fix we're in? All our supplies were in that pack, which at this very minute is probably floating toward the coast. And all you can do is grin like an ass."

She knew she was overreacting, but her head wouldn't stop its incessant pounding. Snapping at someone felt good, and Jess was the only someone handy.

Having had enough of Jess's foolish humor, Gina levered herself up on one elbow. She glanced down at herself and was surprised to find her clothes caked with mud.

Not that being covered in mud was an excuse for his excessive laughter, but the mental picture his comparison to a mud owl brought to mind caused her lips to twitch. She was not going to start laughing! This wasn't the time for silly behavior. Their lives were at stake. They had days of travel before them, and only a smattering of supplies.

Little good was accomplished by listing all the reasons she should keep a serious frame of mind, once she shot another quick look at Jess. Amusement turned his gray eyes to silver as he looked back with a roguish grin, holding his sides while silent laughter shook his body.

His silly grin, so out of place on his rugged face, was her undoing. They both knew she was fighting a losing battle against her own sense of humor. Her smile grew as a chuckle escaped her soft lips.

"I don't look as bad as I think, do I?"

Jess nodded as he bit down on his lip, watching her humor grow as she tried to wipe the mud off her face. She only succeeded in rearranging the mud covering.

"Go ahead, Gina, let go. You can't be serious all the time."

Once started, Gina couldn't stop. Jess's hearty laugh joined hers, and before long they were both rolling in the wet grass, holding their sides, as laughter released the tension caused by fear.

The laughter slowly died as their eyes met and more intense feelings took over. Neither knew who moved first, but they were soon locked in each other's arms.

Jess's hold tightened as he remembered the sensation of helplessness that had flooded him when the weight from Gina's pack almost dragged her off the ledge. He had come so close to losing her.

Gina felt Jess's hold tighten, and had to admit that she liked the safe feeling his strong arms gave her. Admitting she liked being held wasn't easy, and she wouldn't have been able to confess to him that she liked the security of his arms, but enjoying the feeling for a short time wouldn't hurt.

Jess slid his fingers under Gina's chin and slowly raised her face so that he could see into her eyes. He was searching for a sign that she was experiencing the same emotions that were flooding his body with heat.

In her golden eyes he could see the desire she tried to hide behind her sharp tongue, the desire he'd felt as he held her during the storm. He could also see a vulnerability that gave him pause. She was unsure of herself. Treading lightly, so that he wouldn't do irreparable damage to any hopes he had for a future with her, was uppermost in his thoughts. He would show her she had nothing to fear from him.

Gina slowly closed her eyes to keep her feelings hidden. Jess was too astute, and he'd seen enough. Surprise held her immobile as she felt his lips softly brush hers. Feeling no threat in the light touch, she welcomed the kiss as a sigh escaped her lips.

The kiss was so light, Gina knew she could pull away. His hold on her chin was more a caress than a restriction. She knew he would let her go if she showed the least inclination to be set free. Maybe that was why she didn't flee when she felt the touch of his lips on hers. She knew what his kisses did to her. He hadn't been sparing with them last night, and see where that had led her? her conscience questioned. But she wasn't listening to that small voice any longer.

Changing the kiss from light and comforting to hot and passionate met with no resistance as Gina's lips softened under Jess's. The wet grass where they lay wasn't the best place for making love, but they were both beyond worrying about wet grass, or anything else, for that matter—like Gina's being covered in mud. Their senses were filled with each other as their surroundings faded into the background.

Jess rolled onto his back, taking Gina with him, as his mouth devoured her soft lips. This position gave him better access to the hidden curves under her khaki shirt. Lying full-length on his solid body, she fit him like a lost piece of a puzzle. He would never again be complete without her.

Gina's head was pressed against Jess's wet shirt. She could hear the steady beating of his heart as his arms held her tight. She felt protected for the first time in her life, a feeling she could grow to rely on if she wasn't careful. Her thoughts caused her to withdraw as Jess's hands roamed her body.

Sliding his hands down her back, Jess filled them with her gently rounded hips, pulling her into closer contact with his arousal as he searched for her lips. He pulled back, startled, when Gina cried out and began to struggle in earnest. The anguish on her muddy face was genuine.

"I wouldn't force you, Gina," Jess said softly as he brushed a tear from her eye, removing a layer of mud along with the drop of moisture. "I'm sorry if I frightened you."

"The kiss didn't frighten me. You just found one of my sore spots." Gina put her hand on her left hip and slid it down her thigh. When she removed her hand from her sore hip, she discovered a mixture of mud and blood covering her palm.

"Good God! Roll over so I can take a look." Jess gently pushed Gina off balance and rolled her onto her stomach so that he could see where the blood was coming from.

Her mud-covered pants had an eight-inch rip that was surrounded with blood. He couldn't determine the extent of the damage done to her through the tear, and since these were the only pants she had left, he was hesitant to ruin them by tearing the opening any further. Judging by the amount of blood seeping through the ripped pants, though, the cut underneath wasn't a small one.

"You must have landed on a rock. Your pants are going to have to come off before I can see how much damage was done, but you're losing a lot of blood." Jess laid a comforting hand on Gina's shoulder as he searched the slowly clearing sky. "What we need first, though, is some shelter."

They would have a few hours before dark to get settled and take care of Gina's injury. He didn't know whether the daily rain would come after the downpour the night before, but he couldn't take the chance. He needed to find shelter where they could both dry out.

Turning back to Gina, Jess saw a shiver rack her body. Her clothes were soaked, but the shiver might be the beginnings of shock. He retrieved his pack and untied their remaining sleeping bag. At least she would be warm. Without unzipping the bag, he covered Gina as best as possible.

"I can't put you inside, because if that gets wet we'll never get the bag dry again. Try to lie as still as you can, so you don't lose any more blood."

Gina was looking at Jess with dazed eyes.

"Do you hurt anywhere else, Gina?" he asked searchingly.

Wrinkling her brow thoughtfully, she shook her head. She was immediately sorry for the action when the pounding increased and Jess slipped out of focus for a minute. Rubbing the lump on the back of her head, she admitted, "Just a bump on the head. But if my head is as hard as you claim, that bump shouldn't be anything to worry about."

Jess smiled at her silly remark as he softly ran his fingers down her mud-covered cheek. Passing on a feeling of confidence when that confidence was in short supply wasn't easy, and he admired her for it. She was now dependent on him to see to their rescue, and he wasn't sure he had the abilities necessary to get them out of the jungle alive.

Chapter 8

Gina watched Jess disappear into the jungle in search of shelter for the night. Until he squeezed her bottom, she hadn't realized the extent of her injuries. Now her upper left thigh throbbed with pain, while her head pounded where she had been slammed against the bank. Her clammy clothes robbed her body of heat as shivers vibrated through her with the force of last night's thunder. Reaction to her injuries was starting to set in. Pulling the sleeping bag tightly around her, she closed her eyes and prayed Jess would hurry.

To occupy her mind while she waited for Jess's return, Gina ran through a mental list of the supplies stashed in the pockets of her survival pants. Added to the supplies in Jess's pack, the list wasn't very inspiring. They had no alternative but to make do with what they had.

Within minutes, Jess crashed through the foliage, his scouting expedition successful, judging by the pleased look on his face.

"I made reservations for the best room in the house," he said. "So we'd better be going before they rent the room to someone else."

His attempt at humor was heartwarming. The light-hearted banter eased her mind about the success of the rest of their journey.

"I hope they have plenty of hot water. I'm going to need gallons to scrape this mud pack off."

Jess quickly rolled up the sleeping bag before gently removing the pack from under Gina's head and retying the rolled bundle to it. After settling the pack on his shoulders, he helped her to her feet. Bright red blood oozed through the rip in her pants, but he couldn't pack the cut to stop the bleeding through the dirty pants.

Hesitating while he decided how he was going to get her to the shelter, Jess looked down at Gina. Her leg was still supporting her, but he didn't know for how long. He slipped the pack off his shoulders and returned the added weight to the ground. Then he swung her into his arms. The small outcropping he'd found for shelter wasn't very far. He should be able to carry her the short distance.

"Jess, put me down. You're going to hurt your ribs," Gina protested, squirming slightly in his arms.

"Be still. We'll be there in a minute," he softly ordered. Striding toward the shelter, he pulled her tighter into the confines of his arms.

The shelter wasn't more than an overhang of vines over a small outcropping of rocks, but at least they wouldn't be out in the elements if the storm decided to return.

He felt the shivers that racked Gina's body. She needed more than the protection the small indentation in the hillside provided. Easing her out of his embrace, he leaned Gina against the vine-covered bank.

"Will you be all right while I get the pack?"

At her slight nod, he returned to where he'd left the pack, then rushed back to Gina. She hadn't moved an inch.

Jess unfastened the sleeping bag from the pack. After unzipping the soft down-filled bag, he spread it on the ground next to the bank before turning to Gina. She was still leaning against the bank where he'd left her. Her eyes closed, her face pale and drawn under the layers of mud, she looked ready to collapse. Her soft mouth was drawn tight, the only sign that she was in pain. He didn't want to think about the fix they were going to be in if the cut turned out to be serious.

First things first. The mud-caked clothes would have to go. She wasn't going to like him removing her pants, though for one moment he took perverse delight in turning the tables on her. But he would wait until she was patched up before he pointed that fact out to her.

As he lightly touched Gina's shoulder, Jess watched her eyes slowly open. Their beautiful golden depths were dimmed by the pain she was trying to control. Her slim body shook with shivers. Her total exhaustion and pain tempted him to let her lie down without the trouble of removing her clothes, but common sense told him that would be a foolish decision.

The devilish gleam in Jess's eyes put Gina on her guard. He was up to something. Something she had a feeling she wasn't going to like one bit.

"You're almost out on your feet, Gina, but you can't lie down until we get your wet clothes off," Jess said, all seriousness now, his eyes losing their teasing glint. "I can't tell how bad the damage is through the rip."

Gina didn't like his plan, and the glare she sent him clearly told him her thoughts on the idea. But she didn't voice her objections. She'd caused enough problems already with her stubbornness. Still, though she wasn't about to argue, she didn't have to let him think she was meekly submitting.

Jess gave her a cheeky grin before reaching for the buttons on her shirt. Gina slapped his hands away and unbuttoned the shirt herself.

"I'm not completely helpless," she snapped, not looking at him until the buttons were unfastened.

"You know the shirt has to come off, Gina. We only have the one sleeping bag, and you can't get into bed all wet and muddy."

Jess saw her flinch and wished he'd left out the part about their having only one sleeping bag. He hadn't meant to sound accusing.

With one finger under her chin, he lifted her head so that he could see into her eyes. "Losing the pack was an accident, Gina. I wasn't blaming you."

Looking into his warm gray eyes, Gina lifted her chin slightly, breaking contact with Jess's finger. Slowly she began pulling the wet shirt off her shoulders. The mud-caked fabric stuck to her skin, making removal of the stiff material difficult. After a short struggle, she willingly let Jess finish the job when he reached out to help.

As the muddy shirt slid down her arms, Jess sucked in his breath. Under the shirt she wore only a thin white tank top, and it was soaking wet.

Crossing her arms, she tilted her chin at a stubborn angle. Her top was damp and should come off, but she was going to hold on to the flimsy covering as long as possible. The light cotton wasn't as wet as the rest of her clothes, so she could wait to remove it for a while longer.

She turned her attention to the buttons on her pants when she was certain Jess wasn't going to press the issue. She found the buttons caked with mud and impossible to unfasten. Accepting the inevitable, she submitted to Jess's assistance again. Whether he undressed her or not was beginning to be less important by the minute. She just wanted to lie down somewhere warm and dry. How she reached that warm, dry place was immaterial.

Jess watched as Gina dropped her hands away from the buttons on her pants. Resigned to her fate, she leaned her head back against the bank. He understood the significance of the gesture, and, without comment, made quick work of the mud-encrusted buttons.

The pants clung to her slim legs as Jess carefully tugged them down to her ankles while trying to protect her left thigh. Dropping to his knees, he began unlacing her boots. A quick glance upward halted his fingers on the muddy laces. The sight that greeted him trapped the air in his lungs.

The dark green foliage surrounding Gina made her pale skin glow. She looked like a marble statue, lying amid the vines, with rays of sunlight streaming across her skin. Even partially covered in mud, she was a vision to behold. Her next-to-nothing silk panties and clinging wet top did nothing to hide her perfect body from his view. From where he was kneeling, he had an unrestricted view, one he would carry in his memory for the rest of his life.

Berating himself for gawking like an adolescent when Gina needed his help, Jess quickly went back to removing her muddy clothes. As soon as he had her down to her underwear, he gently turned her around so that he could assess the damage. Tugging the leg of her panties aside, he had his first view of the bloody cut.

What he saw did nothing for his peace of mind. The back of her thigh was smeared with mud and blood. A jagged ten-inch cut marred her smooth skin. From what he could see, under the mud, most of the cut was no more than a wide scratch. But where she must have landed the hardest, under the curve of her bottom, the cut was deep, and it was steadily oozing blood.

He could bind the upper part of her thigh to protect the scrape, but the deep cut was in a spot where a bandage wouldn't hold for long, especially with them having days yet to hike through the rough jungle.

With every step, Gina would only tear the cut open and start the bleeding again. Infection was another problem, a side effect of the high humidity. That was why Gina had been so adamant about putting the antiseptic on his cuts.

Now *he* was responsible for taking care of *her,* and he had no idea how to go about mending the tear in her leg. Hell, all their medical supplies were floating somewhere in the river. By now, the pack could already have made it to the coast.

Jess ran a shaky hand through his hair, dragging mud through the overlong wet strands. He didn't know what they were going to do about this new turn of events.

Turning her head, Gina attempted to see what was taking Jess so long. All she could see was him sitting on his knees, looking at her bottom. Having him looking at her almost naked backside was embarrassing.

"Jess, what are you doing?" Gina asked crossly.

She wanted the exam over with so that she could lie down. The spread-out sleeping bag was beckoning.

"I'm trying to figure out what we're going to do to patch you up enough to stop the bleeding." Jess slowly rose to his feet, still holding the leg of her panties away from the oozing cut. "What you need are some stitches, and we don't even have a Band-Aid between us."

"How deep is it, and how long?"

"I don't see what difference that makes. The location of it prevents us from doing much except letting you rest until it heals enough to stop the bleeding."

"Just answer my question, will you? I'm tired. I'd like to lie down as soon as you've completed your examination, Doctor."

Ignoring her sarcasm, Jess hunkered back down. He didn't mind the view from this position. Gina had a fantastic derriere, soft and rounded—a perfect fit for his cupped hands. No, looking at her bottom, encased in pale pink silk, was no hardship.

Damn it, Knight, get your mind back on the job at hand, he silently reproached himself. Couldn't he see that Gina was reaching the end of her rope?

"The deepest part of the cut is about four inches long. The rest isn't much more than a scratch. The cut is right here." Jess ran his finger along the edge of the gash, letting Gina know its length.

Gina jumped when she felt his finger on her bare skin. If he'd seared her with a branding iron, his touch couldn't have felt any hotter. She forced herself to concentrate on his words and not on the fire that licked through her veins, momentarily chasing the chills away.

As soon as Jess removed his finger, Gina turned to face him. Her quick movement caught him on his knees, with his eyes level with her hips. Giving him a fierce frown indicating that she didn't appreciate his position had little effect. All he did was grin at her.

Jess slowly stood, enjoying the scenery the whole way. When his sparkling gray eyes encountered her stormy amber ones, the air was charged with enough electricity to strike sparks.

Gina was the first to turn away. Her cheeks flaming, she searched the ground. "Where did you put my pants?"

Jess shrugged away her testy tone and looked toward where he had tossed her wet clothing. "There." He pointed. "But they're too wet and muddy for you to put back on."

Gina would dearly have loved to sit down, but the throbbing in her thigh told her how much that would hurt. As soon as she could, she was going to lie down.

"Hand them to me, would you?" she asked, ignoring his comment, as she braced herself against the bank, taking some of the weight off her left leg.

Grabbing the muddy mess, which held little resemblance to her pants, Gina sorted through the many zippered pockets.

"Hold out your hands," she ordered as she opened one of the pockets. Taking out a handful of bandages and tape, she dumped them into Jess's outstretched hands before moving on to the next pocket. From this pocket, she brought out foil-wrapped packages. These, too, she dumped into Jess's hands.

Jess watched, transfixed, as if Gina were a magician pulling rabbits out of a hat. His hands were filled with first aid supplies, and she still had pockets to go.

"What else do you have in those pockets?" The baggy pants seemed to have a dozen pockets of various sizes.

"These are my emergency supplies. We'll be able to survive for a few days on the provisions in these pockets. We won't have much in the way of variety, but at least we won't be hungry," she added.

He continued waiting to see what else she was going to pull out of her bag—or rather pocket—of tricks.

The last item was a small waterproof pouch, which she thrust into Jess's waiting hands.

"The other pockets can wait for now. My head is pounding. I need to rest." Gina rubbed her temples as the trees began to whirl around her. Her legs no longer able to support her, she began sliding to her knees.

The next thing she knew, she was lying facedown on the sleeping bag. Now if she could just curl up and get warm, everything would be perfect. But apparently Jess had something else in mind, as she felt him rearranging her legs.

He looked at Gina, where she lay on the dark sleeping bag, with admiration. She was one tough lady. In her exhausted state, she had held out longer than most men would have.

Gathering the scattered medical supplies he'd dropped when he grabbed Gina just before she hit the ground, Jess checked their contents. The foil-wrapped packages contained disinfectant and sterile cleaning pads. He opened the waterproof medicine kit and found inside a small bottle of disinfectant, aspirin and alcohol pads, all wrapped in foil.

The next packet he took out of the kit froze the blood in his veins as the function of the contents dawned on him. The small packet looked like a woman's sewing kit, but the size of the needle and the type of thread told him that this kit wasn't used for sewing on buttons.

Slowly turning toward Gina, Jess found her intently watching him from her position on the sleeping bag. Her golden eyes were expressionless, but her steady gaze told him what she expected him to do.

Jess dropped the small packet as if the pouch had come to life and bitten him. Shaking his head, he began to back away.

"No way! No way, lady!"

As if to emphasize his refusal, he shoved his hands deep into his pockets, where they wouldn't be tempted to reach for the kit. "I'm not going to even attempt *that*." He couldn't even bring himself to say the words.

"Jess, the cut needs to be stitched if we're going to get out of here. And you're the only one who can do it," Gina calmly stated, holding Jess with her steady gaze.

Jess stared at her as if she'd lost her mind. She was so matter-of-fact. Where did she think she was, the Wild West? Just bite the bullet while someone stitched you up and then sent you on your merry way?

Jess broke out in a cold sweat, his heart beating erratically in his chest. Well, he wasn't so tough, no matter what she thought *she* was.

Gina continued to watch Jess struggle with the reality of their situation. She knew he had no choice in the matter, but she would wait for him to come to terms with that fact by himself.

With an abrupt movement, Jess turned away from those all-knowing eyes and looked out through the tangle of trees and vines. For about the thousandth time, he wished to God that he had listened to Virgil and stayed where he belonged.

Drawing a deep breath, Jess tipped his head back and searched the heavens for strength. The bleeding had to be stopped, and he *was* the only one available. Those were the facts, and he couldn't wish them away.

Gina watched Jess battle with the issue, knowing the exact minute he accepted the inevitable. She watched as he let out his pent-up breath and pulled his shoulders back. She didn't know when she had begun to trust Jess, she just did. She had faith in his ability to meet this challenge. Observing him over the past few days, she'd learned that he was the kind of person who didn't run from a problem.

The way he had stood unarmed and battered in that dark cell, ready to meet whoever stepped through the door, told her that he would do everything in his power to confront this problem and come out the victor. He could do no less and still be the man she had come to know over the past few days. The man he had always been—though she had failed to acknowledge it.

Jess turned, meeting Gina's watchful eyes. He cringed when he saw the trust shining clearly in their golden depths. He wished he felt as assured about this ordeal as she appeared to be.

Assuming a poise he was far from feeling, Jess set to work. He had a lot to do before dark, and only a few hours to accomplish everything.

He lined up the supplies from the medical kit along the edge of the sleeping bag. The line was pitifully short for the job ahead. He could feel Gina watching his every move, but she made no comment as to whether he was doing things properly.

The sweat covering his forehead wasn't entirely caused by the jungle heat. He couldn't remember a time when he had been more nervous. To be honest, damned scared was a better description.

Taking a deep breath, he picked up the small bottle of disinfectant. At least he knew the first step. His hands needed to be sterilized, and so did the area around Gina's cut. Holding the bottle up to the light, he frowned. There was precious little of the stuff. The disinfectant wasn't going to stretch to sterilize both areas sufficiently.

"Jess," Gina called softly. She waited for him to look at her before she continued. "Do you think you could find something dry enough to burn?"

The question was so far removed from the problem he was wrestling with that it took a second to register. "I don't know if I can find a dry piece of wood in this whole damned jungle." Jess frowned as he knelt beside her and pulled the edges of the sleeping bag tighter. "Are you cold, honey?"

Jess didn't realize he'd added the softly spoken endearment as he carefully brushed dried mud out of her hair. The tender look on his face was enough to melt the hardest heart, and Gina had no resistance against his power.

"I can feel shock starting to set in. With shock will come more chills, and possibly fever. You'll need hot water to clean my leg. We're lucky you were carrying the pan, or we wouldn't have anything to heat the water in." Her voice faded into silence, and her eyes took on a glazed look before they closed.

Jess tucked the sleeping bag around Gina once more before going to look for dry wood. "Where in the hell am I supposed to find anything dry enough to burn in this wet mess?" he complained under his breath as he headed into the trees. He had no idea where to look, but he was going to do his damnedest.

Jess found dry wood sooner than he expected. Only a few feet from the small stream that trickled down the bank where they were camped lay a large tree that, judging by the split running along the top portion, had been struck by lightning years ago. The tree had landed on another downed tree, which had held it off the soggy jungle floor. Vines and ferns grew out of the trunk, further protecting its interior from the torrential rains, keeping the inside as dry as paper.

Backtracking to where Gina had started her downhill slide, Jess searched until he found where the machete had fallen in the matted weeds. Returning to the fallen tree, he hacked off the drenched outer bark until he reached the more solid chunks that were dry enough to burn.

Once he returned to their shelter, getting the fire going took longer than finding the wood had. After he'd filled the air with words hot enough to start a blaze on their own, a small flame finally took hold. With a lot of patience, and a considerable amount of blowing, the tiny sparks slowly grew into larger flames.

As the fire grew stronger, Jess fed in more chunks of wood, until he was sure it would continue to burn. He would have to make another trip to the fallen tree before dark, so that he could keep the fire going all night. He sure as hell didn't want to have to restart the damned thing.

Once he was satisfied that the fire wouldn't die, Jess turned to Gina. She hadn't moved an inch the whole time he was working on the fire. If she was unconscious, sewing up her leg would be easier on her...and on him. He wouldn't be as nervous if she wasn't aware of what he was doing. Maybe she wouldn't feel the pain he knew was in store.

Jess washed his hands as best he could at the small stream before bringing back a pan filled with water. He balanced the small pan on the rocks near the fire, then poured a small amount of the disinfectant into the water.

While waiting for the water to heat, Jess used Gina's knife to cut his remaining clean undershirt into strips. When the disinfected water was hot enough, he poured a small amount of it over his hands, then wiped them on a piece of the undershirt.

Shooting a look in Gina's direction, Jess was relieved to see that her eyes were still closed. Kneeling on the sleeping bag, he hooked his fingers in the waist band of her lace panties, then slid them down her legs. He was surprised when he felt embarrassment heat his face as he tossed them in the general direction of her muddy clothes. He had performed that simple chore for a number of women in his life without a hint of unease. Gina's vulnerability must be the reason he was so uncharacteristically affected.

Without allowing himself time to think about her naked body lying before him, Jess quickly dipped the cloth into the hot water. As gently as possible, he washed the mud from around her cut. Next he opened one of the antiseptic packets and thoroughly cleaned around the edges.

Gina hadn't made a sound all the while he worked on cleaning her thigh, but he didn't think she would sleep through his next step. The disinfectant was going to burn like hell. She was sure to come around then.

Lifting the little bottle of disinfectant over the cut on her thigh, Jess took a deep breath and quickly poured half the contents over the bloody gash. He watched the liquid mix with blood and overflow the jagged edges, leaving behind a trail that ran bright red.

Rearing up from her prone position on the sleeping bag, Gina let out a tortured scream that tore at Jess's heart. Burying his face in her hair, he whispered soothing words into her ear until she lay quiet once again. He'd had no choice but to do what he had done. He just hoped that if she remembered the intense pain, she would understand.

When Gina didn't move, Jess turned her head enough to see that she was unconscious—not just asleep. With surprisingly steady hands, he reached for the packet of sutures. Before she woke, he was going to have the stitches in place. He couldn't bear to make her suffer like that again.

Jess rubbed his hand over the dark stubble on his face. Exhausted, he settled against the vine-covered hillside and leaned his head back, looking up at the millions of stars filling the clear night sky. He would gladly have given a year's pay for a bottle of whiskey right now. Hell, he would have settled for just one shot. The past two hours had turned him inside out. He never wanted to go through anything like that again.

He'd thought the first stitch would be the hardest, but seeing her body's involuntary twitch each time he punctured her creamy skin had become increasingly difficult. He was thankful the cut had only required six stitches. He would never have attempted the job if the whole injury had needed stitching.

By the time he finished, he had been covered in sweat. His hands still hadn't stopped shaking. Cleaning and dressing the cut had taken forever. He'd felt physically sick by the time he had the bandage covering the stitches and Gina tucked into the sleeping bag.

Jess turned to look into the meager shelter where she quietly slept. He didn't know whether her continued unconsciousness was a good sign or whether it meant something was wrong. She hadn't made a sound other than the soft mews that had torn at his heart with each jab of the needle. An hour had passed since he had finished stitching her thigh, and she still hadn't moved or made a sound.

In his ignorance, he might have done her more harm than good. He'd had no business sewing up her cut in the first place. After all, she was the one with the medical training, not him.

Sure, he could apply a tourniquet and perform creditable CPR, but that was his limit. Surgery was definitely not on his list of accomplishments. Until now.

With his head resting against the ever-present vines that seemed to cover anything that didn't move, Jess closed his tired eyes. He knew he wouldn't sleep. Each time he closed his eyes, he saw the needle piercing Gina's delicate skin. Each little river of blood that ran from a new puncture would haunt him forever. She was going to have a nasty scar; his needlework hadn't been any too neat.

Gina wasn't the vain type, though. She would be the first to shrug off his poor attempt at surgery, but Jess knew he wasn't going to come to terms with the experience for some time . . . if he ever did. The past two hours made what he'd suffered at the hands of the rebels seem paltry by comparison. All you needed to put things into their proper perspective was a more serious problem to contend with. And getting Gina safely to the coast was his most important concern right now.

The only knowledge Jess had of survival in the wilds was what he had picked up from Gina while they were stuck in the cave. He'd thought at the time that she would make a good teacher. She had made their walks interesting, and he'd learned from her—but he needed her. And for more than just getting them safely to the coast.

A soft moan drew his attention. Rising, he went to Gina's side, leaving his worries for tomorrow. No use looking for trouble. He would tackle each new obstacle as it arose.

Gina had thrown off the sleeping bag in an attempt to roll onto her back. Her thrashing would tear her stitches, and he wasn't going to allow that to happen. No way was he going to stitch her cut again.

Jess eased Gina onto her stomach, speaking softly to her until she quieted once again. As he watched her sleep, he smoothed her matted hair away from her damp forehead. She didn't feel overly warm—that had to be a plus. A dozen other problems he didn't know about could arise, but his main concern was the infection she could get from his amateur surgery.

Jess ran his hand lightly over Gina's hair, feeling the long-forgotten tug of caring for someone. She was his responsibility now. He was surprised by the way he accepted that thought without a qualm. Being accountable for someone else was something he had purposely avoided for years. For some strange reason, having Gina depend on him felt good—a little scary, but damned good.

By choice, he'd steered clear of close relationships for years, because of the pain that could come from letting yourself become attached to another person. But Serena, and his reasons for choosing a solitary life, were a thing of the past. She was so far in the past that he was a little surprised to have her memory pop up now when his thoughts were so filled with Gina. The two women were in no way the same.

He hadn't allowed Serena to enter his thoughts for seven years. Long ago he'd put their disastrous relationship behind him and gotten on with his life. The only lingering effect of that association had been his vow to never get seriously involved with anyone again. And he'd stuck to that vow—until Gina walked back into his life.

Jess could still taste the bitterness that had helped him keep the vow all these years, though Serena's leaving hadn't been what had embittered him.

She had been everything he thought he needed in a wife: beautiful, intelligent and sophisticated. He'd met her at an officers' party. She'd come with one of his senior officers. He wouldn't have been at the party himself if they hadn't been wooing him to join Special Services.

When the night was over, Serena had left the party with him. Within a few weeks, they'd been living together. The romance had lasted for over a year, with Jess asking her periodically to marry him.

Serena had been an executive with a thriving computer company and had been looking for advancement to the board. She'd constantly used work as her reason for refusing his proposals, saying the time was never right for them to marry.

Even after she discovered she was pregnant she'd still delayed any plans for marriage. He'd found out why when he returned from an extralong assignment to discover that she had packed up and moved out of their apartment.

He'd found her soon enough, but he'd wished he hadn't. She had moved in with the owner of the computer company, assuring herself of the position she coveted.

His unborn child hadn't stood in her way, either—she'd had the unwanted burden aborted. When she coldheartedly told him what she'd done, he'd realized how much he'd been looking forward to a child and a family of his own. He'd walked away from her without a backward thought, erecting a protective shield around his emotions that held until he met Gina. Without the least effort, she had penetrated his armor, until he had no resistance left where she was concerned.

He didn't know when she had slipped under his guard and into his heart, but he knew that was where she belonged. She filled his heart to overflowing, and it felt right. He was going to do everything in his power to not only keep her safe, but to make her his.

Chapter 9

Dispensing with the ghosts of his past, Jess turned his attention to Gina again. There was nothing more he could do for her tonight, except keep her as comfortable as possible. Carefully lying down beside her on the sleeping bag, he eased her onto her right side with her back against him. She stirred slightly as he pulled the bag over them, but after a small sigh she relaxed and slipped into a deep sleep, her head pillowed on his arm.

Jess felt the results of his foolish actions almost immediately, as her warm body settled more fully against him. Gina's soft bottom was nestled in his lap once again, and his body wasn't tired enough to ignore the signals their intimate position promised. She was a sexy armful, and he was going to suffer the effects of holding her through the rest of the night.

A deep groan escaped his tight lips when she wiggled even closer into his warmth. Smiling dryly, he decided he would rather suffer all night long and be able to do noth-

ing more than hold her close than never be able to hold her
at all.

Jess slid his free hand over her hip and up to cup a full
breast through the thin tank top she still wore. If he had to
suffer, he was going to be rewarded for his good behavior.
Smiling at his selfish thoughts, he settled down to get some
rest.

Gina's thrashing woke him after a couple of hours. She
was still asleep, but even snuggled in his arms, she was
shivering. Jess's heart sank. Had infection already set in?

Easing himself out of the sleeping bag, he ran his hand
over his tired face and through his tangled hair as he muttered a few choice words. What the hell was he supposed
to do now? He had no idea what a person did for infection. Why couldn't she wake up and tell him what to do?

Looking at the glow of the red coals, he decided that the
first thing he had to do was to get more firewood. He'd
planned on making the trip before dark, but had been reluctant to leave Gina. He couldn't put off restocking the
fire any longer, though. After tucking the sleeping bag
around her, he dug the small flashlight out of the pack and
set off for the fallen log.

With the fire burning brightly once more, Jess eased the
covering back so that he could see his handiwork. He
prayed that the stitches wouldn't look all fiery, the way his
cut had looked before Gina started treating him. He carefully removed the bandage. His breath whistled through
his teeth in relief when the narrow beam from the flashlight moved over the cut. The stitches were puckered and
the skin around them bruised, but they weren't the ugly red
the cut on his leg had been. To his untrained eye, the color
around the stitches appeared to be healthy.

He carefully laid his hand on the prickly stitches and was
relieved that they weren't overly warm. Maybe she was
suffering the results of shock and not infection. If shock
was what had her thrashing about, then the only thing he

could do was keep her warm. That was as far as his first aid training had taken him. He sure wished to hell he'd paid more attention to the course.

Using a piece of his torn undershirt, he dipped it into the cool water in the pan and lightly wiped the perspiration from Gina's face. He became concerned when she did no more than sigh. Now what was he to do? Could the bump on her head, coupled with the shock she'd suffered be keeping her unconscious this long? He wished to hell he knew the answers.

As he wiped the cool rag down her throat and across her chest, he racked his brain for any knowledge of concussions. He came up empty-handed. The only treatment he knew about was to keep the patient warm. And didn't everyone always push chicken soup when someone was sick? he thought as he hung the rag on a branch.

Any course of action was better than nothing, Jess thought. And to be on the safe side, he used some more of the disinfectant and liberally doused the stitched area before covering the wound with fresh bandages. He wished again for the medicine case Gina had been carrying in her pack. One of those injections she'd been jabbing him with couldn't have hurt, and it would have eased his mind.

With a half grin, he imagined giving her a shot in her pretty little rear just as she'd been doing to him. Mere days ago he would have relished having her in the position she was in right now. He would have gloated at having the tables turned, but the grin quickly disappeared. Given the chance, he would gladly have traded places with her.

Jess took a couple of aspirin from the first aid kit and added them to a small amount of the drinking water in the canteen. When they had dissolved to his satisfaction, he knelt by Gina's head, placing the cup against her lips. He poured a few drops into her mouth, only to watch them trickle out unswallowed.

After setting the cup on the ground, Jess turned Gina onto her back, careful to keep her off her left hip. Getting no more than a soft moan from her, he lifted her head onto his arm and held it steady with his palm. He held the cup to her lips again, opening her mouth with his thumb as he poured the liquid in. The water and aspirin stayed inside this time. He laid her head back on his arm until he saw her throat work, swallowing.

Jess gently eased her onto her stomach on the sleeping bag and tucked the covering around her. Maybe the aspirin wasn't much, but anything was better than nothing. He'd heard somewhere that aspirin fought a fever. Anyway, aspirin was all he had.

Jess put the flashlight and their small store of medical supplies safely inside his pack and added some more wood to the fire. When he'd done everything he could to make Gina comfortable, he lay down next to her and gathered her in his arms again. She'd stopped shivering and as he assumed his previous position, she settled into peaceful sleep.

As Jess held Gina close, he thought of the fight they'd had before leaving the cave. Morning felt more like days ago than mere hours. The stupid argument over the distribution of the supplies made him feel like a fool now. He shouldn't have challenged her about letting him carry his share. If he'd kept his mouth shut and not harassed her, she might not have gotten hurt. A fat lot of good being the strong male was doing him right now, anyway. He was way out of his realm here.

A throbbing pain woke Gina, and a heavy weight across her waist prevented her from shifting positions to ease the pain. Awakening fully, she realized she was being held down by a muscular arm. An arm that was attached to the hand that was possessively holding her bare breast under her tank top.

Trying to orient herself, she shifted slightly on the hard ground. She was immediately sorry, as a hot pain shot through her body and seemed to settle with an insistent pounding in her head. The searing pain jogged her memory, bringing yesterday's events into full focus.

Careful to keep her leg still, she listed the facts she knew. She had taken a fall off an embankment that had resulted in an injured behind. Jess had found them shelter. He had taken care of her injury. Now she was in a sleeping bag, in the middle of the jungle, with Jess's hand cupping her breast.

She had all the facts straight, but a few unanswered questions remained. Such as, had Jess stitched her cut? How long had they been there? More importantly, what was he doing with his hand under her shirt?

The last thing she could remember was a searing pain shooting through her body just before darkness blanketed everything. Before that, she remembered her head pounding so fiercely that she hadn't paid close attention to what Jess was doing until he began removing her panties. She had felt so exposed with her bare bottom revealed to his gaze that she avoided thinking about what he might do next as she concentrated on fighting her humiliation at her revealing position. All thought of embarrassment had vanished when the black void descended, bringing peace.

Jess murmured soft words in her ear while rubbing his hand over her body in a soothing caress. When his caresses failed to soothe her as they had done many times during the night, he shook himself completely awake to check on her.

He leaned over to find her eyes wide open, intently watching him. The lucid golden eyes, under raised eyebrows, brought bright color to his face as he recalled what he'd been doing before he came fully awake.

The fact that he could be so easily rattled caused him to scowl darkly at her, instead of hugging her, the way he really wanted to do.

"I see you've decided to rejoin the living." The harsh statement, coupled with his scowl, made quick work of ridding his face of any telltale signs of distress.

When all she did was look at him with her eyebrows raised in an unspoken question, he realized he still had his hand under her top, protectively holding her breast. Quickly jerking his hand back, Jess growled a few choice words as he threw back the covering and rose to his feet.

"How long was I out?" Gina asked. The faintness of her voice had nothing to do with her fall. Finding Jess holding her so intimately had left her weak and shocked at first, until her body had begun to react to his touch. If he hadn't been so busy fighting his own embarrassment, he would have noticed how her heart rate had increased and that the heat burning her cheeks had nothing to do with a fever.

If he'd continued with his caresses, Gina knew, she wouldn't have stopped him any more than she had the night of the storm. Where he was concerned, she had no resistance. That thought was enough to chase away the remaining heat his touch had ignited.

She didn't need to be held like some helpless female. She had learned long ago to take care of herself. What she needed now were some answers. In particular, were they going to make it to the coast on time?

Clearing her throat, Gina tried the question again. "How long have I been out?" She was much more pleased with her voice on the second try. She needed to keep her mind focused on their rescue. The boat couldn't hang around in unfriendly waters indefinitely. The local police would start to get suspicious.

Jess gave Gina a sharp look before turning to the remains of the fire. With his back to her, he couldn't see her sleep-flushed body, still warm from his arms, or that she was almost naked under the corner of the sleeping bag that covered her legs. He could almost forget how good she'd felt while he held her during the night. Without too much coaxing, he would willingly have crawled back into that cozy sleeping bag to resume the caresses he'd been torturing himself with all night. His wisest course for now would be keeping his back to her until he regained his control.

"One night. You went over the bank yesterday." As soon as he had the coals stirred and had added some of the smaller pieces of dried wood, he turned to face Gina. "How are you feeling?"

"My leg hurts like hell. And my head is pounding like a construction crew is inside, using a jackhammer on my skull. But otherwise, I'm fine." She looked at him. "How are you doing this morning? Any aftereffects?"

Jess half smiled as he thought of the aftereffects he was suffering from after holding her through the night. He'd run the gambit from intense fear to intense desire during the long hours of darkness. He wondered whether she would like to hear what his thoughts had been while she lay sleeping in his arms.

"I'm fine. No damage done."

Gina studied Jess's bland expression. She hadn't been able to read the thoughts that had flickered so quickly in his gray eyes, bringing the small smile to his full lips. But that secret smile hadn't helped to slow her pulse.

Dark shadows framed Jess's eyes, and his lean cheeks looked a little sunken from lack of sleep. But even rumpled and tired, he still had the power to make her heart beat faster and to rob her lungs of air.

He looked ruggedly handsome with his hair tangled and the dark stubble covering his chin. Gina thought about how she must look with her hair full of mud, not to mention the fact that she needed a bath. Those thoughts reminded her that she had awakened in Jess's sleeping bag,

again wearing practically nothing! Her face flamed as she
realized that she wasn't wearing her panties. She only had
her thin top on...and she'd spent the night sleeping in
Jess's arms!

"Where are my clothes?" she asked, as she belatedly
pulled the sleeping bag around her naked legs.

The question had a familiar ring, and she shot a quick
look at Jess. Judging by the mischievous look on his face,
he was remembering where she had heard that question,
too. This time, she was at his mercy, and she didn't like the
feeling.

"Your pants were caked with mud, so I emptied your
multitude of pockets and swished them in the stream.
They're hanging outside, along with your shirt, waiting for
the sun to dry them. Most of the mud came off, but I won't
make any guarantees about how clean they're going to be."

Jess was enjoying himself immensely at Gina's expense.
But seeing the fire mounting in her eyes also made him feel
relieved. She was back to her old self. She didn't appear to
have suffered any lasting effects because of his amateur
surgery. Her leg would be sore when she tried to walk, but
he knew she wouldn't let that stop her.

"If you're through gloating, you could find me something to wear so I can test my leg."

"All in good time," Jess answered, with a devilish glint
in his eye. "I think I'd better see how my handiwork looks
this morning. And, of course, I'll need to put some antiseptic on your cut," he said, taking delight in using her
very words.

Gina gritted her teeth. He was going to play their reversed positions for all they were worth. Well, let him have
his fun. It wasn't going to last long.

Keeping the sleeping bag around her waist, Gina twisted
onto her stomach, no small feat as the sudden movement
sent a burning pain shooting through her leg. She was go-

Roberta Tobeck   *167*

ing to have to be careful. They had a long walk ahead of them yet.

Jess watched as Gina made herself comfortable on the sleeping bag while trying to preserve her modesty. He waited, building the suspense, before dropping down beside her on his knees. He could see her muscles tense while she studiously kept her head turned away from him.

"Will you just get on with it?" she managed to say through stiff lips. He couldn't just get his examination over with. No, he had to drag the episode out, to get his full pound of flesh.

Jess waited until Gina turned her head to see what was delaying him. Her questioning eyes were met by a bland smile that told her nothing.

"What's so funny?" she snapped.

His glowing gray eyes held hers as he slowly reached for her only covering. Again the mischievous look came into his eyes. He was doing this deliberately, she thought, and she wasn't going to put up with his tormenting her.

She opened her mouth to protest, just as the down-filled covering was being pushed out of the way. Her words froze in her throat as she closed her eyes so that she wouldn't have to see Jess gloat further over the turn of events that had placed her in his hands.

The cool air hit her skin, but only in the small area around her injury. He'd moved the sleeping bag just enough for him to tend her wound, but not enough to expose her completely. Gina's eyes snapped open to see that he was no longer gloating, but was looking at her with such a tender expression that she felt confused.

"I think I've been vindicated enough," Jess said seriously. "The teasing is over."

Without saying more, he turned his attention to removing the bandage on her thigh. She watched as he bent to the task, feeling a moment's disquiet at the expression on his face. Concern had him drawing his brows together when the bandage was finally removed.

He gently touched the tender skin around the wound, as if he were touching the soft petals of a rose. The light touch was surprisingly soothing.

"I'm no authority, but your cut doesn't appear to be infected. The skin around the stitches doesn't look anything like the cut on my leg did." Jess looked at Gina. "You're going to have a nasty scar. My stitching leaves a lot to be desired in the way of neatness."

"Having a scar is the least of my worries. Who's going to see it there, anyway?" She returned his mocking look with arched brows before her eyes filled with serious intent. "I know sewing my leg couldn't have been easy for you, but I'm sure you did a fine job. I know it isn't much, but... thank you."

"Don't mention it. I was simply repaying you for all those times you poked me in the butt with that dull needle. I think we're even now."

Gina let Jess's comment pass. He was deliberately making light of things. And if that was the way he wanted it, she wasn't going to argue with him.

As soon as Jess had replaced the bandage, Gina tugged the sleeping bag into place, covering her posterior from his view. Gingerly she turned onto her good hip and faced him. "About those clothes...at least my underwear should be dry."

Jess slowly nodded as he thought of the little bit of silk and lace he'd rinsed out in the stream, along with the muddy shirt and pants. The little scrap of material hadn't required more than a gentle breeze to blow it dry.

"They're hanging outside, along with the rest of your clothes."

Jess silently retrieved the pink panties, dangling them by one finger as he held them out to Gina. Her cheeks rivaled the color of the silk as she quickly snatched them out of his hand without looking at him.

Gina hid her panties under the covers while she waited for Jess to leave the shelter. When he didn't show any sign of moving, she slowly looked up to find him casually unbuttoning his shirt. Her eyes widened, and her heart rate tripled.

"Are you going to need some help with those?" he asked. He tilted his head toward the hidden panties as the shirt slid off his shoulders, leaving his broad chest bare.

Forcing her eyes higher, Gina pulled the thick sleeping bag up under her chin. Reaching Jess's clear gray eyes, she was surprised to discover that they were devoid of the desire she'd expected to see as he waited for her answer. Gina flushed a darker shade of pink as she quickly shook her head, sending the pounding in her skull into hyperdrive.

Jess nodded in acceptance as he dropped his shirt within her reach, then silently left her to her privacy. She felt like a fool. He hadn't expected to take advantage of her. He'd only been waiting to see whether she needed his help.

Gina threw back the covers, and, without waiting to see whether he was going to return, she shook her underwear out. With some discomfort and a lot of wiggling, she gratefully slid into the minuscule covering. Then she picked up Jess's shirt and gratefully slid her arms into the sleeves. The tails of the overlarge shirt fell to midthigh. The extra length was welcome, since she had no pants to wear at the moment. Jess's scent and warmth clung to the rough material, disturbing her. She might as well have his arms wrapped around her.

When she'd finished buttoning the last button, Jess returned with the pan filled with water. He replaced the pan on the rocks, circling the fire before he turned his attention to Gina.

"How are you doing?" His hooded eyes took in the exposed length of leg and the deep vee in the overlarge shirt that displayed the cotton top underneath. Gina looked like a wood nymph sitting on the rumpled sleeping bag. Her tousled hair and flushed cheeks, still holding a hint of rose color, added to her appearance of wide-eyed innocence. Where had the passionate woman he'd held in his arms gone?

"I'm not going to tell you my leg doesn't hurt, but I think with a little care I'll be able to walk. Now comes the real test," Gina stated dryly as she attempted to stand. "If I'm able to walk, and we have no further problems, we should be able to make the rendezvous. Even moving at a slower pace."

Jess quickly reached out to help her stand, but as soon as she was on her feet, she promptly waved off his helping hand. He shook his head. She was as independent as ever, preferring to chance a fall rather than lean on him.

Being independent was a good trait, but Jess had grown used to taking care of her over the long night, and he wasn't ready to give up that position yet—if ever.

Gina gingerly put her weight on her left leg and felt pain immediately shoot through her thigh, fiercely enough to almost send her to the ground. Closing her eyes, she pulled in a deep breath, holding the air trapped in her lungs until the pain lessened.

Again she put her weight on her left leg. This time she was pleased when the pain wasn't quite as sharp. She stood with her weight evenly distributed and smiled in triumph at Jess.

Her smile continued as she reached for the hand he held out. An answering smile lifted the corners of his mouth, but a shadow quickly passed over his face, dispelling the light mood.

"Why don't you sit down?" he suggested. "You need to take it easy for a while, and I need to see what I can find to eat around here." Gina was so busy congratulating herself on her success that she didn't notice his clipped tone.

"You don't want to overdo it on your first try," Jess added.

He was pleased with her success, but he felt her dependency on him slipping away. She would soon be back to her normal independent self, and would no longer need to rely on him. But for now he would be content with seeing to her care—while she would still let him.

Jess had no idea what was edible in the jungle and what wasn't. The few fruits he recognized weren't much, but with them added to the packets of dehydrated food he'd found in the pockets of Gina's pants, they would survive.

One thing was for certain: When he reached civilization, he was going to have the biggest steak he could find. And he was going to wash the whole thing down with a gallon of cold beer.

Their meager breakfast over, Gina busily filled Jess's pack with their remaining supplies. She could feel him glowering at her as she finished the simple task. Breakfast had gone a long way toward restoring her strength, but she was still dizzy, and her leg throbbed continually.

"Why don't you lie down and rest? We're not going anywhere today."

Jess must have been reading her thoughts, Gina thought wearily as she pulled the edges of the sleeping bag together. She would dearly love to lie down on the soft bag, but that wasn't going to get them to the coast in time to meet the rescue boat.

"Heading out is the only thing we can do, Jess. I don't know how far I'll be able to walk today, but we need to make up as much time as possible."

Reaching the coast in time to catch the boat was important, but Jess knew his father wouldn't let the boat leave without waiting a few days. And he didn't see how she was going to manage walking so soon. She needed rest.

He sat against the outcropping, working on a stick he'd found that was the right length for a makeshift crutch for

Gina. From his position, he watched her struggle with the bag until she had it smoothed out. The long tails of his shirt reached halfway down her thighs, but in her present kneeling position her slim legs were exposed to his greedy eyes. Her awkward movements told their own story—her leg hurt.

"All right, since you're determined to cover some distance today, I'll make you a deal. You lie down and rest until I finish this crutch, and, when your clothes are dry enough, then we'll head out. We can travel until dark. How does that sound?"

It sounded irresistible. "You win. We'll wait until I have dry clothes." Gina sank onto the sleeping bag she'd been attempting to roll up to fit on the pack.

Jess watched Gina protect her injured thigh as she curled up on the folded bag. She rested her head on her crossed arms and closed her eyes.

He finished tying his socks in the juncture of the stick to cushion the makeshift crutch, then set it aside. He frowned as he watched Gina through slitted eyes. The rest would do her good, because the hike ahead of them was going to be a killer. He rubbed his tired eyes. Worrying only succeeded in giving him a headache. It certainly didn't help him to know whether she would be able to make the four-day journey on foot. And if she couldn't, what were they going to do?

Gina watched Jess through her lashes. She read the worry and fatigue on his face. He obviously didn't know what to do with her. Well, she didn't know what they were going to do about her, either. She couldn't let herself slow them up; they didn't have time to spare. Jess's father might hang around for a few days, but she shuddered to think what he might do if they didn't show up. The man was determined to rescue his son.

Jess was a puzzle. As far as she knew, he was a loner. Greg had been his closest friend, but his father obviously loved him very much. The concern he showed for his son's life had been real.

So why had they ended up estranged from each other? What had caused Jess to be such a loner?

"Why did you never marry, Jess?" she asked, the question just popping out of her mouth.

Gina's softly spoken question roused Jess, but he didn't bother to open his eyes. "Came close once."

Now where had that come from? He must have been thinking about Serena too much lately.

Lifting one eyelid to see Gina's reaction to his statement, Jess suppressed a smile when he saw her startled look.

"Well, is that all you have to say?" She raised herself up on one elbow and stared, wide-eyed, at him. "You can't throw something like that out in the open and not explain further. When was this? How come no one knew about it?"

"It was a long time ago. And no one knew because I didn't tell anyone." He smiled at her disgruntled expression, so unlike her normally serious air.

"Why not?"

"The subject never came up."

Gina's brows drew together while she shot a look at Jess that should have fried him on the spot. How could he look so relaxed, leaning against the bank with his eyes closed, as if they weren't discussing such a startling bit of news? It was funny that Greg had never mentioned Jess almost getting married.

"Well, the subject just came up. Who was she? And why didn't you marry her? Did Greg know her?"

"No one you knew." Jess wasn't as relaxed as he looked. Thoughts of Serena no longer brought with them anything more than a faint disappointment. The lingering pain was at the loss of his child. "She found someone more suitable."

A silent "Oh" was Gina's only comment as she studied Jess. He looked detached from the topic, but she had heard the underlying pain he attempted to hide. Maybe he was still smarting about coming in second. She found it hard to believe that any woman would find him lacking. Jess had more than his share of appeal.

For whom? her inner voice asked maliciously. Gina pointedly ignored the question as she lay back down on the sleeping bag, her mind whirling with the information she'd just learned.

"If you aren't going to sleep, why don't you tell me some more about growing up in the great Cascade Mountains?" Jess's question was calculated to get Gina's mind off him while allowing him to learn more about her background.

"I thought we went through this already." Gina resumed her position on one elbow so that she could look at Jess. "There isn't any more to tell."

Jess cocked a dark eyebrow. His disbelieving look had her squirming on her bed. "Five years of living in the woods with a father who spent his time teaching his daughter the fine art of survival cannot be summed up in the few sentences you handed me."

She drew a sharp breath as she realized that he knew there was more to the story than she'd let on and he wanted to hear it—all of it.

The bottom line was trust. Did she trust Jess where her troubled childhood was concerned? The question seemed redundant when she'd trusted him enough to let him stitch her backside.

"Growing up in the Cascades was marvelous. The trees are like giant sentinels guarding their land from intruders. I fell in love with the giant fir trees the first time I saw them. I always look forward to returning home."

Gina thought of her log house, sitting on the side of a mountain, surrounded by towering evergreens. There was a peace in the mountains that she'd found nowhere else in her travels.

"Did you live there alone with your father?" Jess wasn't pretending an indifference to her answers now. He had abandoned his relaxed position to watch her intently.

"Yes. Just the general and me. We lived there for five years. After he was discharged, he took me from Aunt Thelma's house. I never left the mountains again until he died. When I did, I discovered I no longer fit in. I was like a fish out of water. All I'd learned while in the forest was to track and hunt . . . and survive."

Jess could see Gina looking back on a childhood that sounded lonely—too lonely for a teenage girl.

"What did you do then?"

"My aunt was dead, and I was too old for the state to take any notice of. I didn't know what to do until Virgil Carpenter showed up, about two weeks after the general's funeral. I hadn't been to school for five years, so he saw to it that I finished my education. Then he enrolled me in the Agency school, where I finished my survival training." Gina shrugged. "The rest you know."

Yes, he knew. She'd been a naive girl when she joined the Agency, starved for the type of charm and attention that had been Greg's specialty. She hadn't stood a chance. For the thousandth time, he wished he'd seen her first.

"How did Virgil fit into the picture?"

"Sometimes he'd come to visit. He had been in Viet Nam with the general. They trained together, and were on the same squad until Virgil joined the Special Services. He was the only one who ever came into the mountains. I don't know how he learned about my father's death. He just showed up one day."

She'd had enough of dredging up the past—both hers and Jess's. She would do better to put her mind to work on walking than to waste energy thinking about things that couldn't be changed. "My pants should be dry by now."

"It's not even noon yet. There are a few things I think we should talk about, since we seem to have the time and you're not inclined to take a nap."

Jess's words sent a chill up her spine. She watched him as he settled against the bank and drew up his knees. He was nervous. She could tell by the way he clasped his hands together and studied them as if they held the words he needed. She waited, her heart pounding. Was he going to tell her all the reasons why she shouldn't take what had happened between them seriously? Now that the heat of the moment had passed, he must be having second thoughts. Did he think she'd gotten the wrong impression? That maybe she expected more from him than he was willing to give?

Gina couldn't stand the suspense as Jess did no more than stare at his clasped hands. She would rather have the whole episode over and done with. That way, she would preserve as much of her pride as she could. She might as well jump in with both feet, she thought, shrugging.

"You don't have to worry, Jess. I'm not reading more into what happened the night of the storm than I should."

Jess snapped his gaze from his clasped hands to Gina's face. His brow furrowed in question as he looked at the proud tilt of her chin and the determined look in her beautiful golden eyes.

"What are you talking about?"

Now it was Gina's turn to frown, when she met Jess's clearly dumbfounded expression. What kind of game was he playing with her?

"I just wanted to assure you that I didn't get the wrong idea about that night. I know it was just the heat of the moment and the unusual circumstances. Nothing I should take seriously." Her voice trailed off when she saw anger replace Jess's confusion.

"I don't know what the hell you're getting at, but let me set one thing straight right now. You'd better take what happened seriously. I certainly do," Jess growled as he stared into her startled eyes.

Gina didn't know what to say to his declaration. She wasn't going to read too much into his heated words. She must have misunderstood him.

When she averted her eyes to look down at the tail of the shirt she'd been slowly pleating with nervous fingers, Jess drew a deep breath to cool his anger. He wasn't going to tackle that subject until he had the past cleared up. And he wasn't going to get that settled if he continued to skirt the topic. She was more or less trapped at the moment, so now was as good a time as any.

"We'll go into the night of the storm another time. What I wanted to talk to you about now was Greg. And the explosion that killed him."

A slight frown puckered Gina's forehead for a moment as she looked up at him. But her expression quickly turned to polite interest before she went back to watching her busy fingers. She was acting as if he were discussing nothing more important than what they were having for lunch, instead of her dead husband.

"I wanted you to know what led up to Greg's being in the warehouse when it exploded. And the part I played." Jess paused, thinking about the last time he'd seen his friend.

"I'd been investigating the theft of a substantial number of arms from our warehouses for months. Greg's new partner, Rita—"

"Rita? She wasn't Greg's partner. She was yours," Gina corrected him, her eyes accusing.

"No, Rita Tanner was never my partner. She was Greg's partner right from the start. He told you she was my partner to keep you from...being jealous." Jess lamely added the lie as he saw Gina's eyes cloud. This was more difficult than he'd thought it would be.

"Anyway, Rita was already a prime suspect, but I couldn't get any hard proof. I was getting nowhere fast when Greg left me a letter telling me that Rita was Rico's lover. He also told me where the stolen arms were stashed and that he was going to get them. I was supposed to meet him, but I didn't get the information in time. I arrived just as the warehouse exploded, turning the place into an inferno.

"Greg was standing outside, watching the blaze. Then he suddenly ran back in. Later we discovered that Rita had been trapped inside the warehouse. Greg died doing what he'd been trained to do—preventing illegal arms from getting into the wrong hands."

Jess felt a lump lodge in his chest when he finished his flagrantly abbreviated and glossed-over story. Gina didn't need to know about Greg's alleged part in stealing the arms; she needed to know only that he had wanted to make things right in the end, and had lost his life in the process.

Jess cleared his throat before continuing. "I've been searching for Thomas Rico, the ringleader of the arms smuggling operation, for the past two years. The information I got that he was in Central America was the closest I'd ever come to finding him. I was searching for him when I was grabbed by the rebels and thrown into that hole where you found me."

Gina sat as still as stone when Jess's voice came to a halt. She didn't know what to think. She'd accepted that Greg hadn't always been completely honest with her. His death, and Jess's part in it, had ceased to haunt her. She was afraid that their lovemaking in the cave had a lot to do with her feelings. For some reason, her night with Jess made her feel guilty. His explanation hadn't relieved those feelings.

"I don't want to talk about Greg," she said in a tight voice. "I don't blame you anymore and that's all there is to it." She rose up on her knees and started rolling the sleeping bag, dismissing the entire subject. Everything was all muddled in her mind. Every time she thought she had all the facts straight, Jess threw her a curve. If Rita had been Greg's partner, where did Jess fit in? Her head was pounding too much for her to make any sense of it right now.

"I think we'd better start out," she said. Her tone allowed for no arguments.

The firm set of her jaw was an added roadblock. As he watched her roll the sleeping bag and tie it onto the pack, he knew she wasn't going to be deterred this time.

Gina might have said she didn't blame him, but what he wanted to know was, did she believe him? Without Rico, there was no concrete proof. And nothing he could add would change her mind, unless he went into Greg's affair with Rita and revealed the verdict of treason against Greg.

The thought left a bitter taste in his mouth. With Greg not being around to defend himself, he felt he had his hands tied. There was nothing he could do except refuse to admit defeat.

As he helped gather their belongings, Jess ran over what he'd told Gina in an effort to determine what he'd said that had her closing him out. He'd thought telling her the glossed-over story about Greg would ease the tension between them, not intensify the strain. Shaking his head, he moved past her and away from the shelter. When was he going to learn to stop protecting Greg?

Chapter 10

They headed west, Jess taking the lead, machete in hand.

The arrangement suited Gina. Despite her assurance that she could manage on her own, she hadn't gone more than half a mile over the rough ground before she was ready to drop. Her fall had taken more out of her than she'd realized.

Her mind had shut down against the pain that racked her tired body. Concentrating on putting one foot in front of the other took every ounce of energy she possessed.

Keeping her eyes trained on Jess's broad back, she hardly noticed the brush that reached out to grab her clothes or the roots that she stumbled over in her struggle to keep up with him. Her lungs ached with the effort to draw in the heavy, moist air.

They were never going to make the rendezvous at this rate. Jess was going to have to go on without her. As soon as they found a place to stop for the night, she was going to insist that he leave her behind.

After fighting their way through the dense jungle for two laborious hours, they reached the river. They were farther southwest, but the river was the same one that had claimed Gina's pack the day before.

Jess stood on the bank and looked out across the water. Here the river was wide and the current was slower. There was no deep gorge carved out by years of raging water. He might not have to hack a trail through the underbrush anymore, but traveling wouldn't be much easier; it would just be different. There were rocks, trees and refuse that had been carried down-river and tossed on the shore, making their journey just as difficult as the thick underbrush.

As he turned to watch Gina work her way to his side, his heart twisted at the weary sight she presented as she stumbled across the uneven ground. She was beat.

Jess switched the machete to his left hand and slid his arm around her shoulder, drawing her close to his side. When she leaned her full weight against him, he looked down at her in surprise. She must be reaching the end of her rope to be drawing on his strength.

"Let's find some place to sit," he suggested.

Jess examined the bank. He spotted a fairly flat rock a few feet away that would serve as a seat. Tightening his hold, he guided Gina over.

She gingerly seated herself on the rock as comfortably as possible, with only half her bottom on the solid surface. Once seated, she rested her elbows on her knees and lowered her head into her hands.

Jess leaned both rifles against the rock and eased the pack off his shoulders before joining her. Reaching into the pack, he took out the canteen and twisted off the cap. Holding the canteen in front of Gina, he nudged her.

"Have a drink."

She lifted her head from her hands and reached for the water. He watched her drink deeply, though she didn't gorge herself on the water. When she lowered the canteen, he brushed the backs of his fingers across her forehead. She was warm, but with the heat and the taxing hike, he couldn't tell whether she had a fever.

"Do you think you have a fever?" he asked.

Gina ran her hand over her forehead, then wrinkled her brow in thought. "I don't think so. It's just that my head won't stop pounding," she explained as she squinted against the sun.

Now that they were no longer in the jungle, the full sun was beating down on their heads. If she was still suffering from a headache, the bright sun wasn't helping her.

Jess handed the canteen back to her and dug in the pack for one of the foil-wrapped packages that held aspirin. He dumped the two tablets into his hand, then held them out to Gina.

"This might help some," he said as she picked the tablets out of his palm and popped them into her mouth, washing them down with another swallow of water.

"I don't think they'll do a lot of good. Sleep is what I need," she said, wiping her mouth on the back of her hand.

Jess looked up and down the riverbank. He couldn't see a place suitable for them to rest that would give them any cover. And he didn't like the idea of staying out in the open too long.

He looked up at the sky. It was early afternoon. They had a few hours before dark. His first instinct was to make as much time as possible before dark, but he knew he couldn't push Gina hard in her condition. If she had a concussion, as it appeared she did, she was right—rest was what she needed. They weren't making much progress, anyway, and the effort was robbing her of precious strength.

"We'll follow the river until we find some cover for the night. Maybe after you have something to eat and a good night's rest, you'll feel better."

He didn't think for a minute she was going to be in any better condition in the morning. Especially not strong enough to travel the miles they needed to cover to reach the coast in three days.

Judging by the look Gina aimed his way as she rose from the rock, she was as skeptical as he was.

"We'd better get moving," Jess said, ignoring her look. "I don't like sitting out here on this rock."

Together, they slowly made their way along the river. The ground they covered didn't amount to much, and Gina suffered every step of the way. She was leaning on Jess more than on her crutch. If there hadn't been so many rocks and fallen trees in their path, he would have carried her.

Jess stopped in the shade of a tree that had withstood the forces of the river, and enjoyed the breeze that moved across the water. Holding Gina in the crook of his arm, he surveyed the area.

The river was wide and moved at a lazy pace, allowing the jungle to grow right to the water's edge. They would have to move inland. Fighting the dense foliage meant slower going, and he wouldn't be able to help Gina as much while he carved a path through the undergrowth.

"Rest here for a minute, while I see if I can find a place to camp for the night."

He eased Gina against the tree, letting it support her weight instead of her leg.

Gina laid her head against the rough tree trunk and watched Jess climb on top of a large rock. Her leg was on fire, and her pounding head was making her sick to her stomach. Moving one more step was next to impossible, and her balance was gone completely.

They hadn't covered a total of five miles that day. At the rate they were traveling, she knew they would never meet the boat on time.

Jess watched Gina as she eased her weight off her left leg. Her face was deathly white and covered with a fine sheen of sweat.

Turning, he looked at the trees that lined the river's edge. They needed a place that would keep them dry during the rain and would also hide them from any passing patrols—military or drug dealers.

"Ouch!"

Jess had just pinpointed a large tree at the edge of the water when he heard Gina cry out. Turning, he discovered her sitting on the ground at the base of the tree. He jumped off the rock and dropped to his knees. He gently raised her to a sitting position until she could lean against the tree.

"What are you doing?"

"It looks like I'm sitting on the ground," she retorted, frowning as she attempted to rise. "You should have just plopped me on the ground in the first place. It would have saved time, not to mention discomfort."

Jess smiled at the disgruntled look on her face. "It looks like you're developing quite a sense of humor."

"Well, you don't have to look so damned surprised," Gina said, frowning as she rubbed her hip and thigh. She lifted her injured hip off the ground and shifted. It didn't relieve the throbbing in either her thigh or her head.

"Jess, we're going to have to face some facts here. We both know I'm not going anywhere tomorrow. That means we lose another day." She looked toward Jess to gauge his reaction to her words. "We've already lost two. That leaves only two days to cross miles of rugged terrain." Seeing that Jess was about to argue, she hurried on. "You and I both know I won't make it, not in two days."

"Why don't we wait until morning to make any decisions? You get some rest and something hot to eat, and then we'll see how you feel." Jess watched her warily, as if he knew what was to come. "I spotted a place for us to sleep. With a little work, it should be snug and dry."

"That's fine, Jess, but you know tomorrow isn't going to be any different. What rest I gain tonight, I'll lose in the first hour or less, fighting my way through the jungle in this heat." She reached out for his hand. Gripping it tightly, she pulled herself up off the ground, putting her weight on her right leg. Retaining her hold on his hand, she met the mutinous look on his face. "You have to leave me behind, Jess. That's the only option we have."

He released his hold on her hand and captured her shoulders in a firm grip, his determination clear in his gray eyes. "I am not leaving you behind, Gina, and that's final." He continued in a softer tone. "I couldn't possibly leave you here all alone," he said, drawing her into his arms.

"It'll only be for a couple of days, Jess," she murmured into his chest. "If you follow the river..." Her voice trailed off as she felt him stiffen and his arms tighten around her.

"Shhh! Listen."

An unfamiliar noise interrupted the jungle sounds and scattered the noisy birds. Immediately Jess recognized the sound of a motor—the kind that powered a boat!

Looking down at Gina's questioning face, he watched as the sound registered. Her eyes opened wide, and the fatigue that had been etched on her face faded, replaced by professional alertness.

Jess smiled and hugged her tight. A boat was just what they needed. With a boat, they could easily make the coast in time, and Gina would be able to rest the whole way. With luck, they could reach the coast by tomorrow, at least a day ahead of schedule.

Not knowing how close they were to the camp, Gina levered herself away from Jess and tugged his shirtfront until she could whisper in his ear.

"We need that boat."

The words were quietly spoken, but that didn't lessen their intensity. Jess gathered Gina's tired body into his embrace again and leaned down so that he could whisper in her ear.

"My thoughts exactly. We'll just have to devise a plan to relieve them of their transportation."

Jess didn't know which had lightened his heart more, Gina's relying on him or hearing her softly whispered voice in his ear again. Each time she resorted to whispering in his ear, they had managed to escape disaster. He hoped their luck held.

Still holding Gina in his arms, Jess listened until the motor died. The boat was just around the bend. He could take Gina to the tree he'd seen, where she could rest out of danger while he went ahead to see who the boat belonged to.

Smiling to himself, Jess nudged Gina and pointed to a large tree growing on the bank of the river. "With a few ferns and vines for cover, the roots will make for a perfect hiding place."

As with most of the trees in the jungle, the roots grew on the top of the ground. On this tree the dirt had been washed away by the river over the years, leaving a wooden skeleton that resembled a tepee.

Without protest, she let Jess help her into primitive shelter, scooting over to make room for the pack he shoved in after her. He quickly covered the outside with ferns and vines.

Jess poked his head inside and quickly pressed his lips to Gina's. "I'll be right back. I'm just going to have a look," he said, grinning. "We'll have to wait until dark to steal the boat."

Lifting his rifle from the ground, Jess paused to decide which route would be safest to use to find the camp. Since they'd arrived by boat, the men would be camped by the river, so he chose the easiest route and proceeded along the riverbank.

As Jess reached the bend, he could hear voices over the lapping water. The voices were in Spanish, a language he didn't understand but that brought back skin-prickling memories. His guards had spoken Spanish when they weren't firing questions in broken English at him between punches. The thought that the camp might house the rebels still on the lookout for him made his skin tingle with fear.

Logic told him that the rebels couldn't know the route he and Gina would be taking, even if they knew he hadn't been on the helicopter. Assured that the men couldn't be searching for him, Jess eased down onto the ground, cradling his rifle in his arms. He quietly eased through the ferns growing along the bank.

The camp was set up in a small clearing. A large army-style tent and a stack of crates filled most of the area. A fire had been built in a shallow pit, and men were cooking over the small flames. Jess counted five men sitting on the stacked crates, smoking and talking idly in quiet tones.

Tied to a fallen tree that served as a loading dock was a flat-bottomed riverboat. It was built to travel in shallow water without becoming stuck on sandbars and half-sunken logs. He would have no trouble handling the craft by himself. The boat was just what they needed to get to the coast.

Jess watched the group for thirty minutes. No one came or went from the camp, and no one entered or left the tent. If something went wrong with their plans, he and Gina could handle five men. The element of surprise would be on their side, putting the odds in their favor.

Reversing his crawl, Jess eased out of the undergrowth as quietly as possible. Quickly returning to where he'd hidden Gina under the tree, he lifted the ferns and vines and eased himself in beside her.

Finding Gina sound asleep, and having nothing to do until dark, Jess made himself comfortable by slipping his arm around her and gathering her close. Holding her while he slept could get to be a habit, he thought with a smile. One he looked forward to indulging in.

The cry of a big cat in the distance woke Gina with a start. She was cramped, and her leg was throbbing. She was also being held in Jess's arms again. She was surprised that he could have slipped in beside her and taken her in his arms without disturbing her. Either she was losing her edge or she was becoming too comfortable around Jess. She never let her guard down around anyone, and allowing Jess to get too close wouldn't be wise. The kind of hurt he could inflict could prove fatal. She'd already begun to depend on him. Also not a wise move. Not when he wasn't going to be around forever.

Either way, trusting anyone was dangerous. Not to the mission. At this point, he was more in control of the rest of the mission than she was. Her injury made her a liability instead of an asset. As soon as Jess left her in the vine-covered roots, she'd almost passed out from exhaustion and pain. The constant throbbing in her head worried her, too. She must have hit the bank harder than she'd realized.

She wasn't going to be able to make the hike to the coast in her present condition. If they didn't manage to steal that boat, Jess was going to have to leave her behind and go on by himself.

They needed the boat, because without it, she had a feeling Jess would attempt to carry her before he would agree to leave her behind. Especially after encountering whoever was camped beyond the river's bend.

The answering call of another jungle cat, closer than the first, awakened Jess. Night was almost on them. He pulled Gina closer. Sleeping with her nestled in his arms was very gratifying. She was soft and sweet, and he was reluctant to disturb her, but he wanted to be in position before dark so he could see where he was going.

He was surprised to find her already awake. He studied her ashen face intently. She looked better after her rest, but fatigue had painted dark shadows under her eyes, and her face was pale and drawn. He really should leave her hidden under the tree, but that would mean extra time spent returning for her after he'd secured the boat. And extra time was something they wouldn't have.

Lifting one hand, Jess lightly ran his fingers down Gina's cheek. When she didn't pull back, he slowly lowered his head until his mouth covered hers. The kiss was nothing more than his warm mouth brushing gently over her soft lips, but the touch sparked a fire that Jess was growing accustomed to feeling when he was around Gina, a fire stronger than anything he'd ever experienced. And Gina never did anything to encourage him, other than being herself.

Jess lifted his head until Gina could see his eyes. His fingers, lightly resting on her face, were cool as they softly caressed her cheek. Her eyelids felt heavy as she looked up into Jess's warm gray eyes.

She felt as though they had all the time in the world as she watched his eyes roam slowly over her upturned face. He slowly inspected every inch, as if committing it to memory. She wouldn't entertain the thought that he was delaying their leaving because this might be the last time he looked at her. He was just taking advantage of the tranquil moment before they had to leave their sanctuary.

A spark of some indefinable emotion flickered through Jess's eyes. She couldn't read what she saw in the fading light, but his intense look had her heart racing. Gina reminded herself that Jess felt nothing more than animal attraction for her. He'd been locked up without any contact with a woman for too long. All he needed to forget her would be another pretty face passing his way. He might have shown a tenderness for her since she'd been hurt, but that would pass as soon as they were safely out of the jungle.

Gina shook off her dismal thoughts and pulled out of Jess's arms. Looking through the wilting vines, she could see long shadows as the sun sank behind the trees. They needed to get into place before total darkness set in.

"It'll be dark soon," she said.

Jess felt the muscles in his chest tighten as he watched her. Something had turned the soft look in her golden eyes dark and distrustful before she turned away. He sure would like to know what she'd been thinking. And he intended to find out, but right now he would have to postpone delving into her thoughts. They had a busy night ahead.

"You're right. We need to get into position," he said as she pushed the vines aside and crawled stiffly out, not even attempting to hide her pain. When she was standing outside the root enclosure, he shoved the pack out before joining her.

"I counted five men around the campfire earlier. The boat was tied to a fallen tree." Jess slipped the pack on his shoulders as he carefully scanned the riverbank. The silence was disturbed by the shrill cry of a night bird as he hefted both rifles onto his shoulder and turned to Gina.

"It shouldn't be too rough for you, since we have to crawl most of the way. Just stay behind me," he ordered, giving her a cheeky grin.

Gina was concentrating on staying on her feet as the blood pounded in her thigh. Her head was so light, it felt as if it were filled with helium. It felt like one wrong move and her head would disconnect from her shoulders, but she'd heard Jess's remark and seen his grin. At any other time, she would have made a biting comment, but in her present condition, she had to admit he was right. "I might just be able to manage crawling. At least I won't have far to fall," she answered as she forced her feet to move to the edge of the river, where he was waiting for her.

When Jess stopped beside a thick growth of ferns, Gina watched as he dropped to the ground, cradling both rifles in his arms before crawling into the green clump. Carefully lowering herself onto her hands and knees, she followed him into the covering of ferns.

They didn't have far to crawl before they reached the edge of the clearing where the men had set up their camp. The fire was still burning brightly, and the men were laughing as they ate their meal. With darkness settling around them, they wouldn't be able to see Jess and Gina where they lay in the shadows, but Jess wasn't thinking about being seen as he watched the group gathered around the fire.

The five men had been joined by two newcomers, bringing the total to seven—still not overwhelming odds. They still had surprise in their favor. But Jess was surprised as he stared at the two newcomers.

There had to be a mistake!

He'd been searching for one of the newcomers for the past two years, and the other he'd never expected to see again. Enjoying a cozy dinner around the campfire were Thomas Rico and his lover—Rita Tanner.

But she was dead, Jess thought as he tried to digest what his eyes were seeing. No two women could look that much alike. No, the woman snuggled up to Thomas Rico *was* Rita, plain as day.

Jess's insides shook with an anger so fierce that he didn't think he was going to be able to contain himself. She had no right to be alive when Greg was dead, he silently fumed. Hearing Gina's whisper-soft movements behind, he struggled to get his anger under control.

By the time Gina joined him at the edge of the clearing, he had mastered his rage. His main worry was how Gina was going to react when she saw Rita sitting by the fire. Rita's distinctive red hair was as clearly visible in the firelight as her sultry beauty. She looked as if she had just left her lover's bed, which was more than likely why he hadn't seen her, or Rico, during his earlier surveillance.

A sharply indrawn breath alerted Jess to Gina's arrival. And to the fact that she recognized Rita. In the fading light, he couldn't see her face clearly, but, taking no chances that she might do something that would draw attention to their presence, he reached out and gathered her cold hand in his. Squeezing tightly, he effectively drew her attention away from the group around the fire.

Leaning over, he pressed his mouth against her ear. "Easy" was all the warning he could chance whispering.

The simple word must have been sufficient. He felt the easing of Gina's tense muscles where she lay next to him.

If he could have said the same thing about his control, he would have felt better. He wanted to charge into the clearing and tear Rico and Rita apart. The blood pounding in his ears as he watched Rico fondle Rita while his men watched clouded his thinking. These two had killed his best friend. They had no right to be acting like a couple of carefree adolescents when his friend was dead. Lying helpless in the brush while he watched them putting on a show for the five men twisted his guts into knots.

His initial plan had been to wait until the men had bedded down for the night, take care of any guards and then quietly make off with the boat. Now he didn't know what to do about the situation. This was the closest he'd come to Rico throughout his entire search. So far, all he'd had to show for his efforts were pictures and dead-end tips.

He couldn't leave without trying to take Rico—and Rita—into custody. He just needed a minute to come up with another plan of action, one that would ensure that

Gina didn't get hurt or captured. Being a woman wouldn't save her from Rico. Hell, Rico would probably take perverse pleasure in killing Gina to pay Greg back for destroying the arms.

The light was quickly fading, and the group around the fire were showing signs of turning in for the night. Jess didn't have much time left for making decisions. His mind was busily searching for a way to get the boat, as well as Rico and Rita.

Gina didn't feel the numbing pressure on her hand from Jess's grip. The only thing that registered was the woman with the fiery red hair. Her presence didn't make sense. What was she doing here? She was supposed to be dead.

Gina felt as if she'd just walked into a nightmare.

She didn't doubt that the woman was Rita Tanner. She had met the sultry redhead a few years ago, just after Rita joined Greg's department. That Rita liked men had been evident right from the start, and men had definitely been drawn to her. Next to the beautiful woman, she'd felt like an awkward teenager. That one meeting with Rita had made a lasting impression.

Greg had been impressed with Rita, too, singing her praises often. Gina had been pleased when he told her that Rita hadn't been assigned to work with him. A lie, as she'd so recently learned.

How true was his story about Rita having been Jess's latest conquest, then? When Greg had told her that Jess was serious about Rita, she'd felt an unexplainable sick feeling in the pit of her stomach. Now she knew what had caused that feeling—jealousy. And she was feeling it again.

The realization made Gina's heart sink. Peering through the gloom, she tried to see Jess's face. How was he taking the resurrection of his supposedly dead lover? Was the tense grip he maintained on her hand the result of seeing the woman he loved being pawed by another man?

That had to be the cause of the anger she could feel radiating from him. When Gina thought of what had occurred between them the night of the storm, a cold chill shot up her spine. Had Jess known Rita was still alive? Worse yet, had he been thinking of Rita when he made love to her? It was more than Gina could bear, and she tugged at her hand, trying to break contact with Jess.

Jess still hadn't come up with a plan of action, he was so deep in thought that Gina's quick movement startled him. His initial reaction was to tighten his grip, starting a brief tug-of-war that lasted only seconds, just long enough for Gina's rifle to slip to the ground with a thud that sounded like a clap of thunder in the quiet clearing.

Gina and Jess froze. Both pairs of eyes shot to the group around the fire in time to see the men snap to attention. They'd heard the soft thud.

Gina watched in horror as the men reached for their guns, preparing to fire. Everyone moved as if in slow motion, while all she could do was stare.

She and Jess were outnumbered, and the men were armed with blunt-nosed machine guns. The thought had hardly taken hold in her frozen brain when Jess opened fire on the small group.

Gina's sluggish thoughts cleared. They had precious seconds of surprise on their side, and she was wasting them. She grabbed her fallen rifle, and in seconds her shots joined Jess's as the first barrage of bullets hit the brush around them.

With her heart in her throat, Gina continued to pick her targets. She had not often been called on to shoot someone, and never at such close range, but her training had been ingrained in her for too many years for her to lose her head now.

When the shooting suddenly stopped, the eerie silence that filled the clearing was worse than the thunder of bullets. Three bodies lay around the fire. The three other men in the party had disappeared into the jungle. She assumed that Rita escaped with them because she couldn't see her anywhere.

Nothing moved.

After one more sweeping look at the clearing for any sign of life, Gina turned to Jess. He was still holding his rifle trained on the clearing while he carefully scanned the jungle. A lump formed in her throat when she realized how close they'd come to being killed, and all because of her jealousy. Would she never learn?

When Jess didn't turn in her direction, Gina reached out and touched his tense arm. He slowly turned his head to look at her.

"Are you all right?" he asked softly.

Gina hadn't been prepared for the soft question, and when she saw only concern in his smoky eyes, she felt her body sag with relief as she gave him a small smile.

"I'm fine.... How about you?"

Staring into her clear golden eyes, Jess hesitated before he answered her question. He slowly let his eyes wander over her pale face, reassuring himself that she wasn't hurt. He'd been afraid she had been hit by the hail of bullets that swept the brush.

Without saying a word, he brought his lips down hard over hers, taking her mouth with the possessiveness of a conquering hero. The sudden move took her by surprise, but she reacted the only way she could. Instead of submitting, as befitted the vanquished, Gina grabbed a handful of Jess's shirt and arched toward his solid length.

She knew this wasn't the time for distraction. Three men were unaccounted for. They could be anywhere under the cover of the jungle, waiting to pounce on them, but to save her own life Gina couldn't have ended the kiss.

Her fierce response drove Jess a little mad as he deepened the kiss, taking as much as she was willing to give. His mouth devoured her sweet lips, his tongue plunging deep into the secret recesses, staking his claim. She was his. No matter that she would fight him the whole way, he wasn't giving her up.

Releasing her mouth, Jess put a fraction of space between their throbbing lips. "You're mine, Regina Michaels—remember that," he harshly declared, seconds before his lips took hers again for a brief, hard kiss, branding her.

Gina's passion-clouded brain didn't have time to form a response before Jess's fierce kiss chased away all thought. A groan clogged her throat as she tightened her hold on his bunched shirt when he lifted his head, breaking contact with her hungry lips.

The jungle sounds penetrated Gina's foggy mind, and she slowly opened her eyes to find Jess staring intently at her. Her heart stopped at the wondering look on his face, and she quickly ran her tongue over her tender lips before catching her swollen bottom lip between her teeth. She didn't know what to read into his look, but only one word came to mind—*love*.

Before she could respond to Jess's possessive declaration, a moan from the clearing intruded, a reminder that danger was still lurking.

"We haven't finished this," Jess declared, giving Gina a determined look before setting her away from him. Cautiously he eased out of their scant cover.

He congratulated himself on succeeding in deflecting her question about any injuries he might have received. She didn't need more worries right now.

Moving cautiously, Jess circled the bodies lying around the clearing. At a glance, the men appeared to be dead. He moved closer to make sure. He was momentarily jolted when he discovered that one of the three bodies was Rico's. A bullet had entered the upper left side of his chest, and a narrow stream of blood marked a path from the small hole down the front of his camouflage shirt.

Jess bent and placed his fingers over the pulse point on Rico's neck. He could detect no pulse, but he hadn't needed the confirmation. Thomas Rico's sightless eyes were proof that he was dead.

Jess cursed the lifeless body. His search was over, but he still didn't have any evidence that would clear Greg of the verdict of treason that marred his record at the Agency.

The moan came again, and Jess lifted his rifle, turning toward the tent. Rita was lying on her stomach near the opening of the tent, a bright red patch of blood staining the back of her shirt. As he watched, she made a feeble attempt to rise. The struggle brought on a fresh flow of blood and another moan of pain.

Jess quickly checked the other two men to be sure they were dead before going to Rita's side. He carefully rolled her onto her back, propping her head on his arm. The bullet had entered her chest. There was little chance it had missed piercing her lung. Nothing could be done for her; the wound was too severe for her to survive.

Rita opened pain-filled green eyes to find Jess bending over her. "Rico?" she implored with a faint whisper.

Jess cast a quick glance toward where Rico lay by the dying fire. "He's dead," he coldly stated.

Rita turned her head in the direction Jess had looked, but the fire blocked her view. She turned back to Jess, her brow wrinkling.

"How did you get loose?"

"You knew?" Jess stiffened as understanding dawned on him. She knew that the rebels had held him—and lost him. For her to know, she would have to have been responsible for his capture.

Disgusted, he had to restrain himself from flinging the dying woman away from him.

Chapter 11

"You're too damned soft," Rita scoffed, reading his thoughts. "I wouldn't have hesitated if the situations were reversed."

She attempted a laugh that ended with a choke. "You were my first choice, but you weren't interested. Seducing you would have been a pleasure." Drawing a labored breath, she jeered. "Greg's prissy little wife was the only one you had eyes for. That made taking Greg away from her twice as sweet."

Jess looked over his shoulder, relieved to see that Gina hadn't heard Rita's comment. He was surprised that Rita had known of his feelings for Gina. She'd only seen them together once.

"It was Rico's idea to have you snatched and held for ransom. He loved knowing that your hounding him the last two years would finally pay off. You played right into his plans," Rita told him with a touch of malice.

A flash of pain stiffened Rita's body, removing the satisfied smile from her pale lips. Her eyes closed as she fought the pain.

After a moment, she opened her eyes. "How did you escape?"

"Gina Michaels rescued me."

Jess's answer received immediate results, as Rita's green eyes widened further when Gina quietly joined them.

"You!" Pain halted Rita temporarily, but she didn't let it stand in her way, striking out at Gina. "All your fault. If it hadn't been for you, Greg wouldn't have wised up to our operation and tried to turn us in."

Talking was becoming difficult for Rita, but the venom was still heavy in her weakening voice. She struggled to reach Gina, only to collapse in a fit of coughing. When the coughing subsided, her breathing was so shallow it was almost nonexistent. She was so weak her head lolled to the side on Jess's arm.

"How was I responsible?" Gina asked, as if she were in a trance.

Gina's question appeared to revive Rita, and she glared at her before giving a harsh laugh, blood trickling from the corner of her mouth. "You didn't know about Greg and me, did you?" Rita asked in a delighted tone. Gina's startled look was all the answer Rita required, and she drove the truth a little deeper, with obvious glee. "We were lovers. Had been for years." She gave Gina a triumphant little smile that turned into another choking cough.

"Gina, you don't want to hear Rita's ranting." Jess attempted to spare Gina any unnecessary pain. "She's just trying to hurt you."

Keeping her gaze trained on Rita's evil eyes, like a mouse caught before a cobra, Gina laid her hand on Jess's shoulder. "It's all right, Jess, let her finish," she said in a faraway voice.

"She isn't afraid to hear what a cheat her husband was."
Rita sneered at Jess before centering her attention on Gina.
"He was going to leave you and marry me. Of course, he
didn't know I was already married to Rico." A choking
gurgle escaped her bloodstained lips. "That was the real
joke. Greg would do anything for me. He even told me
how they stored the guns until they could be disposed of.
He was too stupid to realize we were stealing them right
from under his nose."

Another fit of coughing interrupted her gloating, but she
struggled to regain herself, knocking Jess's hand away
when he would have halted her efforts. "Get back. I'm not
going to let my chance pass to show Miss Priss what a
sucker she had for a husband."

She turned back to Gina and snarled, "Everything was
going according to plan until you started playing on Greg's
conscience, telling him you wanted your marriage to work.
That you wanted a family." She sneered again. "He started
having second thoughts about us. Then he found me with
Rico, and that blew everything." Rita paused again as she
gathered what little remaining strength she had left.

"Before we could stop him, Greg blew up the warehouse where we had the arms stashed. Two years' work."
With an unfocused look in her glassy eyes, Rita continued
in a rapidly fading voice. "He hadn't planned on getting
caught in the explosion. He heard a woman scream, and
he went back for her. He didn't know the woman was one
of the guards' whores, trapped in a back room." Her voice
grew fainter and her breathing more labored as she fought
to finish, "Everyone thought she was me...."

Jess closed Rita's eyes and laid her on the ground, forgetting her the moment he stood, as the tension ebbed
from his tight muscles. Her words had exonerated Greg of
treason. Though Greg had been guilty of acting foolishly,
he hadn't intentionally betrayed his country.

His feeling of elation lasted only until he turned to Gina. Her silence, along with the stunned look in her eyes, told him that she was having trouble digesting everything she'd just heard. His pleasure in learning of Greg's innocence was an afterthought. Gina was the one he was concerned about now.

He couldn't give her the time she needed to come to terms with Rita's revelations, not with three men still missing. They needed to get to the boat and down river before reinforcements arrived.

Jess took Gina by the arm, pulling her away from the dead woman. "Come on, we need to get out of here. You look ready to collapse." He led her to the fallen log and prodded her until she was safely in the boat.

Gina looked back to the clearing, at Rita and the dead men lying on the ground.

"What about them? Are you just going to leave them here?"

She didn't care about the men, or Rita, for that matter, but leaving them to the jungle animals didn't seem right.

Jess didn't spare the clearing a glance as he gathered up their pack and both rifles.

"Let their friends take care of them. They aren't our worry." After storing the gear in the boat, he went back to the clearing and pulled a burning piece of wood from the flames. With a quick glance around the clearing, he tossed the torch into the stack of wooden crates by the tent. He didn't stay to see whether the wood caught—he couldn't take the time.

Returning to the log, he jumped into the boat and quickly untied the rope from a dead branch. He shoved them away from the bank, and the boat quickly caught the current and picked up speed.

Jess busied himself with starting the motor and steering the boat to the middle of the river. They were too visible close to shore. He wouldn't feel safe until he put some miles between them and the clearing, where a bright blaze could now be seen reaching toward the sky.

Within minutes the night was filled with an explosion when the fire reached the camp's store of ammunition. Well, that was one shipment of guns that wouldn't be killing innocent women and children, Jess told himself.

Darkness had fallen by the time Jess had the motor going. They were far enough away from the clearing that he could breathe a little easier. The small sliver of moon he could see through the clouds wasn't bright enough to give off much light, and in the darkness they couldn't be seen from the shore.

Jess could just make out the dark outline of Gina huddled in the bow. She'd dropped onto a pile of canvas as soon as she boarded the boat. Her inquiry about the bodies had been the last he heard from her.

They needed to talk. Jess had an idea what she was feeling after hearing Rita's poisonous words. He hoped his explanation would counterbalance what Rita had told her. But attempting to communicate over the roar of the engine wasn't what he wanted when he talked to her. He had a lot of untangling to do, and he didn't want any distractions while he tried to make her understand why he hadn't told her about Greg and Rita. His years of waiting were finally coming to an end. He just hoped the ending was going to be the one he'd been striving for.

Jess's eyes burned from fatigue as he watched the sun hit the tops of the trees along the riverbank. In the early-morning light he could see that they were in a rocky gorge, not unlike the one Gina had almost tumbled into. The current made it too dangerous to stop the boat along the bank. If they got caught in the swift current, they would be smashed on the large rocks along the river's edge.

Gina was still sleeping on the pile of canvas in the bow, so even if he found a place to stop, he wouldn't be able to talk to her. And he didn't have the heart to wake her. His confessions would have to wait until they were off the river.

He tied the tiller in place to hold their course and unbuttoned his shirt. A hiss escaped through his tightly clenched teeth as the shirt pulled away from the dried blood coating the open wound on his left shoulder, a souvenir from one of the gunrunner's bullets.

He strained to see the extent of the damage. There was a small hole at the top of his shoulder where a bullet had entered. Since he had been lying on his stomach, the blood running down his back was obviously coming from the exit wound.

With their limited medical supplies, he couldn't do much for the injury, except be thankful that the bullet hadn't entered a little lower. At least no bones had been broken.

Jess fished through the pack until he found the small bottle of antiseptic. Holding the bottle up to the light, he could see that barely any was left. He pulled off the lid and poured the contents into the hole, letting it run down his back. He sucked in a lungful of air through his teeth with a loud hiss as his muscles drew tight when the antiseptic washed over the open wound. It felt as if he'd poured liquid fire down his back.

After pulling his bloody shirt back on, Jess reached for the canteen, half buried under the pack. He watched in dismay as water trickled from a small hole near the bottom. Their lack of medicine wasn't their only concern. If they didn't reach the rescue boat soon, they would have to return to the jungle and look for a new supply of clean water, since the river was anything but.

Jess propped the canteen against a coil of ropes, tipping the container to save what little water remained. He unhooked the tiller and resumed his control of the boat.

Turning the throttle to full, he headed the boat down-river. The sooner they reached the coast, the sooner they would be rescued.

The sun was shining, and a soft breeze moved over the water, relieving the humidity. Controlling the boat was no longer a strain; the current had grown calmer as the river widened. All he had to do was follow the current and watch for the occasional large rock. After the harrowing past few days, the boat ride down the river seemed anticli-mactic.

With traveling easier, Jess had plenty of time to think. At their present speed they would reach the Gulf of Mexico in no time. And once home, he could set the wheels in motion to erase the verdict of treason in Greg's file. Greg might have behaved foolishly, but he hadn't been guilty of stealing the guns from the warehouse.

So many mistakes—both his and Greg's.

He might not be responsible for Greg's death, but he had to shoulder some responsibility for the past. There were things he could have done that would have altered the course of events and saved Greg's life. He could have told him about his investigation of Rita, for one thing.

Had he been afraid to tell Greg for fear he would break off the affair and return to Gina? When Rita said Greg had been having second thoughts about their affair—that he'd been thinking about Gina's desire to make their marriage work—he'd felt his guilt triple. But Greg had risked his life to save the woman he thought was Rita. Even knowing the truth about her, he'd still returned to the warehouse to save her.

It did him no good to try to guess how he might have changed the past if he'd done things differently. He would just have to live with the guilt.

Jess looked toward the bow of the boat, where Gina still slept. Would she understand? Did he have the right to expect her to understand the reason he hadn't tried to stop Greg's affair with Rita? Only time would answer his questions.

He watched the bright sunlight dance on her coppery curls, and he noticed the healthy flush that covered her cheeks. She looked like a child curled up for a nap, with her hands tucked under her cheek. But it wasn't a child he remembered as he watched her sleep.

The woman he'd held in his arms while she slept filled his thoughts. Gina didn't seem to realize that she was more than enough woman for him. She was more woman than most men encountered in a lifetime, and he felt a driving need to call her his own. He had a pretty good idea what she'd been thinking when she saw Rita sitting in the clearing. But she couldn't have been further from the truth. Rita had been the one who was lacking, not Gina. He was going to take pleasure in convincing her of that fact, as soon as he had a chance to talk to her.

Remembering the feel of her satin skin and gentle curves had his hands aching to retrace their path while he watched her eyes darken with passion. The next time he loved her, he was going to watch her every emotion as he spent hours learning her body. He was going to make love to her in all the ways he'd fantasized, and some he hadn't even thought of yet.

With a satisfied smile on his tired face, Jess slid off the small seat beside the motor and settled on the bottom of the boat, resting his head on the edge of the seat. He would close his eyes for just a minute.

Gina's first thought when she woke was that she was safely home in her waterbed, but her bed had never smelled as foul as the bed she was sleeping on now. The crying of gulls and the lapping of water reminded her where she was, as she forced her gritty eyes open to look around.

Jess's sleeping form filled her line of vision, and for the moment she was content to drink in the sight of him. He'd fallen asleep with his head lying on the seat by the silent engine. Gina took the opportunity to study him while he slept. His jaw was covered in two days' growth of beard, and his overlong hair hung over his forehead. He was disheveled, his clothes dirty and torn, not unlike the way she'd found him in the cellar. But to her, he had never looked better.

They were safe. They wouldn't have to traipse through the jungle anymore. No more threats from the rebels or the drug runners. In a short while they would be safely on the boat and heading home. Gina felt her heart sink at the thought. In a matter of days Jess would be headed back to San Francisco, and she would be headed toward Seattle and her home in the mountains. The disaster of this mission was inducement enough for her to make this her last assignment for the Agency. So the chances of their meeting in the future were slim.

Not that she had a reason for wanting to see Jess once he was safely home, she cautioned herself. She had all her answers. Rita had taken care of that.

Gina cringed when she recalled how Rita had gloated over Greg's love for her, and how he'd been planning to divorce Gina so that he could marry Rita.

She felt like a fool when she remembered how she'd begged Greg to stay home that last day. She had even begged him to try to make their marriage work. They must have had a real laugh over her asking him to start a family. She'd even been willing to quit her job and become a full-time wife and mother, if he would just try. But all the while, he'd been making plans to leave her for Rita.

She was wiser now. She knew how little she had to offer a man. Men wanted women like Rita, not someone who didn't know the first thing about being seductive and sensual. All she knew was survival, and to survive, she was never going to entrust her heart to a man again.

Gina attempted to ignore the little voice telling her that she was too late, but the ache in her chest was all the confirmation she needed.

The interruption of the boat's gentle rocking shook Gina back to their present position. They weren't moving. She looked over the side of the boat to see that they had become stuck behind a dead tree partially sunk in the river.

She attempted to lever herself to a sitting position on her musty bed, but her cramped body screamed a protest. She was stiff and sore from being wedged in the bow of the boat for so long, but she was pleased to find that her headache was gone.

She needed a drink. Her mouth was so dry she couldn't swallow. When she straightened, she groaned as pinpricks shot up her numb legs. Her movements also started her thigh throbbing, reminding her of her stitches with a vengeance.

The choppy rocking of the boat as she shifted disturbed Jess's precarious position, and he woke with a start as he began to slide sideways. The first thing he noticed was the silent engine. The motor had been running smoothly when he slipped to the bottom of the boat to rest his head against the seat.

Looking up, he was surprised to see that the sun had disappeared behind the tall trees, which were casting their long shadows across the river. He had eased into a more comfortable position about midday, and now it was early evening.

Moving back onto the seat, Jess checked the engine for fuel. The tank was empty, and he could see no other cans of gas, but he did find a pair of oars lashed to the inside of the boat. At least they weren't stranded.

During his inventory, he noticed that Gina was awake, her serious golden eyes watching him. Their eyes locked, and she shifted restlessly on her makeshift canvas bed as he held her gaze. He saw apprehension flicker in her eyes before she hastily looked away.

She looked defeated, barely resembling the strong woman he knew her to be. He longed to reach out and take her in his arms, to protect her from the pain he saw weighing her down. But Jess's worst fears had materialized. The effect of Rita's words was plain to see in the shattered look on Gina's face.

A sharp pain pierced Gina's heart as understanding dawned—the looks he'd been giving her during their first days in the cave had been of pity. Well, she could do without his pity. But what hurt more than the thought of him feeling sorry for her was learning that he'd known about Greg and Rita's affair all along—and had said nothing. He'd let her go on about how she'd tried to persuade Greg to work at saving their marriage, when he'd known it could never happen.

Pity was what had kept him silent. He was feeling sorry for her even now. And she couldn't face that . . . not from Jess.

The boat gave another lurch, sending Gina tumbling off the pile of canvas. That was one way to get herself moving, she thought dryly as she rubbed her legs to assist the returning circulation.

"Where is the water?" Her dry throat protested the abuse, but at least the question filled the silence. She stretched her back to get the kinks out while she waited for his reply.

"Here's what little is left." Jess carefully passed the canteen to Gina, then turned his attention to removing the oars from their fasteners.

She took the canteen, her brows rising when she felt how empty it was. She didn't bother asking what had happened—the hole in the side was self-explanatory. She took a mouthful and savored it before letting it trickle down her throat. After one swallow, she replaced the cap and set the almost empty container back on the floor.

She looked up as a gull flew overhead, its cry filling the air. "Sea gulls! Jess, sea gulls!" she exclaimed. "We're almost there," she said, turning to him in her excitement.

But Jess was busy tugging the oars from their brackets on the inside of the boat, so he missed the animation on her face. By the time he had the oars in their locks, she had turned her attention back to their situation. He wouldn't be able to make much headway by himself, she realized. The boat was wide across the middle, which made working the oars awkward for one person. She reached for the oar on Jess's right and sat facing the rear of the boat, waiting for him to join her on the wide seat.

"This will go faster with both of us working the oars." Without looking in his direction, she prepared her oar and waited to match his stroke.

"Are you sure you're up to this?"

Jess's question brought Gina's head swinging around until she faced him. The bruised look was gone from her golden eyes, replaced by a fierce, challenging look.

"There's nothing wrong with my arms. It's my butt that's hurt," she answered in a tight voice.

Hiding a smile, Jess slipped into the space beside Gina. He picked up the remaining oar and dipped the flattened wood into the swirling water. At least Gina's fighting spirit was returning. Her spurt of anger was better than the defeated look he had seen on her face earlier.

As Gina met his stroke, Jess increased the rhythm until they were moving at a steady pace. With each pull of the oar he could feel his bullet wound open, letting more blood seep down his back.

His wound hurt, but he could take the pain. The rowing wasn't difficult with both of them working together, but sitting beside Gina as they shared the simple task was distracting. Her soft body was filling his mind with thoughts better left until another time and place.

The constant rubbing of their bodies as they worked the oars helped him keep his mind off his burning shoulder, but it started a burning in another part of his body. With each stroke he could feel Gina's hip and leg pressing against his. The constant reminder of her satin-smooth skin was going to drive him crazy. At this rate, if they didn't reach the rescue boat soon, he would either pass out from the loss of blood or burn up from the fantasies running through his head.

Before long, they could smell salt air and feel the cooler breeze that blew in from the ocean. Knowing they had nearly reached their destination lightened the mood in the silent boat as they encountered a swifter current.

The prospect of reaching the rescue boat filled Gina with mixed feelings. She was torn between wanting to get away from Jess and maintaining the closeness the simple chore of rowing together had created. She couldn't remember when she had last shared a task with anyone. The prolonged closeness was bound to leave her heart aching for something she couldn't have. She'd had a lifetime to learn that handling her problems by herself was the safest course. Now she feared that sharing was something she could get used to all too easily.

"Which way do we go from here?"

Jess's voice startled Gina out of her musing, and she missed her stroke, barely catching herself before she tumbled over backward.

"We head south until we see an abandoned lighthouse sitting off the coast. We should be able to spot the lighthouse easily if we get in range before dark." Gina looked up at the clear sky as she spoke. The deep blue expanse seemed to go on forever without the thick canopy of trees to block her view. On the water, sunset would arrive later than in the jungle, but the light was quickly fading. They didn't have too many hours of daylight left to find the lighthouse.

"The boat is supposed to rendezvous at the lighthouse twice each day. Once in the morning and once at night. If we can reach the lighthouse before dark, we have a good chance of being picked up tonight," Gina said as she checked the position of the sun to see just how much daylight they had left.

She looked down at her hands before she started rowing again. They were red and raw from the unusual strain of working the oar. Carefully she stretched her fingers to relieve the cramps, but her blisters painfully protested. Setting her oar against the edge of the boat, she leaned over and plunged both her hands into the salt water. For a few seconds, the stinging pain was so fierce that tears sprang into her eyes, but she was soon able to flex her fingers.

When she reached for the oar again, Jess captured her hands in his. After turning her abused hands over in his large ones, he slid the knife from the scabbard on his belt and sliced a few inches off the bottom of his shirt.

"This won't work as well as gloves, but it should give you some protection. If rowing becomes too painful, we'll stop and rest."

Gina watched in silence as Jess wrapped her blistered hands in the coarse material. His long fingers were gentle as they wound the torn strips around and around until her hands were covered. She was amazed that such strong hands could be so gentle.

When he finished, Jess cupped Gina's cheek in the palm of his hand, searching her upturned face before settling on her wide eyes. He was pleased to see that the defeated look had disappeared, though she was far from her normal self.

Jess brushed his fingertip over the deep shadows under her amber eyes. They needed rest, and they needed food. They hadn't eaten since their inadequate breakfast the day before, and the lack of food and water was beginning to take a toll on both of them.

Jess's finger slowly traveled down one velvet cheek, coming to rest at the corner of her mouth. At his soft touch, her lips quivered. The slight movement was all the invitation Jess needed. Lowering his head, he replaced his finger with the tip of his tongue.

The contact sent a quiver through Gina's body as Jess toyed with the corner of her mouth for long seconds, awakening a yearning that had her parting her lips as she lifted her head to meet his kiss.

Her soft whimper when he didn't readily comply with her unspoken request tore through Jess's restraint. Closing the distance between them, he held her tight as his firm lips devoured her soft mouth.

Gina's entire body was buffeted by shock waves as Jess alternated between feather-light kisses and kisses that gradually increased in intensity until they burned with fiery possession. The kisses lasted forever, but ended too soon.

Reluctantly, Jess eased his hold on her as he gentled his kiss to no more than a light caress of his lips, until he finally raised his mouth from hers and gazed into her eyes.

"We'll pick this up later, when the time is right."

With those cryptic words Jess set Gina away from him and reached for his oar. Positioning the oar in the water, he waited for Gina to compose herself and commence rowing again.

Working the oar required little concentration, which was good, because Gina couldn't get her mind off Jess's words. Did he think the future was going to hold a "right time" for them? They had no future together. They were too different. They had nothing in common to base a future on. She would never fit into his world, and she had nothing to offer him in hers. Jess lived a far more exciting lifestyle than she could ever get used to.

Wasn't that what she'd been telling herself for years? Jess hadn't changed, not really. Once he was home, he would take up his old ways of flying off to exotic places with beautiful women. She wasn't going to join the platoon of playmates Greg had told her Jess kept.

Gina looked at Jess out of the corner of her eye and felt a niggling doubt. Was that the real Jess? All she knew about him was what she'd learned from Greg. If Greg had lied about his relationship with Rita, wasn't it reasonable to believe he might also have lied about the kind of life Jess led? Especially if he was lying to cover up his own affair?

Questions ran through Gina's mind as she automatically kept her strokes in time with Jess's. She didn't want to think about Jess's promise right now. She had more important things to think about—like being hungry and thirsty and needing a bathroom.

Looking out at the vast expanse of water, Gina knew she would have to wait until they reached the lighthouse. Possibly she would be able to find a little privacy to see to her personal needs while they waited for the boat.

"There it is! Up ahead!"

"What?" came Gina's startled reply.

"The lighthouse."

Gina turned until she could see the remains of what had once been a lighthouse. Only the base of the crude stone building still stood on the small pile of rocks, but the rocks were enough to serve as a marker.

She again scanned the water, looking for the rescue boat. "It's nearly dark. The boat should be in the area."

Jess stifled a groan as he flexed his tired shoulders before he joined Gina in searching the empty stretch of water. In unison, and without comment, they resumed rowing toward the lighthouse, both realizing that if the boat didn't show up before dark, they were going to be spending a long night on the small pile of rocks—without food or water.

As they drew near the crumbling remains, they could hear the waves crashing against the rocks. Gina was debating the best approach to the island to avoid being smashed against the rocks when she sighted an approaching craft.

"Jess, look!" She watched the large boat approach, judging its course. "It looks like it's heading in this direction," she murmured as she frowned in disappointment at the size of the boat. "It looks like a yacht," she added, disheartened.

"Why do you sound so disappointed?" Jess asked in confusion.

"That isn't our rescue boat. It's a pleasure craft," she explained, as if Jess couldn't tell the difference.

He chuckled at her annoyed look. "You said my father was running this show, didn't you?"

"Yes. What's that got to do with it?" Her eyes were glued to the advancing craft.

"If Thomas Knight arranged for a boat to pick us up, that would be his idea of a boat. He wouldn't even consider anything smaller."

Gina turned startled eyes on Jess. "The heat must be frying your brain. That boat is large enough to hold dozens of people. Why would your father send a yacht that large out here for just the two of us?"

Jess put his oar into the water and turned the boat in the direction of the oncoming vessel. "That's the way he likes to do things. With a lot of flash. Gets him the attention he lives for. Besides, it makes good cover."

Gina matched her strokes to Jess's. Even if the approaching yacht wasn't their rescue boat, it would do. Especially if it had a bathroom.

Jess's thoughts were in the same vein as Gina's—any craft would do. He wasn't going to last much longer. They hadn't eaten all day, and their water had been gone for hours. He was bone-tired, and his shoulder felt as if it were on fire.

The yacht hailed them with a blast of its horn. Gina and Jess stopped rowing and drifted as they waited for the large vessel to reach them. They could see the yacht's name, *The Scavenger* painted in big, bold letters across its bow.

Seeing the name of the ship, Jess burst out laughing. At Gina's strange look, he attempted to explain his sudden spurt of insanity. "The name," he managed to get out between laughs, pointing to the bow. "That's my father's yacht. The name fits him." Jess drew a deep breath. "He searches for companies that are sinking and buys them cheap. He fixes whatever's wrong with them, then sells them off, just like a scavenger."

Just then the yacht pulled alongside the smaller boat, so Gina had no chance to ask Jess to explain his curious description of his father.

He caught the strange look she aimed at him and answered with a smug smile.

"Just wait until you get to know him. He likes to run everyone."

The small boat bumped against the side of the yacht. Jess reached out and caught the rope ladder dangling over the side and held fast, stopping the swaying movements so that Gina could safely climb aboard.

"Go ahead, I'll be right behind you," he instructed.

Gina paused as she reached overhead for a rung. This was really goodbye. Everything would change as soon as they boarded the yacht. Her job was finished, and there would be no reason for Jess to continue taking care of her. Turning, she searched his eyes in the fading light. They caught and held hers, but she couldn't read anything in their smoky depths.

Holding his gaze, she leaned over and lightly touched her parted lips to his warm mouth.

Raising his free hand, Jess slipped his fingers around her neck and held her close while he leisurely searched her mouth with his tongue before releasing his hold. At least his kiss had changed the look in her eyes, he thought. They were golden with desire now, instead of shadowed in sorrow.

Jess knew why Gina's eyes were filled with sadness. She thought this was the last time they were going to be together. Well, he would just have to let her think that until he was able to prove otherwise.

He watched her slowly turn and climb the ladder until she disappeared out of sight over the ship's railing.

Then, giving the riverboat a shove with his foot, he followed her up the ladder.

As he was assisted over the railing, he could see Gina surrounded by a small group of men, but only one man held Jess's attention.

He was as tall as Jess, with thick white hair that enhanced his dark good looks. In the fading light Jess couldn't see the color of his eyes, but he knew they were the same iron gray as his own.

Both men appeared frozen as they inventoried each other. Years had passed since their stormy parting, and for a minute neither of them seemed to know how to act.

Thomas Knight made the first move, reaching out to his son. "Jess."

Without hesitating, Jess started across the polished deck, meeting his father halfway—only to collapse in his arms.

"Jess!"

Gina's cry swept through the air when she saw the blood staining the back of Jess's shirt before his father eased his unconscious body onto the deck.

Chapter 12

The gentle rocking motion of the yacht lulled Gina as she stood by the window and watched the glorious display of sunlight on the water. After being cooped up in the jungle for what seemed like weeks, seeing the sun in the clear blue sky lifted her sagging spirits.

She turned from the spectacle outside and let her gaze roam the extravagant room. She'd never been aboard a boat as large as Thomas Knight's yacht. She certainly hadn't been prepared for the opulence of the large vessel.

The light from the windows glowed on the rich dark wood paneling and reflected off the brass fixtures. She shook her head as she looked at the thick carpet covering the floor. Who ever heard of having a carpet on a boat? Or silk sheets, either? she thought as she let her gaze come to rest on the oversize bed where Jess slept amid the dark gray-striped silk sheets and down comforter.

He looked a little pale, but none the worse for wear, considering that he'd rowed a boat for hours with an open gunshot wound.

Gina turned back to the window and her review of the sun over the blue Gulf waters. Drawing a deep breath, she stretched her tired muscles as she listened to the hum of the engines in the silent cabin. They were in U.S. waters now and would be reaching port later today. Before she knew it, she would be back home, alone.

The prospect of returning to civilization didn't hold the same appeal it once had. She'd spent so many nights sleeping on the hard ground that she hadn't been able to sleep in the comfortable bed she'd been given last night. At least, that was the excuse she'd given herself for continually tossing and turning. As soon as she heard the doctor and Jess's father leave Jess's cabin, she'd quietly returned—just to reassure herself that he was all right.

Worry over Jess was one of the reasons she'd been unable to sleep. But on seeing him, she knew she'd really been unable to sleep because he wasn't curled around her as he'd been the last three nights.

Three nights. Such a short time to grow to need someone so that you could sleep. The bed in her room had seemed so empty, and it wasn't nearly as large as the bed she slept in at home. How was she going to survive without having Jess to hold her?

She loved him too deeply to lose him. Awareness of her feelings had been building ever since she'd first seen him in that dark cellar. She just hadn't realized it until his collapse on deck last night.

She couldn't resign from her job, as she'd decided to do, even though her work no longer held any appeal. She needed to get back to work, not to find herself with time on her hands. A new mission would take her mind off Jess.

When she was working, she didn't have time for foolish dreams.

But loving Jess was the only assignment she wanted, and she didn't have the vaguest idea how to go about securing it. After all, he no longer needed her. He was safely on his way home.

Jess watched Gina as she rested her head on the windowpane. The sunlight streaming through the glass lit her mass of red gold curls until they shone like polished copper. She looked as bright as the morning sun in the lemon-yellow sweater and slim dark blue slacks that molded her rounded bottom to perfection.

What was she thinking as she gazed out the window, lost in contemplation? Was she remembering the night of the storm? Did she look back on that night with regret? Or were her memories the same as his? Had she felt their souls meet as their hearts soared together? All those questions had occupied his mind during the night, along with the startling change in his father.

Almost losing his son had been a harrowing experience for Thomas Knight, and it had transformed his attitude. Of course, a great deal of his father's change could be attributed to Jess's newly made decision to resign from Special Services and go into another line of work that would keep him in the country and safely out of the line of fire. He had given a lot of thought to making a career change. Now, he just had to convince Gina that his idea was sound.

Jess eased himself out of the soft bed, wincing as a shooting pain reminded him of his most recent wound. The doctor his father had brought along had assured them that the bullet had passed through the flesh of his shoulder, doing little damage. Little damage, hell! He wished the doctor could feel the burning pain that had him gritting his teeth when he even gently rotated his shoulder.

Looking down at his partially nude body, Jess grimaced at the fading bruises above the band of his white briefs. His body was every color of the rainbow, with a few indeterminate colors thrown in. All in all, though, he felt damned good. A good night's sleep had worked wonders. The best medicine was waking up and finding Gina in his room.

The soft carpet muffled his bare feet as he made his way across the floor. Standing behind Gina, he had a moment to drink in her beauty and the soft fragrance that surrounded her before she felt his presence and turned.

Jess didn't say a word as he intently studied her. Her riot of shining curls was in direct contrast to her pale face. Her shadowed eyes looked immense as they roamed over his face.

Cupping her chin in one hand, he tilted her head back and leaned down to cover her parted lips with his. Jess had meant the kiss to be light and quick, but one touch and he was lost. When his hungry mouth met with no resistance the kiss turned hot and devouring as his tongue slid past Gina's soft lips without pause.

The floor beneath her feet rocked as if they were in the middle of a storm. To prevent herself from falling, she reached out for the only solid thing within her reach—Jess. As her fingers touched the smooth skin at his waist, he closed the small distance between them. Gathering her in his arms, he boldly made love to her mouth with his tongue.

Jess slowly ended the kiss and raised his head to rain light kisses on Gina's flushed face. If he hadn't been holding her, she would have melted at his feet. With her head resting on his solid chest, she could hear the pounding of his heart under her ear. She felt her heart give a little leap when she realized he was as affected by the kiss as she was.

Standing in the quiet room, with the lapping of the water and the hum of the engines the only sounds, Gina felt content.

"Are you all right?" The question rumbled under her ear.

"I'm fine. Now."

She didn't raise her head from his chest when she answered the question, so she didn't see the satisfied smile that spread over his generous mouth. He'd caught the last word, and its significance. Her little slip gave him hope.

Easing his arms from around her, Jess allowed her a little space to stand on her own. He wanted to look at her. Her face had gained a becoming flush, and her lips were swollen from his kisses, but her luminous golden eyes were what held him spellbound. They were the color of newly minted gold, so bright and clear that he ached just looking into them.

Raising his hand, Jess unnecessarily pushed a cluster of bright curls off her flushed cheek. The need to keep touching her was strong.

"Your leg all right?" he asked as he ran his fingers along her jaw and down her smooth neck, never taking his eyes off hers.

"Just fine. The doctor said your stitches were passable, for an amateur." Gina managed a small smile. He was watching her as if he expected her to disappear at any moment.

"How about you?" she asked, looking intently into his eyes "Why didn't you tell me you had been shot?" The mental picture of Jess collapsing on deck drained all the color from her face.

"Hey, it's just a scratch. There's no reason for you to become upset by something so insignificant." He leaned down and gave her a quick kiss on her full lips. "We didn't have anything to doctor it with, anyway, so why worry you?''

His fingers were still wandering. He followed their path with his eyes as they slid inside the neckline of Gina's bright yellow sweater. Her skin was so soft and warm, so inviting. Too inviting, he thought as he moved his fingers to a safer area. Too much touching would get him onto the wrong track, and they had a lot to clear up.

"I'm fine." He continued to study Gina with his smoky gray eyes. "A little stiff and sore, but no worse off than you," he added, dismissing her concern. He let his hand fall to his side and stepped back so that she could see his fading bruises. "If color is any indication of good health, then I'm as healthy as a horse."

The teasing grin that accompanied his remark reminded her of his power over women. One of his devastating smiles was all he needed to have any woman on her knees, begging. Just as she had been close to doing minutes before.

That sobering thought had Gina taking a quick step backward. She looked around the rich stateroom as if she were seeking an escape. She needed distance, if she was going to keep her wits. Jess had a powerful effect on her. When he was near, she seemed to lose all control.

He did look improved. His face wasn't as pale as when he'd passed out last night. And his eyes held a sparkle that was mesmerizing. Her glance slid down to his broad shoulders and on to the corded muscles that stretched across his bare chest.

"You look recuperated," she admitted, as she attempted to swallow the lump lodged in her throat when she realized that his only covering was a tight pair of briefs. Quickly lowering her gaze to the toes of her tennis shoes, she felt heat warm her cheeks.

She was pleased to see him, he knew. That kiss would
have been clue enough, even without her comment. Was
it Greg and Rita's affair that had her shying away from
him?

Giving Gina a thoughtful look, Jess decided it was time
they got their past out in the open. They needed to put
their ghosts to rest if they were ever going to have a future
together.

He glanced around the room. The bed took up most of
the space, but there was a small table, flanked by two
chairs, facing the large windows. They might as well get
comfortable; this could take a while.

"Do you think there's anything to eat on this tub?"

Gina's head snapped up at his question.

"Oh...uh...sure. I'm sorry, I didn't think. You must
be starving." Her hands nervously fluttered in front of her
as she stuttered a response. "There are some clothes in the
closet. Why don't you get dressed, and I'll see what there
is to eat?" she suggested as she gratefully turned toward
the door.

Jess watched her make her hasty escape. That was the
only word he could find to describe her rapid retreat from
the room. His heart sank. What if she was working up the
courage to tell him that she didn't want him to get the
wrong idea about their lovemaking? Was it possible that
she hadn't experienced the same feelings as he had?

He searched the closet for a pair of pants and a shirt,
paying little attention to what he was grabbing. When he'd
dressed, he returned for shoes and socks. He entered the
lavish bathroom and looked in the mirror over the sink. He
rubbed his hand over his smooth cheek, recalling the lux-
ury of the long, hot shower of a few hours ago. He smiled
at his reflection as he remembered the doctor muttering
about infections and other possible side effects of show-

ering with his injury. If he could survive the jungle, a hot shower wouldn't kill him.

Dressed and washed, Jess took up Gina's place at the window. The past month and a half seemed far removed from the extravagant stateroom where he'd spent the night. Or the peaceful scene of the early-morning sun dancing on blue waters.

The hell of it was, after all they'd gone through together, he still didn't know where he stood with Gina. Her hostility had vanished, but it had been replaced by an aloofness that baffled him. When she returned, he was going to find out what was behind her strange behavior. But first he would have to clear up her misconceptions about the past.

Gina silently opened the cabin door, pausing when she saw Jess outlined against the large windows. He stood tall and proud, his head held high, his broad shoulders squared, as if he could meet any problem the world dealt him head-on and win. This was the man who had survived six weeks locked in a dark cellar and had still risen, undefeated, to meet his adversary when he knew he was too weak to fight.

She was seeing Jess Knight in a far different light from the way she'd viewed him while Greg was alive. Her eyes were wide open now, instead of blinded by lies. She'd spent the better part of two weeks struggling to reach safety with Jess, and in that time she'd seen a different person from the one she thought she knew.

Jess turned from the window to see Gina standing in the door holding a covered tray. What had put that pensive look on her face this time? he thought, moving forward to take the tray from her hands.

"Shall we eat here, or would you rather sit on deck?" Holding Gina's gaze, Jess waited for her to decide.

"The deck would be nice, but it's more private here," she suggested in a distracted voice, her eyes locked with his.

Jess turned and set the tray on the small table. The smell of fresh coffee was making his mouth water.

"I hope you brought enough for two," he said as he pulled out one of the chairs for Gina.

"Just some coffee for me," she answered as she sat in the chair he held for her, nervously smoothing a napkin over her lap.

Jess took the other chair and removed the cover from the tray. He poured the steaming coffee into the waiting mugs.

Seeing the food on the tray, he was surprised to discover that he really wasn't hungry and replaced the cover. Lifting his cup of coffee, he took a tentative sip before cupping the warm mug between his hands.

"We have to talk," he stated baldly.

Startled, Gina looked up from studying the coffee in her cup. She watched as Jess settled deeper in his chair, then leaned forward to rest his elbows on his widespread knees, still cradling his cup in his large hands.

Now it was his turn to study his cup as if it held the answers he was seeking in its dark depths. She waited patiently, knowing he had something to say that he was finding difficult.

Mentally she was preparing herself for him to bring up the night of the storm. She remembered what he'd said about his taking their lovemaking seriously and their talking about it later. Now that he was back in civilization, he'd probably changed his mind.

Gina looked as if she didn't have a worry in the world as she sipped her coffee and patiently waited for him to begin. Jess wondered what was going on behind her beautiful golden eyes. They didn't give him a clue.

"About what Rita told you," he started abruptly. He had gone back to studying the contents of his cup, and didn't see the startled look on Gina's face. "I think I should clarify some of the things she told you. I don't want you to get the wrong idea."

By the time Jess looked up, she had herself under control. His inquiring look was met by a tranquil expression of polite interest.

"Rita wasn't completely accurate. And, of course, she didn't know all that was going on in the Agency. I had been investigating the arms thefts for months, but even before that, I had my suspicions about her. Especially after the way she'd made an all-out effort to get Greg. I should at least have tried to put a stop to what was going on before the affair got out of hand."

Jess frowned when Gina's expression didn't change, then continued. "I guess I should start at the beginning." He settled back in his chair and looked into the distance. "Rita transferred to illegal arms investigations out of the intelligence division. She didn't have much experience in fieldwork, so I was assigned to train her. She tried hard to make our assignment more than just field training, but I didn't have the least interest in her type.

"She was too brash for my tastes, and when she didn't get anywhere with me, she quickly asked to have Greg train her. Before the week was out, she had him hooked."

Jess couldn't see what good would be served by harping on Greg's infidelity. He paused, trying to decide how deeply he should go into Greg's involvement with Rita.

"You don't need to spare me, Jess," Gina said as she returned her cup to the table. The coffee had suddenly turned bitter. "I think I've figured out most of what happened. You'll only be confirming my conclusions."

"Well, as I said, Rita hooked her claws into Greg, and it wasn't long before he was spending all his spare time with her. Pretty soon, he was asking to have her partner him on actual assignments. About a year after she joined the Agency, confiscated arms started disappearing from the Agency's warehouses.

"We had no clues to lead us to whoever was responsible. After a number of successful raids on our warehouses over a six-month period, Virgil assigned the problem to me. We knew the robberies were being set up by someone in the Agency. We just didn't know who that person was. My job was to find the traitor.

"We were already looking for Thomas Rico, a known arms dealer. We were sure he was behind the thefts, but we never came close to catching him. Thomas Rico was just a name to everyone at the Agency. No one had ever seen him—except Greg.

"According to the letter Greg left me, he'd met Rico a number of times socially, although not as Rico. He'd been introduced to Greg as Rita's brother. It wasn't until Greg decided to divorce you so he could marry Rita that he found out her brother's real identity."

Setting his full cup on the table, Jess reached out and gathered her cold hands in his large ones. "You have to understand, Gina, Greg was used by a pair of experts. My investigations revealed they'd been pulling this type of scam all over the world. Rico would send Rita in to seduce someone who could tell them where the arms were stored, then he would steal them and sell them to the highest bidder. It was a real slick setup, and most of the time it worked."

Jess gave Gina's hands one last squeeze before laying them in her lap and sitting back in his chair. "It would have worked this time, too, except Greg was having second thoughts about leaving you. Finding Rita and Rico in bed together put an end to her control over him. He was furious about the way they'd used him, and wanted to prevent the guns from being delivered. His one mistake was in not telling me right away. I already had enough evidence to arrest Rita, but I didn't want to accept the evidence that pointed to Greg as her accomplice.

"The letter Greg left me, saying he'd helped Rita, went a long way to proving his guilt, but I just couldn't believe that he'd knowingly help someone steal the arms he'd risked his life to keep out of the hands of men like Rico. He didn't say anything about his not being aware of what she had been doing, so his message was like a declaration of guilt. He went to the warehouse where the arms were stored awaiting shipment. He was going to get rid of them before they could be shipped out of the country. I think he was trying to even the score. He was just..."

Jess ran his hand over his face, as if trying to erase the pictures in his mind. "If only I'd acted sooner, Greg would still be alive."

He looked away, tormented by the thought. "He was so hung up on Rita. When the woman in the warehouse screamed, Greg must have thought she was in there, or he wouldn't have risked his life by going inside when he knew it was going to blow at any minute." Jess paused and stared at his hands before doubling them into tight fists. Drawing a deep breath, he quietly continued.

"I arrived in time to see Greg race back into the warehouse, seconds before it blew. The fire was so intense, I couldn't go in after him. There was nothing I could do but watch the warehouse burn—with my best friend inside."

The sun had risen fully while Jess talked, and it was sending bright patterns across the carpeted floor, but neither of them noticed. The drone of the engines and the gentle rocking of the yacht surrounded them like a cloak but couldn't block out the guilt that hung thick in the room.

Jess knew Gina's guilt was from her doubts about being woman enough to hold on to her husband. She felt she had failed him by not keeping him out of the clutches of another woman. His guilt was another matter. He was going to have to make a clean breast of everything before they could get on with their lives.

Jess gathered his courage, determined to see this to the end, here and now.

"I asked for a transfer from the field division into intelligence so I could track Rico. I wanted to catch him so he could set the record straight about Greg. I've spent the last two years tracking him around the world. That night, in the clearing, was the first time I'd seen more than a picture of him. I was as surprised to see Rita with Rico as you were. Everyone assumed Rita was killed in the fire."

He was no coward. He wanted to see her face when he told her about his feelings for her. Jess reached out and gently turned Gina until she had no alternative but to look at him. He leaned forward, looking into her eyes.

"I didn't care that she was alive. I wanted you. Do you understand, Gina?" Jess gave her a gentle shake before letting his hand fall, releasing her. "Ever since I first saw you, I've wanted you."

The only reaction he got from her was a startled widening of her eyes as confusion knit her brow. Before she could ask the question he saw forming on her soft lips, he continued.

"That's the guilt *I* have to live with."

Finding he didn't have the courage he'd thought, Jess stood and went to the window so that he wouldn't have to see Gina's response to his confession. His eyes followed the Texas coastline without really seeing it.

"I knew Greg was getting involved with Rita and I did nothing to stop him. I was supposed to be his best friend. But I just sat back and watched her work her wiles on him.

I was hoping you would find out about them. That you would leave him, and I'd be the one to pick up the pieces."

Jess hunched his shoulders as he felt the burden of guilt he had lived with for years weigh him down.

"I had the whole thing all worked out in my mind. You'd be heartbroken, and I'd have a convenient shoulder for you to lean on. One thing would lead to another, and I'd get you." Jess turned back to Gina, seeking understanding. "I know what I did was nothing to be proud of, but by then I couldn't stand seeing the way Greg treated you."

Jumping to her feet, Gina restlessly toured the room, fighting to hold back the tears that burned at the backs of her eyes. Had everyone known about Greg? Had they been laughing behind her back all these years? Laughing at simple little Gina, so naive she couldn't see what was going on right under her nose.

She now understood all the times when she'd entered a room, or walked down a hall at the Agency and everyone had stopped talking until she'd passed, when the whispers would begin. Gina swiveled back to face Jess.

Across the room, Jess could see the tears pooled in Gina's eyes, her feeble attempt at anger failing as dismay and hurt took hold. Seeing her distress, he fought the urge to gather her into his arms.

"I'm sorry, Gina."

She flinched as if he had struck her, and he felt a deep, gut-wrenching pain. Smothering a curse under his breath, he slowly went to her. He reached out imploringly, but stopped short of touching her...yet.

"It didn't have anything to do with you. You have to believe that. Rita was...determined. He didn't have a chance." Impatiently he slashed his hand through the air when Gina showed no sign of believing him. "Damn it, he just couldn't resist the chase."

Jess wasn't going to let Gina continue to feel that her failed marriage was all her fault. He put his hands on her shoulders, holding her before him so that he could look into her startled eyes. "It wouldn't have mattered who he married. He still wouldn't have been able to resist Rita."

This statement was forced through clenched teeth as his fingers dug into her soft shoulders. He wasn't trying to restrain Gina so much as he was trying to keep himself from gathering her close.

His resistance lasted until he saw a single tear escape to roll down her pale cheek. With a tortured groan, he pulled her into his arms. Holding her close, he buried his face against the side of her neck, surrounding his face in Gina's silky hair. Gently rocking her back and forth, he murmured in her ear.

"I didn't want to add to your sorrow. I thought by knowing everything you would be free from the past."

Jess's voice was muffled, but she heard his heartfelt words and understood. He thought she was feeling pain at finding out about Greg.

She pushed against the solid wall of his chest until he released her. His torment was plain for her to see. Reaching up, she gently smoothed out the deep furrows in his brow. Her fingers lingered, tracing the bones of his face until they came to rest below his full lower lip.

As if mesmerized, Gina watched her finger. "Sorrow isn't what I was feeling," she said in a small voice. "I think my feelings could be better described as selfish embarrassment. I was remembering all the whispers and pitying glances I'd encountered at the Agency."

Gina let her hand fall to her side and stepped away from Jess. Turning her back, she looked out over the sparkling blue water. "I'm embarrassed to say that Greg and his infidelity wasn't what I was thinking about."

She felt Jess move closer, so close that she was surrounded by the heat from his body and his tantalizing scent. She moved away, not wanting him to touch her. If he touched her, she would be lost, and she needed to clear the air just as much as he did.

"Greg's affair doesn't matter anymore. I just didn't want you to think I was less of a woman than Rita." Gina swung around to face Jess. Did she dare trust him? What if she left herself open to find that Jess didn't want her after all? She didn't think she would survive if she let herself hope, only to discover she'd been no more than a passing fancy. But she didn't think she had the strength to back away, either.

Gina searched Jess's face, and was surprised to see a hopeful glint in his eyes that gave her the courage to softly continue.

"All that matters is you."

As if released from restraints, Jess closed the distance between them and swept Gina into his arms. This embrace was not to comfort, but to celebrate. They were both free of the past. They could move forward from here. All the obstacles weren't out of their way, but at least he now stood a chance with her.

Burying her face against Jess's throat, Gina slid her arms around his neck, pulling him closer. The warmth of his arms, the feel of his solid chest against her breasts, his total maleness, held her as completely as did his steely arms.

Feeling Gina's soft body pressed close, her warm breath caressing his neck, fanned a fire that had been smoldering for years. With infinite control, Jess tipped her head until he could reach her lips. With almost savage fury, he claimed her full lips with his hungry mouth. The kiss was endless. Their lips searched and devoured. His demanding. Hers more than willing to yield, for she knew what rewards awaited her.

The world melted away. To Gina and Jess, locked tight in each other's arms, only the two of them existed.

The first fierce need fed, Jess tempered his kisses with tenderness as he soothed Gina's swollen lips with his tongue. He searched her bright eyes for a sign that he was moving too fast, but they glowed with a desire to match his own.

His heart soared, and he crushed her to him again. His mouth scorched her lips with hot kisses, and his tongue thrust deep, claiming her sweetness for his own. His hands restlessly roamed her back, seeking the velvety skin underneath her soft sweater, before settling on her slim hips. With an uncontrolled movement, Jess pulled her hard against his surging manhood, taking delight in her whimper when she encountered the proof of his desire.

Gina felt her head swim as Jess plundered her soft mouth with kisses that left her breathless with need and had her body straining to get closer. The clawing hunger that his kisses awakened was alien to her. This was a passion such as she had never tasted before.

Drawing a ragged breath, Jess reluctantly ended the kiss. "Oh, sweet, sweet Gina. What you do to me..." He rested his forehead against her silky hair as he moved his hips to demonstrate what she was doing to him. "I want you." He punctuated his words with swift kisses. "The first time was pure heaven, but I want to see you when I touch your soft skin. I want to see your face when I make you mine." He wanted so much more. To see her face when she made that sound deep in her throat that drove him wild. To look into her eyes as he lost himself in her.

"Say you want me, too." Jess was close to pleading, his need was so great, but if she backed away he would find the strength to let her go. He could wait a little longer.

Gina hid her face in Jess's shirt. She could feel the burn of embarrassment heat her face. She wanted him. She just couldn't say the words. Her body throbbed, and her heart raced as never before. She knew Jess held the cure that would ease the tension that was ravishing her. Her answer was in the form of an attempt to mesh her body with his, seeking to cool the flame that licked her sensitive flesh.

Jess could feel Gina tremble in his arms as she molded her pliant body to his. Was this her answer? Did she realize what she was doing? He had to be sure. The first time, circumstances had taken the decision out of their hands and she'd felt regret in the morning. This time, he wanted her to want him just as fiercely as he wanted her.

"Gina, I need to hear you say this is what you want." He kissed the tender skin behind her ear. "I need to hear the words."

"I want..."

The muffled words were barely audible, but Jess heard them, and for a moment his heart froze before threatening to beat its way out of his chest. His arms tightened around Gina. He was content just to hold her until he could gain a little control. They had the rest of their lives together.

Gina didn't remember how they got to the bed. She was floating on a cloud, where mundane things such as walking had no reality. Jess was her only reality.

She watched as Jess sat in the chair near the window to remove his shoes and socks. With heavy eyes, she watched as he stood to remove his pants and shirt, her impatience growing as his body was slowly revealed. He had filled out and changed since the day she'd cooled his fevered skin with a wet cloth. Her fingers throbbed, wanting to seek out those changes, to mold the powerful muscles that corded his chest and long legs. She wanted to feel that power as he merged with her, taking her to the heights she'd reached only with him.

Jess felt Gina's eyes on him as he slid his pants and briefs down his legs and stepped out of them. Her watchful gaze enticed him almost beyond reason, but he crossed the room slowly, giving her plenty of time to become accustomed to him.

Reaching the edge of the bed, he waited until Gina raised her eyes to meet his. He wanted to see her reaction to his arousal. His heart thudded as he watched her run her eyes up his body before stopping at his face. Desire filled her smoldering eyes as her full lips turned up at the corners in a seductive smile that did nothing to cool his raging blood.

Her smile was all the invitation Jess needed to join Gina on the soft bed, where he quickly gathered her in his arms. Hungrily he covered her lips with his eager mouth.

She was still wearing the yellow sweater and slacks, but they were no obstacle for him. With a few swift movements, he had them removed, pausing only to kiss the silky skin he exposed before moving on to remove another article of clothing.

The sweater and pants were soon lying on the floor, and bits of lace and silk caught his eye. Jess paused to chuckle at the pale yellow panties as he slid them down her slim legs.

"These are hardly worth bothering with," he teased as he held them aloft, letting the light filter through the pastel bits of lace on his finger. He watched the rosy color heat Gina's cheeks as he dropped them over the edge of the bed.

"You're beautiful, do you know that?" He gently caressed her flushed cheek, his eyes roaming her face, before moving down her sculptured body. "So beautiful," he breathed as he lowered his mouth to one of the pink tips beckoning him.

They tasted as sweet as they looked. His eager hands moved to caress and mold the lush mounds as he lowered himself to the bed. His senses reeled as he felt the rosy peaks firm to hard points under his laving tongue.

Gina's fingers slid through Jess's thick hair, holding him to her breast, her body on fire. She was melting. She wanted the feeling to go on forever, and yet she needed more.

"Easy, sweet. I don't want to hurt your leg," Jess murmured soothingly when he felt Gina's restless movements. "There's no hurry."

He didn't want to rush. They had all the time in the world to explore. To arouse. To give each other pleasure. He teased her mouth with soft kisses, while stealing her breath as his hands roamed intimately over her body.

Gina didn't give her injured leg a thought as her fingers dug into his back, her world tilting when Jess slipped his fingers between her thighs. His long fingers explored and probed her dewy recesses until her hips were thrusting convulsively as she gasped his name.

"Touch me, Gina. Put your hands on me." Jess's breathing was as labored as Gina's as he anticipated her touch.

Air hissed through Jess's clenched teeth as Gina lightly ran her hand across his firm chest. His response acted as encouragement, and she boldly slid her fingers through the thick hair that covered his broad chest until she encountered a tight nipple.

Jess's entire body jerked when Gina flicked the distended nipple with her fingernail before gently tugging, the way Jess had teased hers. The power she felt when he groaned deep in his throat inspired further exploration.

His body throbbed where her hands touched, and his jaw ached from clenching his teeth while he gave her time to learn his form. He wouldn't be able to last much longer. When her hands found his pulsating manhood, he knew he was lost.

Gathering Gina's hands in his, Jess brought them together over her head, whispering love words to her as he
slid over her warm body. He spread kisses over her face as
he settled between her parted thighs. Pausing, he looked
deep into her desire-laden eyes before lowering his head
until their lips met. Her eyes grew wide as she felt him slip
into her waiting warmth, her body arching to meet his slow
thrust.

Gina felt the fire building to a roaring inferno, and she
rose to meet the heat, lifting her hips to take all that he
would give. With restless movements, she strained to increase the tempo Jess had set. She wanted to find the
pleasure he had given her once before, while he seemed
content to prolong the sweet agony.

Jess's restraint quickly faded when Gina wrapped her
legs around his hips, taking him more deeply, while her
hands gripped his back. He could hold back no longer as
he felt her body begin to tremble with her release. She took
him with her, higher than he had ever flown. For one second, he wondered if they would combust before they returned to earth.

Chapter 13

Gina watched the sunlight track across the stateroom floor as she listened to the even breathing behind her. She was lying on her side, with Jess curved behind her, his arm draped around her waist, his hand possessively holding one breast. The familiar position, begun while they were in the jungle, felt right, although it did nothing to relieve her heavy heart.

Their lovemaking had been glorious—better than the first time. But it had settled nothing. Jess had said all the right words as he kissed and caressed her. Words that didn't mean anything when the loving ended. Not a word had been said about love, only wanting.

Would he stay around until the newness wore off, and then move on to another lover? How would she survive if he left her? She loved him too deeply to have him for a short time, only to lose him to someone else. Someone far more worldly and sophisticated than she could ever hope to be. She would have been better off never to have made love with him at all, she thought as she choked back a sob.

Putting her life back together was going to be next to impossible. Hopefully, once she was back to work, she would see that her feelings had just been the result of her being trapped with Jess for such a long time. They'd simply lost their good sense and let themselves be carried away by the moment.

She would have about as much luck forgetting Jess as she would teaching a pig to fly, Gina reproached herself. What she needed was to put as much distance between them as possible. Maybe she could get an assignment on the moon, though judging by the size of her heartache, that wouldn't be far enough.

Gina eased out from under Jess's arm and slid to the side of the wide bed. She had to get her life in order sometime, she thought as she threw her legs over the side of the mattress and sat up. There was no sense delaying the inevitable. They should be docking soon, anyway.

"Where do you think you're going, pretty lady?"

Startled, Gina tried to pull the sheet over her nude body. She turned to see Jess lying in the rumpled bed, his heated gaze fixed on her. Casting him a dark look, she quickly turned her back on him before the memory of the past hours spent in his arms lured her back.

"We're going to be docking soon. I thought I'd get ready," she stated, running trembling fingers through her tousled curls in an attempt to conceal her exposed feelings.

"There's no hurry," Jess said, frowning as he watched her nervous fidgeting. He'd seen the look in her eyes before she turned away. He had no idea what was causing her anguish, but it gave him a sinking feeling in the pit of his stomach.

Gina's tugging on the sheet in an attempt to cover her nudity didn't help, either. The more she pulled, the angrier he felt. Her delectable body was indelibly imprinted in his mind. He'd spent hours kissing and caressing every inch of her. He could still feel her delicate skin and taste her essence on his tongue.

Realizing that the sheet was trapped under Jess, Gina ceased pulling and held the corner of the sheet over her breasts. As much as she wanted to be totally covered, she didn't want to leave him lying on the bed with nothing over that magnificent body she remembered all too well.

As if reading her thoughts, he tossed away the sheet and got out on the other side of the bed. He reached for his discarded pants and stepped into them. Rounding the end of the bed, he held his shirt out to Gina.

She stared at the forest-green shirt he was offering. The action was so reminiscent of the morning after Jess had doctored her leg that it brought tears to her eyes. Furious at the show of weakness, she refused to allow the tears to fall. She wasn't going to cry! she commanded herself as she reached for the shirt.

When Jess didn't release the garment, she sent him a questioning look. A mistake, she was soon to discover, when her tear-filled eyes were caught by his smoky gray ones. He continued to hold her gaze as he slowly released his grip on the shirt.

"What's wrong?" he asked with an edge to his voice as he watched her slip into the shirt, fastening the buttons in proper order. "You're back to acting like I took advantage of you again." Her concentration on the simple task infuriated him. "Will you at least give me an answer?"

Gina could feel the tremors building inside at Jess's angry questions. What could she say? *I want you to love me?* That would make him laugh. She had to get away before she made a complete fool of herself by begging him to love her.

Finished with the buttons, Gina smoothed the soft fabric over her hips and squeezed her eyes closed. The light scent that clung to the shirt was almost her undoing. It was like being back in Jess's arms.

She could feel his piercing gaze as he studied her. She rose from the tangled sheet and moved to the window, keeping her back to him as she watched the docks of Galveston grow larger on the horizon.

"Gina?" Jess called, attempting to control his anger.

She continued to ignore him. Why wouldn't she tell him what was troubling her? Had nothing changed? Was he right back where he'd started? Even the lovemaking they had shared hadn't erased the shadows from her eyes.

"You're driving me crazy. One minute you're all warm and loving, and the next you're silent and sullen. After all we've been through, don't you trust me enough to tell me what's troubling you?" Jess rubbed the knotted muscles in his neck that were causing his head to pound. "Say something, damn it!"

"I won't be one of your women," Gina quietly stated, not taking her eyes off the fast-approaching shoreline.

"You what?"

Jess's question was a near shout, and it stirred Gina from her post at the window. "I won't be another of your collection of women. The ones you pick up during your travels around the country."

"What the hell are you talking about? There are no women, here or anywhere else. That was Greg talking, remember?" Jess's sharp retort dripped with sarcasm.

"Greg?" Gina asked, dazed and unsure.

Standing in front of Gina, Jess held her shoulders and looked directly into her startled eyes. "Why do you continue to believe everything Greg told you? You should realize by now that Greg and the truth were worlds apart.'' Almost touching the tip of her nose with his, he continued, ''Listen, and listen good—I do *not* make a habit of collecting women. Is that clear?'' he growled, giving her shoulders a sharp shake.

Wide-eyed, Gina nodded.

''Good!'' Still holding her captive, he growled between clenched teeth, ''And just for the record, no other woman has meant a damn to me since I met you.''

Gina's eyes widened again as she searched his face for the truth. What she found stopped her heart. Could she believe what he was implying? She wrapped her arms around herself, attempting to control the erratic rhythm of her heart.

''What are you trying to tell me?''

Dropping his hands from her shoulders, Jess stepped back, giving her some space. He ran a heated glance from the top of her head to her bare toes.

''When I first saw you, I thought you were the loveliest woman I had ever seen. Your copper curls, your big golden eyes and your sweet shy smile captivated me. I fell in love with you right then.'' He didn't hear her gasp, as his memories were coming alive. ''Then Greg introduced you as his new wife, and I felt sick. All I could think was 'What is Greg doing with someone as sweet and innocent as her?' He was used to the polished sophisticates of the world, women who knew the score and didn't hesitate to play the game.''

Jess drew a deep breath before he continued. ''I told you about Greg and Rita, so I won't go into that again.'' Hunching his shoulders, he shoved his hands into his pockets. ''I'm not proud of my feelings for my best friend's wife, but I was powerless to stop them. I could have stopped seeing you,'' he said, looking at Gina with smoldering eyes, "but I didn't have the strength to do that, either."

Gina's heart was pounding so hard, she was sure Jess could hear it. His words had triggered her memory of the first time she'd met him. Greg had told her they were going to meet Jess at a party given by one of the other operatives. He had gone into lengthy detail about how Jess was a womanizer, so she wasn't to take what he said seriously. He had elaborated about Jess's power to attract women.

Jess had arrived late. When he entered the room, every head had turned. His hair had been windblown, lying casually over his forehead. In a dark shirt with the sleeves rolled up, revealing muscular forearms, and tight jeans that hugged him like a second skin, he was every woman's ideal man.

He seemed to have spotted her right away. Holding her startled gaze, he'd headed in her direction—or so she had thought, until she realized it was Greg he was in a hurry to meet, not her.

Had that spark she remembered seeing in his smoky eyes as he'd looked down at her before Greg introduced them been for her alone? The glowing silver had been replaced with an icy gray so quickly that she'd thought she was mistaken. Especially after he abruptly said a polite hello, then left.

Over the years, he would sometimes come to the house to see Greg, or they would happen to meet at the Agency. He'd always been very polite. Never once had he gotten out of line. In all those years, he hadn't once attempted to flirt with her or flatter her with flowery compliments.

Frowning, she realized that she hadn't been outraged at the thought of being treated like one of Jess's women. She'd been disappointed. She had been attracted to Jess from the moment she'd seen him enter the room.

Maybe her fascination, for that was what it had been, was partly Greg's fault. He'd talked about Jess continually. The picture he'd painted of him was larger than life. Exciting, especially to someone who led a very quiet, secluded life.

"You loved me?" she finally asked.

Jess looked up when he heard the amazement in Gina's soft voice. She was staring at him with wonder in her clear golden eyes.

"Yes, I love you. I think I always have, but it wasn't until you fell over that cliff that I realized just how much."

"Then why didn't you flirt with me or flatter me like you did other women?" The question was stupid, but it had bothered her for years.

Jess frowned at her question. "What other women?"

"Greg said I wasn't to believe the flowery things you said. That you said them to all women, and I shouldn't let them go to my head."

Jess threw back his head and laughed. He couldn't believe how stupid both he and Gina had been. "Greg sure knew how to play the game." Shaking his head, he paused to catch his breath and control his laughter.

Gina was eyeing him as if he'd lost his mind.

"He told you I fed women flowery compliments?" At her nod of confirmation, he laughed again. "Well, he told me you didn't like compliments, you thought they were sexist."

Gina's mouth dropped open as her brows shot up. "He said that?"

Jess's smile grew at her dumbfounded expression. "Yes, among other things I think it would be wise to disregard. Most of them I have discovered for myself are untrue."

Gina's face flamed when she understood his implication, and she turned away in embarrassment. Jess was quick to turn her back to face him, taking her hands in a firm hold.

"No more hiding, Gina," he said seriously. "You have nothing to be ashamed of, and neither do I. We were both innocent pawns in Greg's games, and it's time we put Greg, and the past, behind us."

Jess rested his forehead on Gina's as he stared down at their clasped hands. "The night I played doctor, I made myself a promise. I was going to settle things between us, then I was going to sweep you off your feet and marry you so fast you wouldn't have time to come up with any reasons why we shouldn't." At Gina's sharply indrawn breath, Jess looked up. Her eyes were shining like polished gold, and her cheeks were lightly flushed. "If you want to continue working..."

Gina put her finger over his lips, halting his words. "Is that a proposal, Jess Knight?"

"A roundabout one, but yes, it was a proposal. Will you marry me, Gina?"

"Oh, yes, I'll marry you." She slipped her arms around his waist and gave him a fierce hug before setting him free so that she could look into his eyes. "About working... I don't need to continue at the Agency. I would much rather be a full-time wife and build us a home."

Gina's eyes turned dewy at the thought, letting Jess know she didn't feel she was being forced to give up her career.

"I would like that, too, but I thought you might like to try something new." The glint in his eyes caught her attention. "Since I seem to be without a job, and you're planning to quit yours, I thought we might start something together."

"You don't have a job?" Gina's mouth fell open, and she stared at Jess with obvious skepticism. He was the best operative the Agency had. "They fired you?"

"I quit."

"You did?"

"I did. Last night. After the doctor finished patching me up, I called Virgil." Jess smiled as Gina struggled to follow what he was saying. "I planned to explain everything to you, but we got sidetracked." He loved the way she turned red when he referred to their lovemaking.

"How would you like to start a survival training school?" he went on. "That way we could put our talents to good use, and we would be together."

"Oh, Jess, that would be perfect. We could build a training field in the mountains around the house. I wouldn't have to travel around the world." Gina's features became even more animated as she thought about Jess's suggestion.

Jess pulled her into his arms and pressed a kiss on her smiling lips. "The sooner we get you home, the sooner we can start on that house you want." He kissed her again, this time with more passion.

"Not a house. I already have a house," she murmured against his lips.

"Then what *do* you want?" Jess asked, puzzled.

"A home. I've never had a home, not a real home. One filled with love, and laughter... and babies," Gina whispered, a blush staining her cheeks. "That's a real home."

"A real home," he murmured, feeling a glow warm his body. Hearing her say the words made him realize he'd been looking for a place to call home all his life. And now he had found his home—with Gina.

"We can have all those things. And we may have already started building."

At Gina's questioning look, Jess pulled her closer. "We may have already started those babies."

Gina's brow wrinkled in confusion until understanding dawned. Wrapping her arms around his neck, she flashed him a seductive smile.

"No sense leaving anything to chance."

* * * * *

This October, be the first to read these wonderful
authors as they make their dazzling debuts!

Women to Watch

THE WEDDING KISS by Robin Wells
(Silhouette Romance #1185)
A reluctant bachelor rescues the woman he loves
from the man she's about to marry—and turns into
a willing groom himself!

THE SEX TEST by Patty Salier
(Silhouette Desire #1032)
A pretty professor learns there's more to making love
than meets the eye when she takes lessons from
a sexy stranger.

IN A FAMILY WAY by Julia Mozingo
(Special Edition #1062)
A woman without a past finds shelter in the arms of
a handsome rancher. Can she trust him to protect
her unborn child?

UNDER COVER OF THE NIGHT by Roberta Tobeck
(Intimate Moments #744)
A rugged government agent encounters the woman he has
always loved. But past secrets could threaten their future.

DATELESS IN DALLAS by Samantha Carter
(Yours Truly)
A hapless reporter investigates how to find the perfect
mate—and winds up falling for her handsome rival!

Don't miss the brightest stars of tomorrow!

Only from ▼ *Silhouette*®

Look us up on-line at: http://www.romance.net   WTW

Take 4 bestselling love stories FREE

Plus get a FREE surprise gift!

Special Limited-time Offer

Mail to Silhouette Reader Service™

3010 Walden Avenue
P.O. Box 1867
Buffalo, N.Y. 14240-1867

YES! Please send me 4 free Silhouette Intimate Moments® novels and my free surprise gift. Then send me 6 brand-new novels every month, which I will receive months before they appear in bookstores. Bill me at the low price of $3.34 each plus 25¢ delivery and applicable sales tax, if any.* That's the complete price and a savings of over 10% off the cover prices—quite a bargain! I understand that accepting the books and gift places me under no obligation ever to buy any books. I can always return a shipment and cancel at any time. Even if I never buy another book from Silhouette, the 4 free books and the surprise gift are mine to keep forever.

245 BPA A3UW

Name	(PLEASE PRINT)	
Address	Apt. No.	
City	State	Zip

This offer is limited to one order per household and not valid to present Silhouette Intimate Moments® subscribers. *Terms and prices are subject to change without notice.
Sales tax applicable in N.Y.

As seen on TV!

Free Gift Offer

With a Free Gift proof-of-purchase from any Silhouette® book,
you can receive a beautiful cubic zirconia pendant.

This gorgeous marquise-shaped stone is a genuine cubic
zirconia—accented by an 18" gold tone necklace.

(Approximate retail value $19.95)

Send for yours today...

compliments of ▼ *Silhouette*®
™

To receive your free gift, a cubic zirconia pendant, send us one original proof-of-
purchase, photocopies not accepted, from the back of any Silhouette Romance™,
Silhouette Desire®, Silhouette Special Edition®, Silhouette Intimate Moments®
or Silhouette Yours Truly™ title available in August, September or October at your favorite
retail outlet, together with the Free Gift Certificate, plus a check or money order for
$1.65 U.S./$2.15 CAN. (do not send cash) to cover postage and handling, payable
to Silhouette Free Gift Offer. We will send you the specified gift. Allow 6 to 8 weeks for
delivery. Offer good until October 31, 1996 or while quantities last. Offer valid in the
U.S. and Canada only.

Free Gift Certificate

Name: _____

Address: _____

City: _____ State/Province: _____ Zip/Postal Code: _____

Mail this certificate, one proof-of-purchase and a check or money order for postage
and handling to: SILHOUETTE FREE GIFT OFFER 1996. In the U.S.: 3010 Walden
Avenue, P.O. Box 9077, Buffalo NY 14269-9077. In Canada: P.O. Box 613, Fort Erie,
Ontario L2Z 5X3.

FREE GIFT OFFER
084-KMD

ONE PROOF-OF-PURCHASE

To collect your fabulous FREE GIFT, a cubic zirconia pendant, you must include this
original proof-of-purchase for each gift with the properly completed Free Gift Certificate.

084-KMD

Continuing in October from Silhouette Books...

This exciting new cross-line continuity series unites five of
your favorite authors as they weave five connected novels
about love, marriage—and Daddy's unexpected need for a
baby carriage!

You loved

THE BABY NOTION by Dixie Browning
(Desire 7/96)

BABY IN A BASKET by Helen R. Myers
(Romance 8/96)

MARRIED...WITH TWINS! by Jennifer Mikels
(Special Edition 9/96)

And the romance in New Hope, Texas, continues with:

HOW TO HOOK A HUSBAND (AND A BABY)
by Carolyn Zane (Yours Truly 10/96)

She vowed to get hitched by her thirtieth birthday. But
plain-Jane Wendy Wilcox didn't have a clue how to catch
herself a husband—until Travis, her sexy neighbor, offered
to teach her what a man really wants in a wife....

And look for the thrilling conclusion to the series in:

DISCOVERED: DADDY
by Marilyn Pappano (Intimate Moments 11/96)

DADDY KNOWS LAST continues each month...
only in *Silhouette®*

DKL-YT

The collection of the year!
NEW YORK TIMES BESTSELLING AUTHORS

Linda Lael Miller
Wild About Harry

Janet Dailey
Sweet Promise

Elizabeth Lowell
Reckless Love

Penny Jordan
Love's Choices

and featuring
Nora Roberts
The Calhoun Women

This special trade-size edition features four of the wildly
popular titles in the Calhoun miniseries together in
one volume—a true collector's item!

Pick up these great authors and a chance to win
a weekend for two in New York City at the
Marriott Marquis Hotel on Broadway! We'll pay
for your flight, your hotel—even a Broadway show!

Available in December at your favorite retail outlet.

NEW YORK
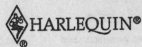
MARQUIS

A brutal murder.
A notorious case.
Twelve people must decide
the fate of one man.

Jury Duty

an exciting courtroom drama by

Laura Van Wormer

Struggling novelist Libby Winslow has been chosen to sit on the jury
of a notorious murder trial dubbed the "Poor Little Rich Boy" case.
The man on trial, handsome, wealthy James Bennett Layton, Jr., has
been accused of killing a beautiful young model. As Libby and the
other jury members sift through the evidence trying to decide the fate
of this man, their own lives become jeopardized because someone
on the jury has his own agenda....

Find out what the verdict is this October at your favorite
retail outlet.

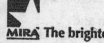 **MIRA** The brightest star in women's fiction

MLVWJD

Look us up on-line at:http://www.romance.net

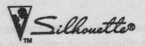